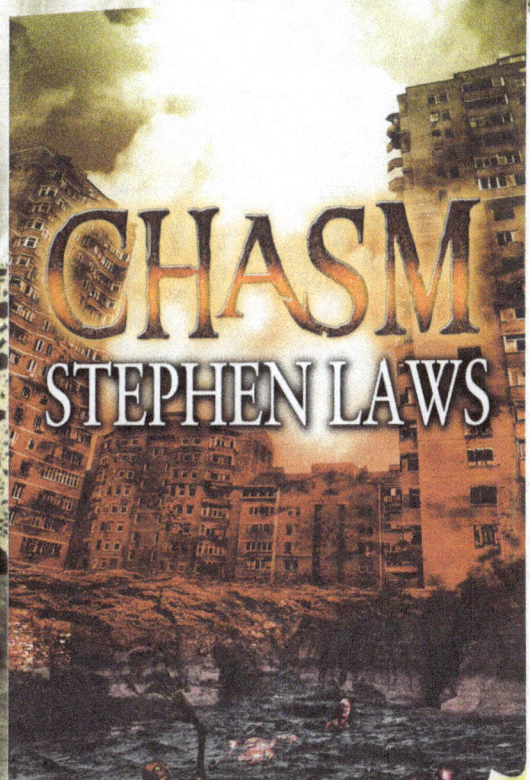

Updates from the Dark Beach: Guest Editorial

Welcome to the guest editorial of this very special issue of *Dark Discoveries* magazine.

Allow me to introduce myself.

My name is Aaron J. French. I joined *Dark Discoveries* as an associate editor a few issues back, around the time JournalStone Publishing picked it up. I'm a member of the Horror Writers Association, as well as an up and coming supernatural fiction author and the editor of three small press anthologies: *Monk Punk*, *The Shadow of the Unknown*, and *Songs of the Satyrs* (forthcoming).

I'm also a fan of *Dark Discoveries* and have been since its premier issue back in 2004. When the opportunity to join this editorial team came my way I jumped on it, and I couldn't be more pleased. I'm thrilled to have co-edited this special dark fantasy issue with Editor-in-chief James Beach, whose insights into the publishing biz have been a big help to my career. And let me tell you something, we've worked very hard at collecting the stack of hundred plus pages you hold in your hands, and I promise that you won't be disappointed.

This quarter's theme, Dark Fantasy, is very close to my heart because much of my own writing strives toward a similar balance between the magical and mundane. The fiction we've chosen this time around pulls off this balancing act with grace, and the nonfiction articles here explore the meaning of this enigmatic term—Dark Fantasy—by highlighting relevant authors and their material.

But enough throat-clearing, let's get down to business.

We have an 8000 word vintage reprint story from New York Times bestselling author Jonathan Maberry, as well as a brand new interview with the author, in which he shares some thoughts on his successful career.

Horror legend Ramsey Campbell completed several unfinished Robert E. Howard manuscript fragments many years ago, and without much trumpet blowing to announce this collaboration, a lot of fans remain unaware. We've managed to secure one of these tales, "The Castle of the Devil," for your reading pleasure. We also have a brand new dark fantasy western story from Steve Rasnic Tem and a new sword and sorcery horror tale from Angeline Hawkes.

As if that wasn't enough, rising star Weston Ochse, author of *Seal Team 666*, gives us a piece of meta-fictional writing, detailing a strange interplay between himself and the destructive tendencies of his creative muse.

Joe McKinney complements Ochse's weirdness by offering his own quasi-meta-fictional story about an obsessed fan who loves horror icon Robert McCammon just a little bit too much. McCammon, indecently, is also 2013's recipient of the HWA's Lifetime Achievement Award, along with Clive Barker.

Speaking of the HWA and the Bram Stoker Awards, JournalStone Publishing's President Christopher C. Payne got it in his head to release this special issue of *Dark Discoveries* magazine in conjunction with The Bram Stoker Awards® Weekend 2013 Incorporating World Horror Convention in New Orleans, Louisiana. A brilliantly insane idea! So we have included a section specifically devoted to WHC, the Stokers, and the HWA, including a comprehensive list of every past convention and its location, and every past Stoker award winner. We've also got quotes by all the best professionals in the field who express their gratitude for the Association and all the work it's doing.

But we're not finished!

This issue introduces several new columns which will become regular additions to *Dark Discoveries*. Former *Cemetery Dance* editor Robert Morrish revives his celebrated feature "Where Are They Now?" and this time the object of his inquiry is horror author Sean Costello. We also added author Yvonne Navarro who will offer her unique perspective on, well, whatever she feels like, and a new young adult section that will feature reviews, along with Dr. Michael R. Collings's regular contribution.

There are interviews with Boris Vallejo and Dark Horse Comics' Scott Allie, as well as nonfiction features on Robert E. Howard, Karl Edward Wagner, and Brian McNaughton. Finally, we round out the issue with an extensive sword and sorcery filmography and a recommended reading list.

Lastly, on a sad note, we lost three of the good ones while we were putting together this issue. First off a great editor, writer and all-around good guy (and Hellnotes editor and facilitator) David B. Silva passed away on March 13th at age 62. He set the bar high with his landmark magazine, *The Horror Show*, back in the 1980s and subsequent anthologies he produced. Many a writer's, editor's and publisher's career was launched in, or influenced by, *The Horror Show* and David's example. His own writing was excellent as well, but sadly he never became as big as he should have been. Our own Editor-in-chief has openly and frequently acknowledged Silva's huge influence on the magazine you hold in your hands. In honor of David, we have assembled a number of tributes to him in this issue. Second, bestselling British horror author James Herbert passed away on March 20th at age 67. Herbert was one of the pioneers of "Splatterpunk" with landmark novels like *The Rats*, *The Fog* and *The Spear*. And lastly, HWA Lifetime Acheivement award-winner Rick Hautala passed away on March 21st at age 64. Rick was a native of Maine and went to school with Stephen King. The author of numerous books like *Moondeath*, *Little Brothers* and *Occasional Demons*, he was slated to have two books published soon by our publisher JournalStone. Look for features and tributes on Herbert and Hautala in issue #24 as well. Too young for all three and they will be missed!

I hope you enjoy this special issue as much as we enjoyed assembling it. And be on the lookout for more exciting things to come from *Dark Discoveries* and JournalStone Publishing.

—*Aaron J. French*
Dark Discoveries, Hellnotes
Associate Editor, Reviews Editor

DARK DISCOVERIES

Publisher
JournalStone Publishing, LLC

Editor-in-Chief
James R. Beach

Assistant Editors
Aaron J. French
Chuck Caruso
Elizabeth Reuter
Lacey Friedly (Submissions)

**Art Director,
Layout, and Design**
Cyrus Wraith Walker

Contributors
*Robert E. Howard &
Ramsey Campbell
Angeline Hawkes
Jonathan Maberry
Weston Ochse
Joe McKinney
Chuck Caruso
James R. Beach
Aaron J. French
Trever Nordgren
Joel B. Kirkpatrick
Robert Morrish
Yvonne Navarro
Michael R. Collings
Amy Shane
Steve Rasnic Tem*

**Contributing
Artists/Photographers**
*Vincent Chong (Cover Image)
Cyrus Wraith Walker (Various Interior)
Allen Koszowski (pg. 9)
Nick Gucker (pg. 91)*

Special Thanks
*Robert E Howard Estate
Boris Vallejo
Andy Golub
Scott Allie*
_____

DARK DISCOVERIES
(ISSN 1548-6842) is published (Qtrly)
by JournalStone Publications, 199
State Street, San Mateo, CA. 94401

**Christopher C. Payne
Dark Discoveries Publications
199 State Street, San Mateo, CA. 94401
U.S.A.**
christophercpayne@journalstone.com.

Please make check or money order payable
to: JournalStone Publishing and send to the
address above.
Credit/Debit cards via Paypal at:
christophercpayne@journalstone.com.
Advertising rates available. Discounts for
bulk and standing retail orders.

Fiction

Non-Fiction

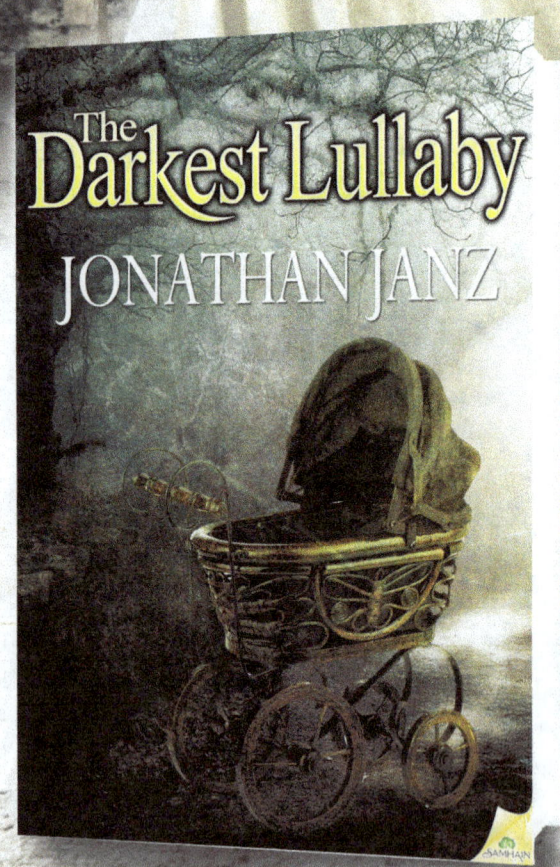

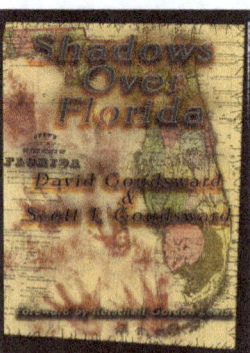
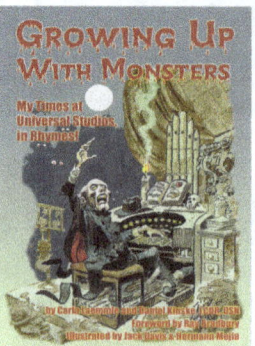
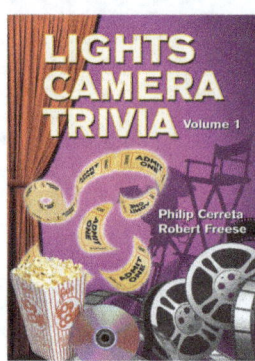
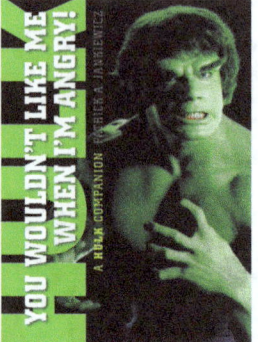
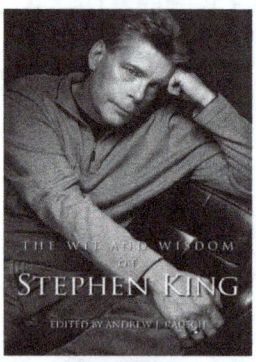

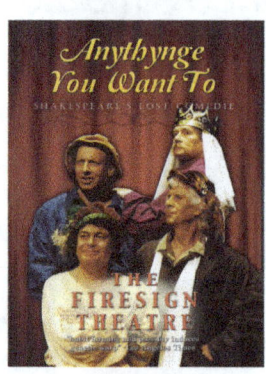

"The Mad Exultation of Battle": The Sword & Sorcery Legacy of Robert E. Howard

By Chuck Caruso

"Howard's writing seems so highly charged with energy that it nearly gives off sparks."

—Stephen King

Most of us growing up in the last half-century or so first encountered the dark fantasy of Robert E. Howard through the lurid cover of a Conan paperback or comic book. For me, I think it must have been one of the Lancer/Ace editions featuring cover art by Frank Frazetta – these illustrations are so deeply woven into my adolescent consciousness that I cannot fathom a time when they did not haunt and thrill me. The cover of *Conan of Cimmeria* shows the mighty warrior swinging his sword against two red-bearded, axe-wielding barbarians in a battle to the death on some icy mountain top. The cover art of *Conan the Adventurer* depicts the densely-muscled hero standing triumphant atop a pile of the dead while a barely-clad beauty clings to one of his legs. The publisher re-issued nearly all of Howard's Conan stories in this series, publishing his original works alongside the authorized Conan tales of L. Sprague De Camp and Lin Carter who had both carried on building the legendary figure of Conan.

When you're thirteen years old and you run across one of these paperbacks in the bookstore, there's no way you're going home without it. You read it first thing when you get home too, burying your nose in the musty smell of cheap paper and black ink. Howard's words come alive on the pages and your mind explodes with the images of Conan striding bold and fearless through a world stripped of its veneer of polite society, a world that belongs to the strong and the brave, a world where your inner savage runs free, slaughtering enemies without remorse, plumbing the darkest mysteries of primordial chaos and blackest magics – and hoping you might survive so long to experience the secret joys within the perfumed chambers of harem girls. Before you know it, you've read all the stories in this book and you're hungry for more. You circle back and read it again while you begin plotting chores you can perform for neighbors. You need to secure enough pocket cash for the next time you scour the shelves of the local bookshops for more of Howard's work. In the meantime, you start to research and share information with friends. Here's what you learn:

A native of small town Texas, Robert E. Howard (1906-1936) became one of the greatest writers of pulp horror and dark fantasy during an amazingly prolific career that lasted just over ten years – from the first fantasy story he sold at the age of 18 until his sudden and tragic suicide at the age of 30. Howard wrote at a blisteringly fast pace, sometimes staying up all night or even two nights in a row, the incessant clatter of his typewriter keeping his neighbors awake into the wee hours. He let his native talents and his raging subconscious do all the work of myth building for him while he focused on keeping the action lively.

You can sense the writer revealing something of his savage vision already in the opening paragraph of that first professional story, "Spear and Fang" (*Weird Tales*, July 1925). Describing a primitive man named Ga-nor painting a mammoth on the wall of a cave, Howard writes, "With a piece of flint he scratched the outline and then with a twig dipped in ocher paint completed the figure. The result was crude, but gave evidence of real artistic genius, struggling for expression" (*Shadow Kingdoms*, 12). Not surprisingly, "Spear and Fang" recounts a violent struggle between its artist-hero and a brutal Neanderthal who has kidnapped a beautiful woman. The hero triumphs in battle and wins the girl. It's a tale as old as that cave painting, but Howard brings it vividly to life.

Sharply intelligent and remarkably well read despite relatively little schooling, Howard encountered at a young age many of the works that would most influence his own writing in the coming years. He devoured adventure stories by Jack London (especially *The Star Rover*) and Rudyard Kipling (particularly *The Jungle Books*) as well as steeping himself in the historical volumes and collections of mythology (such as Lewis Spence's *Atlantis in America*) that would weave their strands into his own worlds of intense

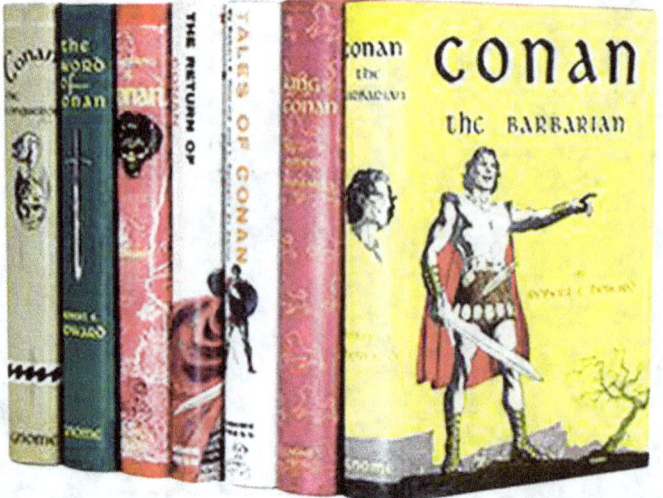

savagery and endless war.

Howard knew Shakespeare and the other classic writers well and could apparently memorize long passages of verse after only a few readings. Still, his formal studies ended pretty much with high school and his early twenties mostly found him working trivial jobs until he started making regular professional sales to *Weird Tales* and other pulp magazines. He developed a long friendship with H.P. Lovecraft, becoming an active member of the "Lovecraft Circle," a collective of like-minded authors who discussed their work largely through correspondence. Sadly, Lovecraft and Howard never met face-to-face, but doubtless Lovecraft's generous praise and lively engagement provided the young Howard with a great deal of encouragement for his writing even while the two argued over a wide range of topics in their letters. It was through this circle that he earned his nickname "Two-Gun Bob." For those with more than a passing interest in this correspondence, editors S.T. Joshi, Rusty Burke and David E. Schultz have collected the whole works into a two-volume set from Hippocampus Press called *A Means to Freedom: The Letters of H.P. Lovecraft and Robert E. Howard* (2011). In fact, this trio of scholars – Joshi, Burke and Schultz – have done, individually and collectively, a great deal of excellent work related not only to Howard but to Lovecraft, Clark Ashton Smith, Ambrose Bierce and others in the weird fiction realm.

Later strong influences on Howard's writing include the romantic fantasy novels of James Branch Cabell. Howard had a particular enthusiasm for Cabell's *Something About Eve* (1927), an admiration that reveals much about Howard's own portrayals of women. As the authors of *Dark Valley Destiny: A Life of Robert E. Howard* (1983) explain, "What most appealed to Robert Howard was Cabell's classification of women into the Evadne type, the dangerous vampire or enchantress, and the Maya type, the 'good wife,' who spiderlike traps men in a sticky web of domesticity" (221). While Howard's work remains undeniably sexist and quite often racist, such observations are too obvious to be more than mundane. Howard's dark fantasy taps into a male adolescent view of the world that is all throbbing red blood and raging testosterone. Because his writing does not function in the manner of realist fiction (though it borrows some of realism's tools) any ignorance or bigotry Howard seems to betray in his stories must finally be understood merely as the unfortunate by-products of archetypal fantasy.

While De Camp offers a nice overview of Howard's career, as well as a few critical insights, such as the above summation of the pulp author's main female archetypes, Mark Finn's recent *Blood & Thunder* (2006) offers a better and more recent biography of Howard. It not only includes an excellent introduction by Joe R. Lansdale but also serves as something of a corrective to the superficial treatment provided in De Camp's biography. For whatever good he may have done to enhance Howard's reputation and ensure his ongoing publication and enduring appreciation by future generations, De Camp has long been criticized by those who have see more than a little cynical manipulation in his financial control of Howard copyrights.

With the publication of "Red Shadows" in the August,

1928 issue of *Weird Tales*, Howard introduced the first of what would become his trademark sword and sorcery stories with epic, larger than life heroes. Set in the imaginary wilds of West Africa and originally titled "Solomon Kane," this story introduces that holy warrior, but it also signals the arrival of Howard's characteristic style of long, poetic sentences, alliterative phrases, dramatic action verbs and well-turned metaphors. Consider this description of Kane:

> All his life he had roamed about the world aiding the weak and fighting oppression, he neither knew nor questioned why. That was his obsession, his driving force of life. Cruelty and tyranny to the weak sent a red blaze of fury, fierce and lasting, through his soul. When the full flame of his hatred was wakened and loosed, there was no rest for him until his vengeance had been fulfilled to the uttermost. If he thought of it at all, he considered himself a fulfiller of God's judgment, a vessel of wrath to be emptied upon the souls of the unrighteous. Yet in the full sense of the word Solomon Kane was not wholly a Puritan, though he thought of himself as such.

There is a desperate and driving pulse to Howard's characterization here. Yes, the poetic cadence of his prose is reminiscent of his influences, but it also carries a quality entirely its own, a hot-bloodedness that few of Howard's heirs and imitators have fully captured in their own writing. Howard continued Kane's adventures in "Skulls in the Stars," "Rattle of Bones" and three more stories published in the pages of *Weird Tales* during the next few years. Kane is also featured in a couple more stories, a handful of fragments, and several poems – all of these published posthumously.

In the 1970s and '80s, Marvel Comics printed a number of comic books featuring Kane, and in the last few years Dark Horse Comics has taken up the mantle by issuing several Solomon Kane mini-series. In 2009's dark film adaptation, Michael J. Bassett delivers a rousingly violent and period-capturing portrayal of the fighting Puritan. James Purefoy gives the lead role a dirty and dangerous turn, sneeringly delivering the central ethos of Solomon Kane: "If I kill you, I am bound for Hell. It is a price I shall gladly pay." Much stylishly bloody swordplay and dramatic firing of cap and ball pistols ensues. It's a good film if not a great one, but at last Solomon Kane has found his way onto the big screen.

Robert E. Howard experimented with several other larger-than-life heroes during the next few years of his writing career, penning stories about King Kull and Bran Mak Morn, but in 1932 he wrote and published "The Phoenix and the Sword" (December 1932, *Weird Tales*), the first of his tales featuring Conan the Cimmerian. Perhaps sensing that he had finally hit upon the ultimate character to express what he had been relentlessly pursuing for years, Howard found Conan absorbing his imagination in a way that no other character had down before. In a letter to Clark Ashton Smith dated December 14, 1933, Howard wrote:

> For weeks I did nothing but write the adventures of Conan. The character took complete possession of my mind and crowded out everything else in the way of story-writing. When I deliberately tried to write something else, I couldn't do it. (quoted in *Dark Valley Destiny*, 267)

Once Conan took hold of his mind, Howard cranked up his already furious rate of production, publishing five more Conan stories in 1933, another six in 1934, and three more in 1935. In December 1935 Weird Tales printed the first of five installments that would make up "The Hour of the Dragon," later collected and published as a novel called *Conan the Conqueror*. The next year, Weird Tales published "Red Nails" in three installments, beginning in July 1936, the month of Howard's sudden suicide upon learning that his chronically ill mother would not recover from her coma. Mother and son were buried on the same day in a dual funeral. The last two portions of "Red Nails" were published in the August and September numbers of *Weird Tales*.

In later years, De Camp and Lin Carter would revise or complete a number of fragmentary Conan tales that Howard left unfinished at the time of his death. Since that time, more than a few other authors have tried their hands

THE DARK MAN AND OTHERS

ROBERT E. HOWARD

utpatel

at Conan tales and novels, most notably Steve Perry, Andrew J. Offutt, John Maddox Roberts, and Karl Edward Wagner. Both Harry Turtledove and Robert Jordan also wrote Conan pastiches, though they remain better known for their own work. Jordan wrote seven Conan novels, including the novelization of the *Conan the Destroyer* (1984), the second Conan movie starring Schwarzenegger. Notably, Jordan also compiled *A Conan Chronology* (1987) that catalogued all the published works set in the Conan universe up to that point. Already impressive, the list of works featuring Howard's heroic Cimmerian has continually expanded since that time.

Howard's quintessential creation of Conan, the king of kings in the sword and sorcery genre, continues to reign supreme in dark fantasy. The potent cinematic duo of *Conan the Barbarian* (1982) and *Conan the Destroyer* (1984) not only brought the character and his world to life in a way that readers of the stories and comic book could only fantasize about before, but they established Arnold Schwarzenegger, a relatively unknown Austrian body-builder, as a legitimate Hollywood star. However campy and dated the films may seem in retrospect – especially the second one, directed by Richard Fleisher with supporting roles played by Wilt Chamberlain and Grace Jones – they did serve to show that sword and sorcery could be a box-office draw for mainstream audiences. And they did so mostly by trying to keep the scripts faithful to Howard's writing. Oliver Stone's original script for the first film was based on "Black Colossus" and "A Witch Shall Be Born." After Stone left the project, John Milius took over directorial duties and revised the script to include more elements of Japanese samurai films such as Kobayashi's *Kwaidan* and Kurosawa's *Seven Samurai*, but he retained several scenes that Stone adapted closely from Howard's stories.

Red Sonja (1985), with Brigette Nielsen in the title role and Schwarzenegger reprising his Conan, was the third entry in this 1980s Conan series. Also directed by Fleisher, this film suffered from bad reviews and poor box-office returns. The film was so bad that it was nominated for several Golden Raspberry Awards, and its own stars turned to disparaging it publically. Fortunately for Schwarzenegger, other commitments prevented him from starring in the next planned film *Conan the Conqueror*, and after years of development problems its abysmal script was finally turned into the entirely forgettable *Kull the Conqueror* (1997), starring Kevin Sorbo and Tia Carrere.

In 2011, *Conan the Barbarian* got a cinematic re-boot with a slick hack-and-slash epic in the vein of *Gladiator* and *The 300*. Directed by Marcus Nispel and starring Jason Momoa, the film suffered from a lukewarm box-office reception and garnered mostly negative reviews, largely based on its lack of character depth. Still, some reviewers admitted to enjoying the CGI gore-fest, and even at its worst the film remains more watchable than many action films.

Indeed, Conan remains one of the great gifts Howard bestowed upon the world during his too-brief career. Whether you manage to locate one of those battered old paperbacks or plunk down more serious cash for the reissued collected works of Robert E. Howard in massive and lavishly illustrated volumes, one thing remains the same – when you immerse yourself in this great pulp writer's stories those realms of dark fantasy come vibrantly and violently to life. What more could you want?

As Conan himself says in "Queen of the Black Coast" (1934): "Let me live deep while I live; let me know the rich juices of red meat & stinging wine on my palate, the hot embrace of white arms, the mad exultation of battle when the blue blades flame crimson, and I am content."

FIRST PAPERBACK PUBLICATION
BY ROBERT E. HOWARD
CREATOR OF CONAN
SOLOMON KANE
SKULLS IN THE STARS

THE CASTLE OF THE DEVIL

By Robert E. Howard
and Ramsey Campbell

A rider was singing down the forest trail in the growing twilight, keeping time to his horse's easy jog. He was a tall rangy man, broad of shoulder and deep of chest, with keen restless eyes which seemed at once to challenge and mock.

"Hola!" He drew his horse to a sudden stop and looked down curiously at the man who rose from his seat on a stone beside the road. This man was even taller than the rider—a lean somber man clad in plain dark garments, his features a dark pallor.

"An Englishman? And a Puritan by the cut o' that garb," commented the man on the horse. "I am glad to see a countryman in this outlandish domain, even such a melancholy fellow as you seem. My name is John Silent and I am bound for Genoa."

"I am Solomon Kane," the other answered in a deep measured voice. "I am a wanderer on the face of the earth and have no destination."

John Silent frowned down at the Puritan in puzzlement. The deep cold eyes gazed back at him, unswerving.

"Name of the Devil, man, know you not whither you are bound at the present?"

"Wherever the spirit moves me to go," answered Kane. "Just now I find myself in this wild and desolate country through which I journey, doubtless drawn hither for some purpose yet unknown to me."

Silent sighed and shook his head.

"Mount behind me, man, and we will at least seek some tavern in which to spend the night."

"I would not overtax your steed, good sir, but if you will permit, I will walk along by your side and converse with you, for it is many a month since I have heard good English speech."

As they went slowly down the trail, John Silent still gazed down at the man, noting the stride that was long and cat-like in spite of Kane's lank build, and the long rapier which hung at his hip. Silent's hand instinctively touched the long curved hanger in his own belt.

"Do you mean to tell me that you journey through the countries of the world with no goal in view, caring not where you may be?"

"Sir, what matters it where a man be if he is carrying out God's plan for him?"

"By Jove," swore John Silent, "you are even more waywardthan I, for though I rove the world also, I always have some goal in mind. As now I come from the command ofa troop of soldiery and am going to Genoa to go on boarda ship which sails against the Turkish corsairs. Come withme, friend, and learn to sail the seas."

"I have sailed them and found them to be little to my liking. Many who call themselves honest merchantmen be naught but bloody pirates."

John Silent hid his grin and changed the subject.

"Then, since the spirit has moved you to traverse this land, 'tis like you have found something to your liking herein?"

"No, good sir, I find little here but starving peasants, cruel lords and lawless men. Yet 'tis like that I have done somewhat of good, for only a few hours agone I came upon a wretch who hung on a gallows and cut him down ere his breath had passed from him."

John Silent nearly fell out of his saddle.

"What! You cut down a man from Baron Von Staler's gibbet? Name of the Devil, you will have both our necks in a noose!"

"You should not curse so hotly," Kane reproved mildly. "I know not this Baron Von Staler, but methinks he had hanged a man unjustly. The victim was only a boy and he had a good face."

"And forsooth," said John Silent angrily, "you must risk our lives by saving his worthless one, which was already doomed."

"What else was there to do?" asked Kane with a touch of impatience. "I beg you, vex me no more on the subject but tell me whose castle it is that I see rising above the trees."

"One which you may come to know much more thoroughly if we make not haste," Silent answered grimly. "That is the keep of Baron Von Staler, whose gibbet you robbed, and who is the most powerful lord in the Black Forest. There goes the path which leads up the steep to his door; here is the road we take—the one that leads us quickest and furtherest out of the good Baron's reach."

"Methinks that is the castle which the peasants have spoken to me of," mused Kane. "They call it an unsavory name—the Castle of the Devil. Come, let us look into the matter."

"You mean go up to the castle?" cried Silent, staring.

"Aye, sir. The Baron will scarce refuse two wayfarers a lodging. More, we can ascertain what sort of a man he is. I would like to see this lord who hangs children."

"And if you like him not?" asked Silent sarcastically.

Kane sighed. "It has fallen upon me, now and again in my sojourns through the world, to ease various evil men of their lives. I have a feeling that it will prove thus with the Baron."

"Name of two devils!" swore Silent in amazement. "You speak as if you were a judge on a bench and Baron Von Staler bound helpless before you, instead of being as it is—you but one blade and the Baron surrounded by lusty men-at-arms."

"The right is on my side," said Kane somberly. "And right is mightier than a thousand men-at-arms. But why all this talk? I have not yet seen the Baron, and who am Ito pass judgement unseen. Mayhap the Baron is a righteous man."

Silent shook his head in wonder.

"You are either an inspired maniac, a fool, or the most courageous man in the world!" he laughed suddenly. "Lead on! 'Tis a wild venture that's likely to end in death, but its insanity appeals to me and no man can say that John Silent fails to follow where another man leads!"

"Your speech is wild and Godless," said Kane, "but I begin to like you."

Kane rode along the track that rose between the fir trees, toward the castle. Silent followed on his horse, its hooves clattering on shards of granite. When it threatened to stumble, he dismounted and led the beast.

The path doubled back constantly. Huge ferns made the depths of the forest seem dismal and primeval. Again and again the Puritan thought they had reached the approach to the castle, but always the building mounted higher above the trees, as though striving to rise above the world.

The innumerable firs threshed and groaned softly, like a gathering of mourners. Otherwise the track was heavy with silence, which made their harsh footfalls violent and unnerving.

At last, when even Kane's easy stride was faltering a little, they came in sight of the castle. Their climb had kept pace with the light; here on the granite height it was still not entirely dark. The castle looked one with the rock on which it stood. Granite towers and battlements massed against the gloomily luminous sky.

But Kane was not concerned at that moment with the building. Among the firs beside the track a horse waited silently. Even in the twilight he sensed that there was something wrong with it. Silent made to follow him, but his steed balked, and he had to tether it to a tree.

"Methinks this castle is aptly named the abode of a devil," Kane muttered furiously, gazing at the still horse. It was long dead, and decayed; chains held it standing. But decay could not account for the fact that it had been crudely blinded.

Silent gripped Kane's arm fiercely in his anger. "By the bones of the saints!" he swore. "What kind of monster wounds a poor beast so?"

His violence distracted Kane momentarily. In that moment Kane knew that they were not alone among the trees. Before he could act, several men surrounded them, silent as ghosts. But the men were solid enough, for their sword-points pricked the Englishmen's throats, while one of the swordsmen disarmed them.

The oldest swordsman confronted them. Like the rest, he was tall as Kane. He wore no armor, but was dressed in gray rather drab clothes. He carried only a sword. Beneath his thick gray hair his broad wizened face looked weathered as the granite. His expression seemed less menacing than sadly resigned. "What business have you on the lands of Baron Von Staler?" he demanded in a deep cracked voice.

"Why," Silent replied before Kane could voice his wrath, "we are Englishmen abroad in the Black Forest. Seeing the Baron's castle from afar, we thought he would not refuse two weary travelers hospitality."

The old man scrutinized his eyes, as if he might be using the twilight to obscure the truth. "Perhaps that is so," he said at last. "You must tell your tale to my master."

The men—a dozen of them, Kane counted—sheathed their swords almost noiselessly, but did not return the Englishmen's weapons. They paced their captives stealthily. "Bring the Englishman's horse," the old man told the youngest, a lithe but broad-shouldered youth. "You need not fear," he told Silent, glimpsing his expression. "No harm will befall your steed."

As they reached the courtyard, Kane saw that the castle was overgrown and, in places,

crumbling. It seemed on the edge of ruin, as though relinquishing its shape in order to merge again with the rock. He shivered, not only from the chill of granite that enclosed him. The castle felt to him as though it had lost its soul.

They entered the castle. He observed that the great door was almost soundless. "Please remove your shoes," the old man said.

An Oriental practice, thought Kane. But the man explained, "My master requires quiet. Never raise your voice here, for you would be risking your life."

He led the way into dimness. Kane had never seen an inhabited building so dark. On the walls, a few torches struggled with the shadows. The granite smelled damp as a cave. He sensed that the passage was high, but dank blackness hovered lower than the ceiling. Beside him Silent glanced rapidly about, wary as a trapped beast.

At last they emerged into the main hall. There was more light here, for a great log fire blazed in an immense hearth. On the walls, weapons flickered in a parody of combat, bathed in the glow as though in blood. Among them were the heads of many animals. Firelight panted in their mouths and glared from their dead eyes.

Beside the hearth stood a man dressed in black. He was large-boned, and taller than Kane. He turned to the men as they entered, stooping toward them as though burdened like Atlas. He was bald; his face seemed pared down to skin and massive bone. "There are two strangers with you, Kurt," he said, almost whispering.

"Two Englishmen, Herr Baron," the old man said.

"Englishmen." He lingered over the word as though it were a rare delicacy. "And what is your name, Englishman who moves like a great cat?"

He was staring at Kane; flames filled his eyes. Something about him disturbed Kane; he had dignity and quiet power, yet these qualities seemed spoiled, perhaps turned into cruelty. And there was something else—"My name is Solomon Kane," the Puritan said, remembering to restrain his voice.

"You name yourself with pride, as a man should. And what is your name, strider?"

"John Silent," he said, speaking low.

"Indeed! Well, if you are aptly named, you will be welcome here. But what mission—Hark!"

He had frozen, extending one hand to command silence. Kane could hear nothing except the crepitant song of the fire. The men-at-arms were intent as their master, and hardly breathing. "She is calling, Kurt," the Baron said.

The old man hurried away, up a wide staircase in the further reaches of the hall. The Baron straightened up a little; he looked like a leaning tree whose roots were losing their grip on the earth. The men-at-arms relaxed, but remained silently watching the Englishmen.

"You were speaking of your mission here," the Baron said to Kane, as though it had been the Puritan who had interrupted.

"I have but one mission, wherever Providence may choose to take me," Kane said, in a low voice more intense than any shout. "To seek evil and relieve the world of it."

The Baron stared at him, and Kane was sure that there was something odd about his eyes. "I have not heard a man speak so frankly here for years," he said. "You sound to be a man of honor, Englishman. And has your search of my lands been rewarded?"

Silent made a surreptitious gesture to Kane to take care. Without looking at him, the Baron said, "Control yourself, my silent friend. I believe your companion cannot lie."

He had the measure of Kane, who said, "I found a boy choking on a gibbet in the forest. He was too young to hang so, and I cut him down."

"Indeed? Well, no matter," said the Baron indifferently.

His nonchalance angered Kane. "If his survival is of so little consequence," he demanded, "why was the poor wretch treated so at all?"

"These are my lands. Do not question my laws here!" The Baron's whisper was vicious as a snake's hiss. "And do not think that my laws are so easily flouted," he said ominously.

He turned to the shadows beyond the tide of firelight. "Ah, Kurt." Kane had not heard the old man return, nor any sound that might have hinted at the nature of his task. "Tonight I will dine with my guests," the Baron said.

Then, with a leap of theme that made Kane suspect madness, he demanded of the Puritan: "So you came in search of evil, eh? No other reason? None at all?" His voice sounded both menacing and disturbingly wistful.

"None," Kane said quietly.

"I suppose I must believe you. You will lodge tonight in the Castle Von Staler," he said in a tone that made it unwise to refuse.

Kurt ushered the Englishmen upstairs. Two passages led from the wide landing. One, which was wholly dark, he avoided, and guided them down the second, infrequently lit corridor. He lit torches in brackets outside rooms facing across the corridor, and withdrew.

Though Kane's apartment was crowded with furniture, it was so large as to seem bare. The curtains of the great four-poster were damp and, in places, stained. The tapestries that cloaked the walls were ashen and blurred with dust. Some of the heavy furniture smelled of pine, and seemed in danger of decaying. Two of the men-at-arms entered, bearing logs, and built a fire in the deep hearth. Even the generous flames could not rid the apartment of the sense of decay that pervaded the castle.

Silent appeared, shivering perhaps from the chill of the passage. "By the holy saints, Kane," he muttered, "there's deviltry here. D'ye think as I do, that he has a wench locked up?"

"Aye, mayhap. Or mayhap she has a sickness, and keeps to her rooms."

Silent shook his head and made to speak; then he swore savagely. "Blast the man, he's got me afraid to speak my mind! I feel he can hear me through yon stout wood door!"

They were staring morosely at the fire, and Kane was musing on their ill-defined dilemma, when Kurt announced the Baron's summons. In the hall, the mountainous fire flung shadows behind the long laden table and heavy carved chairs. Counting quickly, Kane saw that places had been set for the Baron, his guests, and the men-at-arms—but for nobody else.

The Baron motioned his guests to sit on either side of him. His eyes were bright, nervous with firelight. At a word, Kurt ushered in the men-at-arms, bearing an entire cooked wild boar. Their stealth made Kane uneasy; apart from Kurt, they seemed to have less presence than specters.

The Baron sampled the meat approvingly. "Well done, Kurt." To his guests he explained: "We have no servants here. They are too loud and too inquisitive."

Kurt filled a plate with choice portions of food and carried it upstairs. "My friends, you are agog to have this mystery solved," the Baron said smiling. "It shall be done. Kurt has taken the plate to the Baroness, who keeps to her rooms."

"Is she unwell?" Kane asked.

"By no means. She is perfect. But none may look upon her."

The bald head turned to Kane, then to Silent. "Those who venture near this castle do so to look upon her perfection," the Baron muttered. "Still, I believe that such is not your mission. It would be ill if it were so, for those who dare must perish. So the youth whom you found on the gibbet learned, as you saw."

Kane was silent, brooding on this unfamiliar evil. His companion said, "But why do you hoard such perfection, Baron, for your eyes alone?"

"Not for these eyes, my friend." Smiling bitterly, the Baron touched his eyes, out of which flames glanced. "They see nothing at all."

For the rest of the meal Kane could hardly bear to look at the bright empty eyes; they seemed soulless as the castle. The Baron chatted throughout the meal, and afterward told them of his hunting exploits, though in a bitter tone. But Kane was constantly aware that he was listening to sounds elsewhere in the castle.

At last he bade Kurt show the Englishmen to their apartments. He stood before the hearth, hands stretched out to the fire, as though the fierce heat might conjure back the sight of the flames. Kurt led the men to their doors, and hesitated. "Do not judge my master too harshly," he said in a whisper they had to strain to hear.

He seemed willing to say more. Kane gestured him into his room, and closed the door carefully. The room was chill, despite the fire; he thrust logs into the flames. "Then tell us what possesses him," he demanded low.

"He was not always as you see him. Once he was a great huntsman. Then one day, chasing a boar, his favorite steed threw him. The fall damaged his brain—it robbed him of his sight. That changed him utterly. You saw what he did to his steed."

Kane remembered the blinded horse, and his face grew hot with fury. "But he has never mistreated us," Kurt said hastily. "Before his ill luck, he was the noblest lord of the Black Forest. While others persecuted the peasants for their beliefs, my master offered them sanctuary on his lands, whatever their creeds, and was willing to protect that sanctuary. We who are loyal to him are some of those men, or their sons. The peasants admire him, or fear him. They know nothing of his blindness."

"And what of the woman who cannot be seen?" Silent demanded. "Is she here from choice, as you are?"

Momentarily the faith in the old man's eyes flickered. "She will come to no harm," he said curtly. Before he could be questioned further, he withdrew.

"Name of the Devil, Kane," Silent mouthed, "there's a prisoner in this castle to be set free, and I'll not sleep until it's done." The parting of his lips made more sound than his whisper. "Are you game to help me?"

"Aye," Kane replied. "But we must be stealthy as shadows."

"I've tracked savages through jungle without their hearing me," his companion said, with a silent laugh.

They eased open the door of the room and crept to the top of the stairs. The Baron sat before the sinking fire, apparently asleep. Otherwise the hall was deserted.

Silent lifted a torch and explored the lightless passage, while Kane returned to the passage from which their apartments opened, to search its depths. Kane's unshod feet had grown almost used to the bare stone. But the dank chill of the reaches of the passage seized him. The doors of the further apartments seemed to have rotted away; the doorways gaped. Within, framed paintings on the walls were black as mud; furniture was overgrown with dust and fungus. The sense of death was claustrophobic here, and he was glad to retreat to his room, having found nothing.

Silent was standing by the fire, as close to the warmth as he could manage. His face looked pale and drawn; his eyes gleamed uneasily. "By God, I heard her," he whispered. "She's there, in a room at the end of that dark corridor. She was singing to herself. I've never heard anything so beautiful, or so lonely."

Kane could see that the incident had disturbed him. But Silent rallied now that his companion had returned. "Pray God her door is not locked," he whispered. "I did not dare to try it, lest the blind one awake. D'ye think we can smuggle her out of this place without wakening him?"

"I think not," the Baron said beyond the door.

His whisper reached into the room like the chill drifting mist. Kane snarled, and leaped for the door. But he fell back, for ten of the Baron's men waited there, swords drawn.

The Baron stood among his men. His vicious smile made one side of his face look palsied; his eyes were dead. "You have taught me a lesson, Solomon Kane," he said softly. "My ears can deceive me. I thought you were a man of honor, not a common thief who preys on men's hospitality." Kane started, ready to match wits with the man if he could. The swords drove him back. "Pray go to your window," the Baron whispered smiling. "I have prepared a spectacle for you."

Beneath the window was an inner courtyard. Dismayed, Kane saw that from the opposite wall dangled a hangman's noose. The Baron appeared in the courtyard. Smiling crookedly, he gestured like a conjurer. At once two men-at-arms dragged a youth into view. It was the boy whom Kane had saved from the gibbet.

"Did I not say that my laws would not be flouted?" The Baron sneered at Kane's gasp of rage. "Why, this fellow was brought back to me before you arrived here."

He gestured the men to begin. They obeyed at once, efficiently. Though the boy struggled and cried out, the noose was quickly about his neck. They hauled on the rope, and he jerked in midair, choking.

"See how he entertains his lord. He sings for me, and dances." The Baron cupped one hand at his ear, the better to hear the choking. "But your crime is greater," he hissed, pointing straight at the Englishmen. "I think you will lose your eyes before you hang. First we must make sure that no gallant knight comes to rescue this criminal," he said, and dragged at the legs of the hanged boy until he died.

When the Baron turned purposely and entered the castle, Kane knew they had no time to plan. "Quickly," he hissed at Silent. Seizing the unburned end of a blazing log from the fire, he rushed at the men in the doorway.

They crowded forward, swords bristling. But the narrowness of the doorway aided him. No more than two men could enter abreast. The first man fell back, clutching his seared face; the second retreated screaming, his hair ablaze.

Both had dropped their swords. Silent seized one weapon, Kane the other—though Kane had to dodge the whistling slash of a blade, which nonetheless chopped flesh from his shoulder. But it was not his sword-arm, and as he rose his sword ripped open the man's torso. The man slumped against the wall, trying to press the wound together as it poured away his life.

Kane had battled his way into the passage. Two blades hacked toward him, and he saved himself only by falling. But his sword bit deep into one man's sword-arm, and while the other was raising his sword to chop Kane down, Kane impaled him through the groin. He caught up the man's fallen sword with his free hand, which still functioned, though painfully.

Silent had reached the corridor now. One of his adversaries tottered back, trying to gasp through his slashed throat. With a two-handed blow he opened the skull of another. "Kane!" he shouted, alerting the Puritan to the rush of the man behind him, his sword poised spearlike. Kane dodged aside, and his sword hacked deep into theman's neck, like an axe into a tree.

Kane dropped his second sword, for his injured arm was exhausted. The floor was slippery with blood, which soaked through to his feet. The feeling maddened him, and made him frantic to be done with the fight. He was disturbedtoo by the fanatical silence of the men. Except for the youth who had screamed, they uttered no sound. The walls resounded with the clash of swords; he would never hear the Baron if the blind man crept behind him.

He whirled. But the man behind him was Kurt, hurrying away down the passage—no doubt to protect his master. The last of the ten was chopping at Silent's blade, trying to break through his guard. Silent knocked the blade aside and thrust his sword into the youth's heart.

"Now to our mission," he said grimly to Kane.

They strode to the top of the stairs. Kurt had not hastened to protect the Baron after all, Kane saw; he was guarding the second corridorthat led to the Baroness' room. The Puritan advanced on him, hoping he would yield; it would grieve him to harm the old man, whose only error was an excess of loyalty.

But the Baron's whisper came hissing upstairs. "Even such indomitable heroes as you will not be able to break down her door. I have the only key."

He stood beside the great hearth. Firelight trembled on the key which he drew into sight by a chain around his neck. No longer was he stooping; he towered like a heroic statue, dwarfing the hearth. A sneer twisted his lips, but his eyes were empty. He had taken a saber from the wall, and brandished it before him.

"If you will not yield up the key willingly," Kane said, "I must take it from you."

The rise of the saber-point was the Baron's only reply. Kane began to descend the stairs. At once the two remaining men-at-arms appeared and rushed at him. But Silent ran his gory blade through one while Kane dispatched the other, who reeled backward down the stairs, practically decapitated.

The Baron's sword-point moved as though questing like a snake. Kane felt uneasy, almost dishonorable, for challenging a blind man. Perhaps he could disarm the Baron at once. He stole forward, sword poised—and had to leap back, for the saber had whipped down, cutting flesh from his sword-arm.

He had thought the Baron might hear his approach, but never that his perception could be so accurate. He had no time to marvel, for the blind man came noiselessly at him, and the saber clanged against his sword with a shock that jarred his arm painfully. Before he could recover, the saber sprang toward his neck. He almost fell as he recoiled, and even so, blood gushed from a new slash in his neck.

He tried to hold his ground and to attack, but could do no more than parry. Feinting helped him not at all, for the Baron ignored such ruses as though he was unaware of them. More disturbingly, he seemed able to anticipate Kane's moves with unnerving accuracy. In his blindness he had developed a sixth sense.

Kane's arm ached from parrying. Again he was forced to retreat, as the saber nicked flesh from his side; had he not fallen back, it would have opened his heart. He observed, as best he might as sweat burned his eyes, that the Baron appeared to be suffering. Though Kane's sword had not touched him, the blind face was clenched and twisted. Yet the violence of his blows did not abate.

But Kane had some purpose in retreating. Beside the staircase, out of sight of Kurt above, Silent waited, sword poised. Kane's retreat would take the Baron within reach. Kane cared little for the ruse—but he had no time for scruples, for the Baron was forcing him back. The blind man's sword-point hissed past his eyes, an inch away. Silent raised his sword, his face purple from holding his breath lest it alert their adversary—and the saber clanged against his blade, slamming it against his jaw and hurling him backward onto the stairs, unconscious.

The Baron's face winced as though he had swallowed poison. But the saber swept viciously at Kane. Taken off guard, the Englishman stumbled against the stairs, and fell. The impact of the fall jarred his sword from his hand. The Baron reared above him and lifted the saber to chop the life from him, wincing again at the clatter of the fallen sword.

At once Kane saw where he was vulnerable. As the Puritan twisted aside beneath the saber, he drew a deep breath and uttered a prolonged savage roar such as might have emerged from the throat of an enormous beast.

The Baron covered his ears with his hands, moaning. He staggered backward, and a chair tripped him. His forehead crashed against the table. Kane seized the fallen saber and advanced on the stunned man. Flickering firelight made the Baron's eyes seem to follow the movements of the blade.

At the top of the stairs Kurt cried, "No, in God's name!"

Despite the anguish in the man's voice, and the throbbing of his own sword-arm, Kane hesitated only for a few moments. But in that time the Baron struggled to his feet and stood gazing foolishly about the hall. What his mishap while hunting had done, this fall had undone. His sight had returned, after a fashion.

He stumbled toward the stairs, clumsily as a drunkard or an infant, ignoring both Kane and the fallen weapons. Uncertain now, Kane let him go, and stooped to examine Silent, who was stunned but whole.

He heard Kurt gasp at the spectacle of the sighted Baron. Then there came sounds of struggle. "No, master," the old man was pleading. "You should rest now. You must grow used to your sight again."

"Stand aside, fool!" Kurt was hurled to the floor. Kane gathered that for some reason, the old man was anxious to prevent his master from seeing the Baroness. He heard the Baron's footsteps floundering down the passage, then the sound of a key fumbling in a lock.

There was a breathless silence. Then the Baron's voice resounded down the passage, cracked and wailing. "Traitors! You have stolen her!"

Kane heard a woman's scream, cut off immediately. Kurt tottered to his feet, sobbing dryly. He was unarmed; the Baron had taken his sword. Before Kane could arm himself and seek upstairs, Kurt had stumbled into the dark passage—but almost at once he emerged, with the sword-point at his throat.

The Baron loomed over him, eyes glaring like ice. "You at least I thought would not betray me," he whispered."But you took her for yourself and put that thing in her place."

Kurt shook his head helplessly but made no sound, not even when the sword thrust between his ribs and sprouted from his back. His hands clutched the Baron's shoulders in what might have been an attack or an embrace. The two men struggled at the edge of the stairs. Still embraced, they crashed the length of the stairs to the hall,
and lay unmoving.

Kane seized a torch and went in search of the woman who had screamed. At the end of the dark passage a door stood open. Soft light flickered within. He dodged into the room, and halted aghast.

It was a woman's apartment. Delicately embroidered tapestries softened the walls; elaborately woven lace was spread over the furniture. But dust paled everything. In a great four-poster, whose hangings were delicately sewn, a woman lay. A widening stain of blood from a sword-thrust covered her breast, like an opening flower.

She was pale, and enormously swollen as a termite queen. Even in life she would hardly have been able to move. Her face was aged, its features scarcely distinguishable amid collapsed fat. A key on a chain was almost hidden between her massive breasts. But at the end of arms like pipes, her hands were small and delicate.

The sense of death, or of suffocating inertia, was most powerful in this room. Kane hurried back to the hall, glad to be free of the lightless passage. The Baron was dead, his spine broken; but Kurt still had breath in him, though his eyes were dimming.

"What else could I do?" the old man faltered. "She was my sister; she had not long been a widow. When the Baron fell blind I brought her here to nurse him. He became obsessed with her voice and her touch. For him she became the most beautiful of all women. When he grew well, he insisted that she stay. Of course it was an honor; but he confined her to her apartment, and she became as you saw. Her mind and her body grew dull. But how could I have told him? What else could I do?"

He seemed to be pleading for reassurance. Kane shook his head sadly, which appeared to satisfythe old man. And so he died.

Silent regained consciousness snarling, and grabbed for his sword. Kane told him what had happened; but he must see for himself. Shortly he returned, his face ashen. They left the castle and its smell of blood, to search for the stables where they found Silent's horse and a steed for Kane. The other horses they set free.

As dawn reached between the firs, illuminating tracks of mist, they rode away. Above them trees closed about the castle, which grew blurred, as though decay were progressing more swiftly now that all life was gone. They were glad to reach the forest trail. They would ride together for a while, until Silent headed for the wide sea, while Kane went wandering again until evil drew him.

(Originally Published in 1978 in Solomon Kane: Skulls in the Stars)

Talking Shop:

Dark Horse Comics' Scott Allie on Robert E. Howard, Hellboy and Abe Sapian

By James R. Beach

Scott Allie is the Editor-in-Chief of Dark Horse Comics, and is coming up on his 19th year with the Oregon-based company. He got into publishing back in college, by getting involved with a defunct imprint and reviving it. **"I started the group because I wanted to get my own writing out there, but both the publishing of books and the writing became equally attractive to me. When I got out of school, all I cared about was getting a job in publishing."** Scott interviewed for a couple of jobs back east but eventually came out west to Portland to look for work. Eventually he hooked up with Glimmer Train Press, who does a literary journal/magazine, and worked into a regular part-time job with them – which he still does on the side. **"I love them personally, I love the magazine and I have fun. I'm their copy-editor and they're a very important part of my life to this day."**

After a short stint with self-publishing comics (including a horror anthology), he crossed paths with some people who worked for Dark Horse. Not long after, he was interviewing for an assistant editor spot and after missing out the first time, he finally landed the job and went right into working on *Hellboy* with Mike Mignola in the fall of 1994. **"That was a real boost for me career-wise. And working with (Mike) Mignola has been *the* most important part of my career. There have definitely been other significant ones, but the work I have done with him has overshadowed most other things."** Hellboy became a very successful franchise for Dark Horse with a large number of comics and books in the series and two successful movies. **"We've grown it from this little book that only the two of us were really paying attention to into a really big seller for Dark Horse."**

He's also worked on the popular *Buffy the Vampire Slayer* series based on the TV show. **"Buffy is like a close second as far as career defining jobs. Everything I feel I**

know about storytelling I've learned from Joss (Whedon) or Mignola. It's been to my great benefit to work directly with them like I have."

How did Scott get started writing for Dark Horse? **"When I started at Dark Horse I was the kid at the front of the office opening packages. Editorial assistant evolved into Assistant Editor and the VP of Publishing asked me to write a series for him that didn't work out, but I did write a short story in Dark Horse presents and that kicked things off."** It's significant because it shows a lot of Scott's influences that came to play in projects as time went on. **"My story was very influenced by the**

old *Weird Tales*. It was an H.P. Lovecraft/Robert Bloch homage. I actually found the older guys through Stephen King. I lived in New England and read his books as a kid. I connected with his work very deeply because it felt like it was set in my town. And that led me to Lovecraft."

For a while now, Scott has been helming a successful series of Robert E. Howard based comics. He's not only done Conan comics, but also Solomon Kane and Kull. Have he and his collaborators stuck close to the source material? "I think that's one of the unique attributes to what we've done. I have to give credit to the Howard estate and also the modern fandom. There's a sense of purism today. Back in the sixties and seventies it made sense that back in Lin Carter's day, you needed guys like that to complete the fragments as I think people didn't really have much interest in that sort of thing. But today there is a resurgence there. People are hungry for the real thing. Imperfect though it may be. We've done our best to stick to what Howard did – expanding on fragments, doing original stories - as well as do a study on what Howard was all about. When we first started the series back in 2002/2003, it had been fallow for about 6 or 7 years. We really tried to stick close to our main influences and that was words Howard wrote and (artist Frank)Frazetta." Why Frazetta in there? "For me to get my head around creating a Conan comic I needed a visual and Frazetta was it. He created an indelible image that hangs over everything that is sword and sorcery and particularly Howard – for me at least."

Were there challenges to doing these comics? "When I started writing Solomon Kane I knew all along that he was eventually going to Africa. And that presented some problems for me with the weird racism in Howard's work. How do you handle that sort of thing without being dishonest? It seems to me, though, that with Howard it was less how his white characters interacted with his black characters and more about how he described the black characters. Even though his main characters were white, Howard did create heroic black characters. And I found that there was some profound truth in that. That a guy who grew up in a small Texas town and probably didn't have much interaction with black people could do that. But I think Howard had a pure attraction to heroism and could see that in anyone."

Dark Horse is also doing reprints along with the newer stuff - much like their successful *Creepy* and *Eerie* revival. "We're doing a number of different books in the Howard series. Some are the newer comics and others are reprints of the older stuff. Savage Sword of Conan is an archival series and we're also reprinting some of the old Kull comics for example. There's a huge audience for the classic, archival works." And the newer works? "Brian Wood is doing some of the brand new graphic novels. *Conan: The Hour of the Dragon* is anew adaptation of the Howard novella. *Queen of the Black Coast* is a long running adaptation of the Howard novella. *Chronicles of Conan* is an archival of the newer Conan comics. With Kane and Kull there have also been reprints as well as new stuff."

There's been a number of great artists and writers working on the Howard series. Who are some of the guys involved? "Brian Wood that I mentioned before is a young, hot writer who is very popular. He's probably about 35 or 40. Made his name in the

independents and also working on X-Men. He's got a ton of integrity and has carved his niche by doing original work. Mike Mignola has done some covers and things and has lent his unique touch. Marvel legend Roy Thomas has been involved. He did a year-long run with Conan with us. Tim Truman and Joe Lansdale did a series together which was pretty Gonzo."

Is the new stuff more popular than the older stuff? Is there one character more popular than the others? "It's all a bit of a different audience and the packaging is a little bit different. With the Kull stuff there's a smaller audience than there is for the Conan stuff. Kull and Kane are pretty similar and Conan is 2-3 times as popular. But with the archival stuff, we're selling to a different type of crowd. The older collector tends to be more interested in that, whereas the newer stuff appeals to both the younger and older audiences."

How does Scott feel the impact has been for the Robert E. Howard based comics? "Keeping Conan alive and vital is really important work. In 2003 or so when I was involved in launching the first Conan comics, we did really well. It sold well, we won awards and it felt really good to be part of a thing that was so unique when it launched. It changed genre fiction in my opinion. Howard changed it in a huge way."

Does it satisfy Scott's interests in the darker stuff? "I've been a horror geek my whole life. There have been some movies and other things have worked for me outside of it, but for the most part I just want monsters." Is Howard's writing horror? "When I started getting into Howard I asked myself that. His writing is fantasy overall, but it's really horror/adventure I think. Most of the dark fantasy stuff has a romantic bend to it. Howard's stuff is dark and grim and scary. You have these protagonists running around fighting monsters. And there's moral ambiguity."

What else is going on for Scott at Dark Horse? "The *Abe Sapien* series is very big for me now that I'm doing with Mignola. Hellboy left the *B.P.R.D.* (Bureau of Paranormal Research and Defense) in 2001 and it continued without him. The characters go through various changes. We're not afraid to kill off major characters and radically change things. About a year ago the end of the world happened. Hellboy got killed off and things started going very badly. Abe Sapien got shot by a young woman and they put him into

a water tank to keep him alive and he started to transform. Then he woke up and he finds out the world is completely going to hell. You've got Lovecraftian monsters and all sorts of stuff going on. I get to take Abe across the country trying to figure out what's going on getting involved in one crazy thing after another. It's sort of like *The Incredible Hulk*. It's kind of like *The Hitchhiker*. You're going to see some big Monster stories, some Zombie stories, some Mayan mythology. It's a lot of fun. It's honestly my dream book."

Sounds very cool! Any last words? "I had a conversation with Gahan Wilson one time when he was doing an intro for *Hellboy*. He told me about meeting some of the real old guys back in the 1970s. I said it's amazing how you grew up reading those guys, then met some of those guys and passed the torch on to others. Through your work and guys like Stephen King, I was led back to Lovecraft and earlier artists. You were able to take your influences and push that forward. And he said to me 'Yeah, and now you're doing the same thing.'"

KARL EDWARD WAGNER

By Aaron J. French

Many good editors and authors do not receive the credit they deserve. All too often good fiction and book publishing slips through the mainstream's cracks.For those in the horror world and in the word of the small presses, this is a familiar scenario. Whatever the reason (well there are, in fact, *many* reasons), the struggle to break into popular culture—to be *canonized*, as it were—is the most daunting task a writer or artist can undertake. In the case of horror, I'm willing to bet I can count the number of authors/artists who've succeeded in doing this on both hands. The rest become, sadly, something like ghosts haunting the aisles.

And this is where we come to find Karl Edward Wagner. I'm not approaching this article as *"someone in the know."* Fans and practitioners of horror and fantasy will be familiar with Wagner's work—and not only familiar, but reverent. The recent "A Book of Horrors" edited by Stephen Jones, a project attempting to bring horror back into mainstream light, was dedicated to Wagner. And the man is fondly remembered by those who worked with him, and his stories are often anthologized. But mention his name to someone on the street, someone who is not a horror bibliophile, and I suspect you'll draw blank gazes. So this is written with them in mind.

Casual Reader, this is what you need to know:

Karl Edward Wagner was born on December 12, 1945, in Knoxville, Tennessee to Aubrey J. Wagner and Dorothea Huber. As a boy he was (and remained) an avid reader, obsessed with the pulps, and he would later go on to accumulate a sizable library of that material. Although he earned a psychiatry degree from University of North Carolina-Chapel Hill he eventually abandoned his medical career to focus on what he considered his legitimate career—writing.

With the birth of the "sword &sorcery" genre in the 1960s, Karl's first novel *Darkness Weaves with Many Shades* found publication in an abridged and altered form in 1970 by West Coast porn imprint Powell Publications (text was later restored and reprinted in 1978). This book was the public's first introduction to one of Wagner's many well-known creations—Kane, a version of Robert E. Howard's *Conan the Barbarian* redrawn with a rich, mystical, biblical background and granted more intellectual cunning. With Kane, Wagner married the brains and brawn duality and forged one of the most memorable characters in sword & sorcery fiction. He completed several books using this character, and even went on to write an actual Conan novel, *The Road of Kings*(1979), as well as *Legion from the Shadows* (1976) which was based on another of REH's creations—Bran Mak Morn.

In addition to fantasy writing Wagner did a significant amount of editing, anthologizing, and short horror fiction. He edited three volumes of Robert E. Howard's original Conan tales, restoring them to their original, unaltered form, and his own anthology series of weird fantasy fiction, *Echoes of Valor*. This series featured some restored versions of the pulp-era fantasy tales; authors included Fritz Leiber, C. L. Moore, Ray Bradbury, Henry Kuttner, Forest J. Ackerman, Nictzin Dyalhis, and Manly Wade Wellman.

Incidentally, Wagner became close friends with Wellman, and later on when he started his own small press during the 1970s, Carcosa (which produced only a handful of books), Wagner published two of Wellman's collections, *Worse Things Waiting* and *Lonely Vigils*. But unfortunately Carcosa's vision of replacing Arkham House was never fully realized, and the imprint was forced to close its doors prematurely.

But Wagner excelled at his editing work, and although he never produced a horror novel, he did produce a lot of books for the horror community, namely the acclaimed *Year's Best Horror Stories*. Wagner took over the series from Gerald W. Page in 1980 and continued it right up to his death in 1994 (volumes 8-22), at which point the series was discontinued. Some of the most exceptional horror fiction of the '80s and early '90s was reprinted in these volumes and Wagner did a tremendous service to young writers by targeting small presses and attempting to discover and nurture new talent.

But personally, the aspect I enjoy most about Wagner's career is his short horror stories. Over the years, Wagner penned close to 50 of these, and their theme, content, and style is across the board: a testament to Wagner's versatility as a writer. It's a shame he never composed a fully orchestrated horror novel; his career might have jumped a step closer to commercial success if he had; but among horror and fantasy fans, his short fiction is stuff of legends.

I'm only going to mention three of these, in order to illustrate the vast scope of Wagner's writing style. The first, and perhaps the most well-known, is "Sticks." The story was first published in the March 1974 issue of *Whispers*, then reprinted in Stuart David Schiff's excellent anthology of the same name. The bizarre lattices of twigs in the tale were inspired by the work of *Weird Tales* artist Lee Brown Coye—who also illustrated Manly Wade Wellman's two Carcosa volumes that Wagner edited.

"Sticks" also earned an August Derleth Award by the British Fantasy Society.

The story centers on an artist, Colin Leverett, who comes across a series of bizarre stick bundles and lattices scattered around a particularly feral section of wilderness. Leverett follows the sticks to a ruinous house and ventures inside, discovering an altar in the basement where old ritual practices had been performed. Incidentally *The Blair Witch Project* follows the basic plot of "Sticks" and this story remains one of the unsung inspirations for that popular film.

"The Slug" (1991) first appeared in Ellen Datlow's *A Whisper of Blood,* and now Wagner in a more humorous, less Lovecraftian style paints the horribly tragic, while amusing, portrait of a struggling writer named Keenan Bauduret who is harassed on a daily basis by a noisy overweight visitor. As his work starts to suffer, Keenan becomes convinced that his visitor is a slug who will not leave him alone, and who is sucking the creative energies out of him. At last Keenan decides to kill the slug, and he does so by pouring copious amounts of salt over him. This tale has more of a psychological bent, and it reveals the suffering tendency of the artist who is ever pressed for his time and inspiration.

Finally, "The Kind Men Like" (1991) appeared first in *Hotter Blood* edited by Jeff Gelb and Michael Garret, and was reprinted by Windling and Datlow in their *The Year's Best Fantasy and Horror* (volume 5). Wager displays a much more extreme style here, penning a tale that would be at home among the splatterpunk enthusiasts. I won't go too much into it, save to say that the main character becomes an inverted, dildo-stuffed, leather-bound cocoon during the climax.

It's no question that Wagner's short horror stories are a treat, but while they have been collected several times, they are still not readily available to the reading public. Some of these collections currently go for as much as $200 on Amazon. Not to suggest they aren't worth every penny, but readers trying to get their hands on some of these tales will be hard pressed. Just to mention the most relevant editions here: *In a Lonely Place* (1983), *Why Not You and I?* (1987), and the posthumous *Exorcisms and Ecstasies* (1997) edited byStephen Jones. Centipede Press recently brought out *Masters of the Weird Tale: Karl Edward Wagner*, *Where the Summer Ends*, and *Walk on the Wild Side*—all beautiful editions. Wagner also collaborated with well-known fantasy and science fiction author Drake on *Killer*, a science fiction horror novel set during the Roman times.

Karl Edward Wagner was 49 when he died in 1994, thought to be the result of a lifelong struggle with alcoholism. While he was never fully accepted by the mainstream reading public—like King, Koontz, and Straub—his influence and legacy in the horror and fantasy communities remains very active, and his fiction and editing work endure as testament to his craft.

If you haven't familiarized yourself with Wagner's worlds and characters, you truly are missing out. If you require further convincing, then I leave you with these words from some of Karl's longtime friends and colleagues.

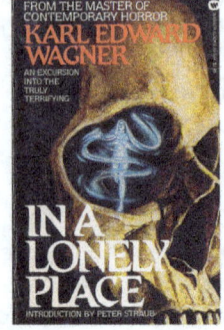  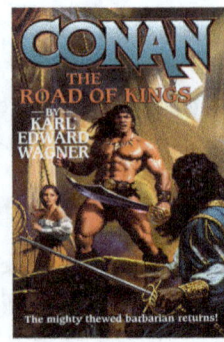

"I met Karl and Manly Wade Wellman in 1971. I'd been selling for five years; Karl had been selling for three; and Manly had been selling since the 1920s.

Karl and I weren't Manly's students, but we gained enormously from knowing him and simply from knowing one another. All three of us wrote very different things, even when we were in the same sub-genre. (Compare Manly's *These Doth the Lord Hate* with Karl's *Sticks* and my *Firefight*.) Knowing other writers, chatting with other writers over dinner, and just friendship were very important.

I'd like to think that Manly gained something as a writer from us as we certainly gained from him."

—David Drake, author of the *Hammer's Slammers* series

"When I was in college, in the late 1970s, I started reading Karl Edward Wagner—specifically his early Conan and Bran Mak Morn work—and was quite taken with it. Some years later, I got acquainted with him through *Deathrealm*; he regularly contributed a column called 'The View From Carcosa', which really was one of the most original and engrossing features the magazine ever ran. I found it a rare pleasure to share a few drinks and shoot the shit with him. You never knew when he would be subdued and soft-spoken or as sharp-tongued as Kane, his most famous creation. I loved his short stories, and I remember him reading an early draft of 'At First Just Ghostly' at a local con, which really gave me a charge; it certainly fired up my desire to write. Of course, sadly, he departed way, way too early. I do think of him often."

—Stephen Mark Rainey, author of *The Monarchs*

"Despite being a self-taught writer, Karl was a stylist, first and foremost. His fantasy and horror fiction was often more brutal, more sexy and also more subtle than the genres had been used to up to that time. His characters were fully formed on the page, and his plots took both those genres into areas that other writers had not previously explored.

He was one of a number of writers and editors who was consciously pushing the boundaries of the genre in the 1980s. He was a maverick, an iconoclast, who wasn't afraid to bite the (publishing) hand that fed him.

Karl would never put up with second-best. He genuinely loved and respected the genre he worked in, and he did not suffer fools gladly. That's what made him different—he lived and worked on the edge: his writing was classy and dangerous, and he didn't care what other people thought. That's what I love and miss about him."

—Stephen Jones, editor of *The Mammoth Book of Best New Horror*

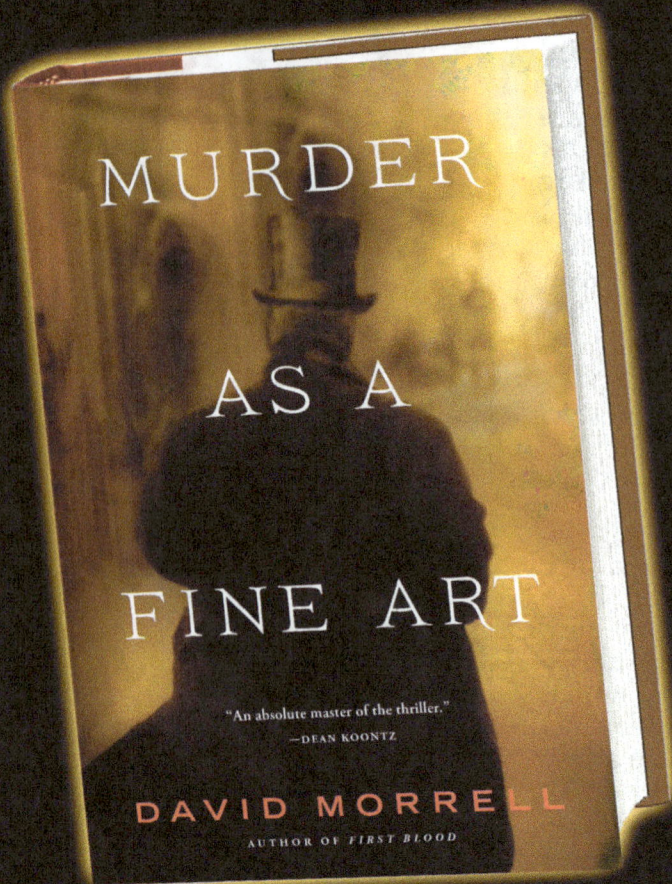

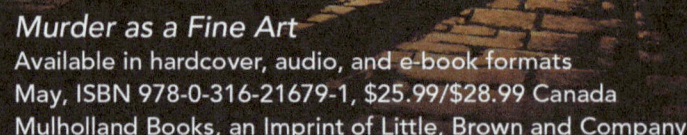

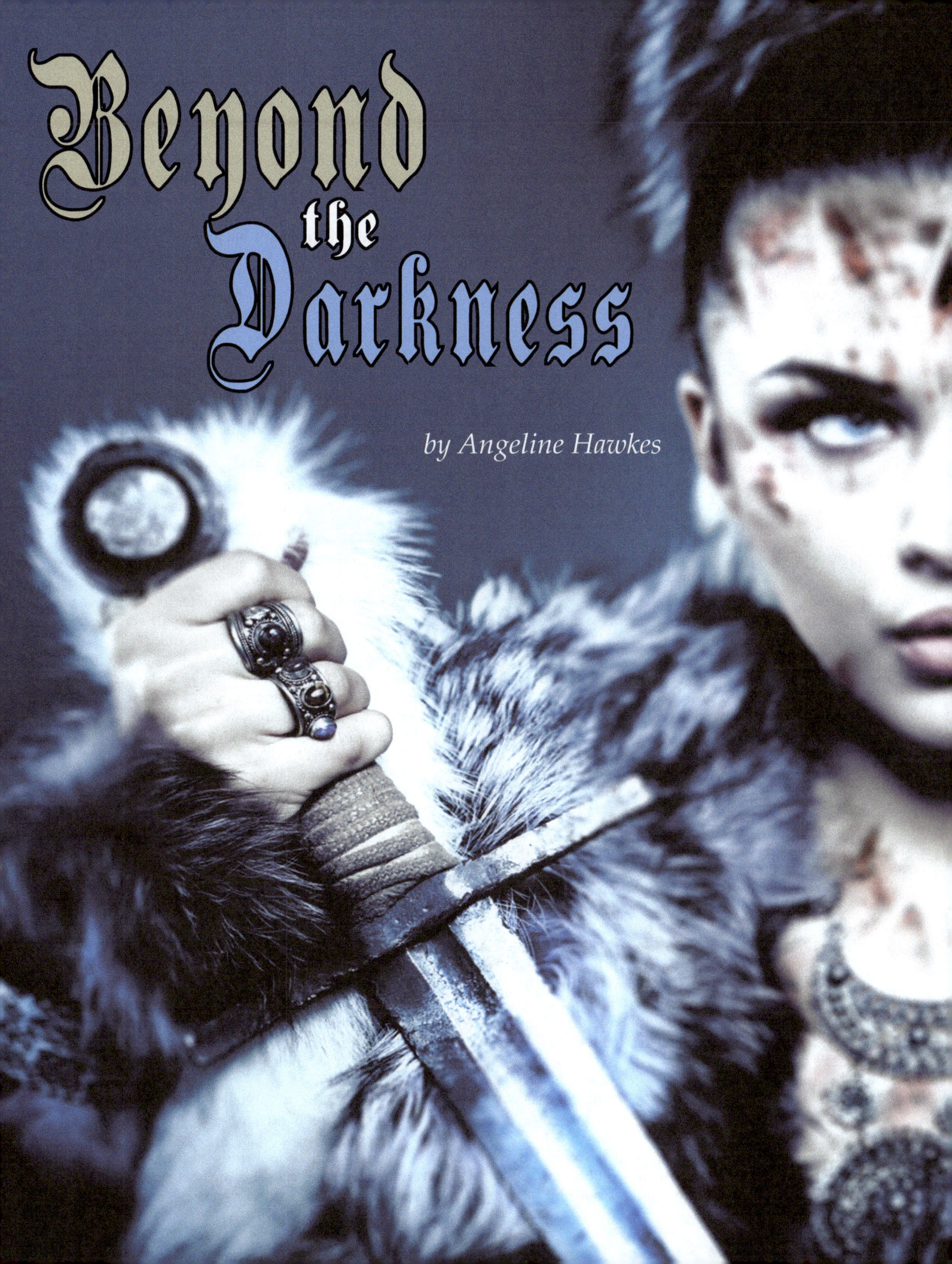

Beyond the Darkness

the

Darkness

by Angeline Hawkes

The warrior Adina stood before the stone fireplace with her back toward the great hall. She heard the approaching footsteps of King Shaddon, but did not turn around. He was not her king and she had little use for protocol here in the wilds of Woldenstag. Leaning against the stone with one arm, Adina pushed her fur robes behind her as she studied the dancing flames – waiting for Shaddon to speak.

He cleared his throat. "Perhaps, you are unaware of who stands behind you?"

Adina slid a hand to her sword hilt beneath her furs, but still did not turn around. "I am aware of everything that happens within the walls of Woldenstag, Shaddon. I've been waiting for you. Your messenger arrived earlier." Slowly, she turned to face the battle-weary, aging king. "I trust your ride was uneventful?"

"It was," he answered. "If my messenger has already arrived, then you know that I seek the help of your husband, Kabar?"

"He is not here." Adina walked to a leather chair, and waved to the other seat opposite her for Shaddon to sit.

He sat in the chair offered and tried to conceal his growing aggravation. "What do you mean Kabar is not here?"

"Exactly that. My husband is in Ur at his mother's bidding. I'm permitted to act in his stead."

"You?" Shaddon laughed. "Surely, you don't expect me to believe the tales of your abilities? You're nothing but a pampered princess in barbarian furs."

"I don't know what you have or haven't heard, but if it's a princess you expect here, your sources are gravely mistaken. Whether you believe this or that is of no concern to me. It is not my brother languishing in Queen Summu-ramat's dungeon. If he dies, the tears shed for his demise will not be mine."

"Hmpf."

"When is the last time you held a sword, old man?" Adina waved to a servant standing in the shadows and wine was swiftly poured. She took the wood goblet from the tray and drank deeply, watching Shaddon over the cup's rim.

"I—"

"The Festival of Moons comes swiftly. You and I both know that the vile harlot Summu-ramat will ravage and sacrifice your brother on her bed of stone exactly on schedule. Ishtar waits for no hero. What was it your brother Korsas did to catch Nineveh's great slut's eye?"

"He killed twenty-six of her soldiers before capture in the Battle of Berossis." Shaddon's voice sounded weary, full of sorrow.

"She has chosen lesser men."

Shaddon nodded. "He is a great warrior. He deserves a better death than to be raped like a street whore and gutted by Summu-ramat's sorcerer. If only I were twenty years younger—"

"Time comes for us all, Shaddon." Adina's voice was gentle. "Let me help you."

The king scratched his hoary beard and looked around as if Kabar would suddenly appear.

"He isn't here. I can tell you, he'd be insulted to know you doubt me. I am a warrior in my own right. Kabar would not consider me a worthy wife if I were not."

Shaddon exhaled. "I have no more time and no one else to help me. I see no other options but you."

"Good. Now that that's settled, what do you know that will help me secure your brother?" Adina beckoned the waiting servant, whispered into his ear, and the man hurriedly left.

"Where's he off then?"

"Preparing my mount. I plan to ride immediately. Ishtar's Festival of Moons will be soon upon us. Korsas is running out of time."

Shaddon drank his wine. "Summu-ramat's fortress is carved, on one side, into the craggy cliffs. The grandson of a stone mason working on the fortress sold me a map of an entrance known only to him, his father and grandfather before him." He pulled a leather tube from his robes and passed it to Adina.

She unwrapped the cylinder and removed a rolled piece of hide. Unfurling the stiff map, she saw a crude inked sketch. "*This* is the map?"

"He was a stone-cutter, not a cartographer," Shaddon snapped. "The tunnel takes you into the fortress. That slut of a queen has a sorcerer, Utu-nah, an ancient wielder of black magicks. He and his ensorcelled monstrosities guard the dungeons where Korsas is held."

Adina studied the map with a scowl. "How can I be sure the passageway still exists?"

Shaddon shrugged. "There are no assurances. The man who drew this map and his son after him are in their graves. The man who sold me it is at least as old as I am." He put a hand into his robes again and withdrew a heavy purse. "This is for your troubles." The purse clanked as it landed in Adina's lap. "Gold."

She rolled the map, replacing it in the leather cylinder. Then she hefted the weight of Shaddon's purse in one hand. "I will send word to Kabar of my travels and I will leave for Nineveh within one hour. You are welcome at Woldenstag until I return, or I will send word to your palace, whichever pleases you." She stood, taller than most women, and wildly more beautiful.

"May your gods go before you," Shaddon said, and clasped her hand in his. He moved to kiss it, but Adina withdrew.

"My hand soon brings death; surely to kiss it would bring bad fortune. Reserve your kisses for your brother – or his corpse." She turned and walked to the main doors, leading to the outside. "Pray to *your* gods. *Mine* might need their assistance."

(2)

The hot, dusty ride to Nineveh quickly faded from her mind as Adina cupped her hand to her brow and stared upward at the craggy mountainside. The sun beat upon her as she pulled the map from the leather cylinder tied at her belt. Not much had changed in the terrain since the crude map was sketched. There was more vegetation, erosion, and a steeper incline than indicated in the illustration.

She scanned the mountainside for evidence of the tunnel entrance. Clumps of periwinkles grew from crevices, blowing softly in the breeze. According to the map, there should be an abundance of scrubby tamarisks growing tightly together, covering the tunnel entrance. Scanning the rocky ledges, she found a niche in the stone protected by dense Juniper shrubs, tamarisks and other vegetation. The shape of the depression matched the one on the map.

She swung from her saddle and strapped her sword and scabbard to her back. An axe, protected by a leather sheath, was secured to her belt, along with a small waterskin and a purse of smaller items. For the most part it was a simple climb, but if the tunnel proved

not to be where she was assuming it should be, she'd have start again. Adina prayed to her gods, and then began her ascent.

In some places she found she could jump from ledge to ledge, but finally she found herself crawling up the rocks on her belly. When she finally landed on the jutting shelf before the tunnel entrance, her hands were cut and bloody.

"By Shar, this place is accursed!" Adina poured water on her hands and wiped them clean with her tunic. She then took a long drink and turned her attention to the barrier before the entrance. Wiggling between two ancient bushes, she was able to scurry beneath the branches and come out behind. Before her, the dark, narrow passage stretched into the darkness.

She needed a torch. Removing the firestone from her purse, she gathered wood and sat on the rocky ground. It was good to rest her legs while she struggled with the flame. Once she got the fire started, she located a solid, dry branch and ripped fabric strips from her tunic's hem. Adina studied the shadowy entry. The last thing she wanted was to be stuck in a tunnel, feeling her way in the darkness, hoping it led her inside the fortress before she became lost forever. She returned to the small fire, examining the nearby shrubs. Fresh and dried Juniper branches lay

in heaps beneath the bushes. She gathered a cluster and trimmed them even with a knife from her purse. Using the fabric strips she wrapped the Juniper branches near the tops in a bundle.

Once she lit the torch, she would need to move fast. She only had a rough idea how long the passage was and she didn't know how long the flammable Juniper would last.

Taking one last look around, she returned her possessions to her purse, lit the torch, and kicked dirt and rocks over the fire. Without hesitating, she began her journey through the tunnel.

The passage went deep into the mountain. She traversed the steep, downward slant of the path before it leveled again. Her torch sputtered and popped, burning closer to her hand.

Up ahead, several tunnels were obviously aborted, ending in dead ends, but one small opening was straight, and Adina could see a speck of light at the far end. She would have to crawl most of the way.

She stooped to enter the passage, and soon found herself on her hands and knees, holding the torch in front of her. The flame licked dangerously close to her fist. Brown, tarry sap melted and bubbled from the wood, splattering on her flesh. It stung, but she held firm and pushed onward. A gust of wind blew from the nearing opening, sending sparks from the fire to her hand and wrist. Dust and rocks fell from the tunnel ceiling, and Adina froze, fearful of moving lest she cause a cave-in.

Her heart beat wildly as she inched forward, more rocks raining upon her. "By Shar, this tunnel will fall in on itself with me in it!" She quickly scurried onward, eager to get out. Suddenly, a cloud of dirt and dust gusted and rocks and earth filled the tunnel behind her.

Adina choked, wiping dirt from her eyes and nostrils with the back of her hand. The torch was sputtering, suffocating by the dust clouds enveloping her.

"Fire be damned!" she cursed and tossed the torch aside. It quickly extinguished in the rocky debris.

Moving fast, she used the dim light ahead to guide her. As she neared the opening, a wafting fragrance of incense tickled her nose. *The palace!* The perfume spurred her onward, faster than before and soon she found herself looking through an iron grate into a dark, chiseled stairwell that led upward into some chamber in Queen Summuramat's fortress.

A ventilation shaft! That's where she was. She brushed

the dust from the grate's edges and discovered it wasn't bolted. Holding firmly to it, she pushed against it and the grate popped free. She slid it out of the way.

Adina strained to see up the stairs. The ventilation shaft was positioned beneath a large table against the wall. Rusty swords and cast off weaponry were stacked atop the table. From somewhere she heard the drip of water and muffled tones of music, but no voices. Slowly, she crawled from the tunnel, out from under the table, and stood, pulling her sword from the scabbard with a silvered whisper.

Up the stairs she climbed, coming to a heavy door with a barred window. Incense poured through the bars in curling tendrils. She gave the door a push and it creaked on ancient hinges, but swung open.

Harem-chamber or temple, she wasn't sure, but there was a profuse amount of burning incense and it irritated her nose. "Damn Ninevites," she whispered, but cautiously stepped through the door, immediately looking for shelter.

She rushed behind a large vat, and surveyed the room.

A dancing girl, long ebon tresses covering her near-nakedness, lay sprawled on a silken couch in deep slumber. Cast aside, over a satin cushion, lay her satin dimije with gold gilt embroidery – so light and fluttery the billowing pants would feel like wearing air. Beside the dimije lay a jewel-encrusted *choli*.

Adina crept stealthily to the clothing, silently gathering the items, along with the girl's satin shoes, and then made her way out of the chamber. In the corridor on the other side of the incense-fogged room, she ducked into a recess and changed from her clothes into the beautiful dancing ensemble. She affixed her accessories, not willing to leave behind weaponry or the supplies she brought. The map became even less detailed at this point. Simple lines with no other markings directed her from the mountainside tunnel and toward the fortress dungeons. She followed the map as best she could, finally relying on her nose to seek the pungent odor of sweat, filth, feces and death to take her the rest of the way through the dimly-lit corridors and to the piss holes holding Korsas.

Down a flight of stairs she tread, careful to mind her step. Each stair was worn to a dull slant from centuries of use. In places, chunks of stone were missing. The clank of chains and the moan of death throes menaced her ears as she stepped from the last worn stair. Quietly, she moved close to the wall, watching, ever aware of imminent danger. Where were the guards?

Never before had she seen a fortress so unpatrolled. Not a single guard had passed her on her trek through the vile queen's abode. The only creature encountered, beside rats and insects, was the sleeping girl who was none the wiser.

A foul odor smacked her in the face, instinctively causing her to gag. She fought the urge to retch as she covered her mouth and nose, peering into the shadows for the source of the offensive stench. She saw nothing.

Pushing on, she clung to the walls, listening to the sounds around her. The corridor opened into a large square chamber that held a stone table fitted with leg irons. Around the top of the far wall, several barred windows allowed slivered light to pour in. A crudely hewn bench was shoved into a corner beneath one of these windows. Two doors led to chambers unknown, one on the right and one on the left wall. She consulted the map, but neither door was featured. The square chamber was in the illustration though.

She turned around to back track her steps, when the odor blew into the room again. Adina heard shuffling and a hissing sound that reminded her of a basket of snakes. Crouching behind the stone table, she watched the corridor.

A massive creature – hideous to behold, half slithered and half skittered into the room, sniffing the air with seven serpent heads. Adina felt her heart slam into her rib cage. Shaddon had warned her of ensorcelled monstrosities. She reasoned this abomination was why there was no need for soldiers within the queen's walls.

The beast looked like a hydra, but different. Each serpent head had a distinctly human-like quality to it, but yet, when each head moved and flailed, it looked very much the serpent.

The beast exhaled loudly.

"I smell you, human," it said in a booming voice that pounded against Adina's ears. The monster moved about the room. "You can't hide from me. I know every crack in every stone of these walls. I am as old as the foundation, perhaps older. No one leaves or enters this fortress without my knowledge."

Adina knew that was a lie. She had made it this deep into the belly of the fortress without detection.

The creature sniffed the air again. "What do you seek? No one –" It stopped talking. "A *woman?*"

Adina sucked in a sharp breath.

"You are a *woman?*" The monstrosity rumbled with laughter. "Well, never have I encountered a woman thief within these walls. You must be brave indeed."

She watched it slither closer. She remained still, hand ready on the hilt of her sword.

"I am intrigued. Face me, and I might let you live. If you're pleasing to the eye, there are places you can be useful. Death need not come to you if you possess beauty or other – talents." It laughed again. "Come now! I am Lotanis, son of Lotar. I am the guardian of the fortress and the protector of the temple. Show yourself, so I might decide if you should live or die."

The seven serpent heads gyrated through the air, tongues darting from each mouth. When Lotanis breathed, his nostrils wheezed. He moved his body over the uneven stones of the floor, searching for her.

Without warning, one of Lotanis's heads reached behind the stone table and grabbed Adina by the leg of her harem pants. Pulling, the serpent dragged her into the open, while the other heads laughed in mockery.

Lotanis's center head narrowed its eyes and studied her. "There is no way into this fortress without detection. What kind of sorcery do you use?"

Adina swatted at the serpent head clutching the fabric of her pants, but it did not let go. "I'm not a sorceress. I entered through the use of my strength and my wit. It is not my fault if your walls are so easily breached. Perhaps you've gotten too old, Lotanis."

The creature laughed. "Let her go," Lotanis's center head said to the one holding the prisoner.

The head lifted her into the air and let her fall to the floor. Adina stood, brandishing her sword.

"You're no thief. Who are you working for?"

"Is it so hard for you to believe a woman might be working alone?" Adina scooted to the other side of the stone table, trying to put it between her and the serpent-headed monstrosity.

"Working alone for what? What is it you are looking for?" Lotanis asked. "There's no treasure here. This is a military fortress."

Adina inched toward the hallway, sword before her, hoping to outrun Lotanis once out of striking distance of the heads. She grew impatient waiting for Lotanis to make his move. Angrily, Adina slapped the head on the right across the snout with the flat edge of her sword, and lunged for the corridor. Lotanis was agile and fast. The heads struck simultaneously, knocking Adina onto the floor.

She grasped the wall and stood, kicking the striking mouths of the seven serpent heads of Lotanis.

"Now I will have to kill you, you insolent girl!" Lotanis bellowed. The farthest head on the left darted in a blur of motion, grasping Adina by the hair, as another head wrapped its long serpentine neck around her legs.

She brought her sword down in a powerful slash, sending the neck and head entwined with her legs, tumbling to the ground in a spray of gore and crimson. The neck stump went limp. Lotanis flailed his center head and let rip an angry wail. Not waiting for the monster to finish his lament, Adina lashed at the head holding her hair. She cut her own hair, freeing her from the serpent. Falling to the ground, she found her footing, stood and ran through the hall, away from Lotanis.

But, Lotanis was behind her – half slithering in a snaky movement, and half darting like a desert lizard. "You will not escape me, woman! There are horrors within the chambers of this fortress the likes of which you have never even imagined!"

"You're probably wrong about that." Adina leapt upon a bench and jumped toward the iron candelabra hanging over Lotanis. Clinging between the melting candles, she struck another of Lotanis's heads, delivering a deep gash to its throat. Whimpering, it collapsed to one side. Lotanis raged.

Still he came for her. As she tried to devise a killing strategy, another head seized her thigh. The monster sunk sharp fangs into her flesh. Adina sliced the head from the neck with a forceful blow. *How to*

stop it? She pried the mouth from her leg, tossing it to the floor. Blood seeped from the wounds, but she could not afford to pay her injuries any attention.

Lotanis moved closer. She was trapped between the monster and the wall. With one head in the center, two heads on the right and one head on the left, Adina saw no escape. She charged him, ramming her sword deep into the scaly torso, but nothing happened. Quickly, she yanked her sword free, and ducked beneath the one screeching head on the left. Lotanis spun around, as Adina attempted to run away. A head whipped between her legs, knocking one leg out from under her.

She rolled over the floor, jumping to a defensive crouch. Lotanis growled, and came for her again. Adina used one of the writhing heads to the right as a step, and ran up the monster's neck to face Lotanis's center head. The other heads moved in, striking with stinging bites, but at last, Adina's sword found its mark. She lopped off the central head, while shouting a warrior's cry. The head bounced against the soot-besmeared walls, and rolled across the corridor floor. Lotanis dropped to the stones with a heavy thud, and moved no more.

Adina jumped free of the gore-encrusted monster, panting, and wiped her face with the back of her arm. Seizing a torch from the wall, she jogged through the corridor in search of the dungeons. She had wasted enough time. Korsas had precious little left.

(3)

Save for the moans of prisoners, the dungeon was quiet. Flies buzzed through the iron bars over the slits of windows bordering the walls. One long corridor ran alongside a dozen cells. Each cell was strewn with filthy straw, and contained two buckets: one for water and one for waste. Most of the cells were empty, and those occupants Adina saw were in no condition to fight.

She waved her torch toward the iron bars, searching the faces, looking for the warrior that should stand out from the common thieves and ruffians chained to the floor.

She heard a man hiss: "You! Woman! Who do you seek?" He moved within the glow of the torch.

Adina looked him up and down. "From the looks of things, I'd say, you. Are you Korsas, brother to King Shaddon?"

"Well, half-brother."

"Half, full, who really knows who is or isn't their father?" Adina shrugged.

Korsas laughed. "Shaddon sent a *woman* to rescue me?"

"I'll pretend I didn't hear that," Adina said, and looked behind her, surveying the corridor. "Is there a jailer? Does he leave his keys?"

"There are two jailers: one in the morning and one at night. Both keep the keys."

Adina looked into the cell. "Who else is with you?"

"Only the beast."

"Beast? What are you on about?" She tried to shine the light into the shadows of the far corner of the cell. She only made out a dim silhouette.

"His name's Ziz-nei. He's an ancient creature. Summu-ramat has held him captive for many years. Something to do with a curse and as long as Ziz-nei is within the fortress walls, no harm can come to her."

Adina raised her eyebrows. "Is this that bastard of a sorcerer's doing?"

She heard a low growl. "It is written in an ancient prophesy."

"Are you Ziz-nei? Show yourself," Adina said into the darkness.

The shuffle of feet and clank of chains were her answer.

"I can help you," she said.

Ziz-nei laughed. "I am beyond help, but it is good to look about such beauty again."

Korsas laughed too. "My brother – he has good taste, does he not?"

"I haven't introduced myself," Adina said, lowering her voice and pausing to listen to the dungeon. It was still silent. "I'm Adina of Woldenstag."

Korsas let out a low whistle. "The legends are true?"

Adina slipped her knife point into the key hole and wiggled it around. "I don't know what legends those might be, but I do know I am working on a new one today."

"I was a legend once," Ziz-nei said, sorrow heavy in his voice. The creature moved closer, into the golden haze of the torch.

She gasped. Before her stood a gryphon. Ziz-nei had the body of a lion, and the forearms, wings and head of an eagle.

He hung his head. "My wife was also a gryphon. It was foretold that I would bring down the queen. And so, she killed my Tai-nia, leaving me alone for eternity – imprisoned me here in gold chains, so I might never escape. As long as I am captive, no harm can come to the Queen of Nineveh."

"Well, then we'll have to see about getting you out of here. Together we are stronger," Adina said, checking over her shoulder.

"I have a son. My only wish is to look upon him before

dying."

"When does the jailer come?" Adina asked.

Korsas looked to the light coming from the window and to the shadows stretching over the straw-strewn floor. "Soon. The shadows grow long. The day jailer comes once the sun has risen. The night jailer comes as the sun sets."

Adina studied the contents of the cell and glanced around at the other prisoners. "Can they be trusted not to tip off the guard then?"

"Most of them have no tongues left."

"Unfortunate."

"Maybe not for us, so much," Korsas said.

"Ziz-nei: are your talons still sharp? Can you kill a man? Or will if offend your gods?" Adina asked.

Ziz-nei growled a rumbling purr. "My gods would be offended if I did *not* kill a man to gain my freedom. There is no place in this world for the weak of heart."

"When the guard comes, allow him to enter the cell. Don't be startled by anything I do, but be prepared to act," Adina said, and then turned to Korsas. "We must away before Summu-ramat can take your seed and give your heart to Ishtar."

An empty iron sconce was secured on the wall opposite Korsas and Ziz-nei's cell. She dropped the torch into the loop and made her way to the end of the corridor. A small storage recess was carved into the stone wall. Rows of hooks held chains and other implements. She crouched, sword ready, and waited.

The guard entered the corridor as the setting sun's last slivers of purple-hued rays bathed the darkening dungeon. The sky outside was a frosty silver, and the dancing flames of the torch cast an orange tint to the brown straw on the flagstones. Adina peered cautiously around the edge of the niche, watching the jailer's every move.

Holding a bucket of bread over one arm, he looked into every cell, stopping before the one holding Korsas. "You there? I'm to bring you to Utu-nah."

Korsas feigned sleep and snorted, rolling over to face the guard, but not opening his eyes.

"Wake up!"

"He appears to be in slumber," Ziz-nei said in a sleepy voice. "Shut up, monster." The jailer threw a chunk of bread through the bars, and it bounced from the gryphon's head. Ziz-nei said nothing.

"Lazy bastard." He fumbled with his keys and the bucket, and finally unlocked the cell. As he entered the cell, he heard a noise behind him and turned, startled, to see who was there.

Adina stepped from the gathering shadows and into the torch's light – as naked as the day she was born. Sword in hand, she spread her arms, giving the guard full view of her charms. The man dropped the bucket, gawking.

Immediately, Korsas retrieved the bucket and slammed it over the jailer's head. Dazed, the man stumbled, holding his bleeding head, as he was shoved into the waiting arms of Ziz-nei. With a shrill eagle's shriek, the gryphon seized the jailer with his forelimbs, bit into the man's skull, and raked talons across his tender throat. The jailer slumped in a puddle of crimson beneath the form of the gryphon.

Adina brought her sword down over the ensorcelled gold chains the gryphon was powerless to break, and then tossed the keys to Korsas. She threw on her clothing, and eyed the corridor for soldiers. None came. Korsas tossed the keys to a nearby prisoner as he and Ziz-nei followed Adina through the hall.

"I came through a ventilation shaft, but it caved in. We'll need to find an alternate escape," Adina said, pressed against the wall. "Ziz-nei, my friend, do you know of another way?"

"There is a balcony in the chamber of the dancing girls. I can take flight from there. Perhaps you and Korsas can climb down the wall? The fortress is known for its hanging gardens. The outside has a tiered construction. Directly below the balcony is an unmanned gate workers use."

"We will part there. Is the gate ever patrolled?" Adina made her way up the worn stairs, sword ready.

"My information comes from the slop-boy. He changes the straw and removes waste. We used to talk. He said it was unmanned. That is all I know," Ziz-nei said.

The fortress was eerily quiet as the three entered the chamber of the dancing girls.

"Where *is* everyone?" Adina whispered.

"They ready themselves for the Festival of Moons," Ziz-nei hissed.

A balcony was visible behind lengths of silken drapes which fluttered softly on the night's breeze. Adina and Korsas turned to Ziz-nei.

"Farewell, my friend. May your gods go before you," Korsas touched Ziz-nei's shoulder.

"And before yours – and yours as well," he said to them.

The gryphon ran through the marbled chamber and took a flying leap from the balcony, soaring into the ebony night amidst a background of twinkling diamond-stars.

"Shar be with you," Adina whispered. "I hope you're good at climbing," she said to Korsas as they walked to the balcony, eager to be gone.

(4)

Adina sheathed her sword in the scabbard on her back. She grabbed the colorful swathes of silk draping the arch leading to the balcony and pulled them down. "Help me tie these together."

Korsas found the ends. They tied them into tight knots and secured one end around a lion sculpture which was part of the balcony railing. Korsas leaned backward with all of his weight, testing the strength of the silk and the knots. "Grab hold behind and pull with me." They made sure the fabric would hold both their weight at the same time.

"You go down first," Adina said. She gave him her knife. He clutched it in his teeth and held firm to the makeshift rope, slipping over the rail.

Adina watched him descend. Then she hopped onto the rail to follow him.

Someone grabbed her ankle. She shouted and twisted around, leaping to the floor. She heard Korsas call to her, and saw him coming back up the silk drapes.

"I am insulted. I have a guest and there were no introductions." A gnarled man, his beard black shot with silver, stood before her.

Korsas leapt over the railing, knife brandished.

"Oh, and I see you have the queen's new pet with you as well." He glanced in Korsas's direction, but seemed unconcerned.

"She has an ill way of treating her pets," Adina said, pulling her sword free of the scabbard. She stood battle-ready, legs akimbo.

The old man laughed. "So, I have a woman with a sword and a half-starved man with a paring knife. How amusing."

Adina exchanged glances with Korsas.

"Who are you old man?" Korsas demanded.

"Why, I'm Utu-nah. I'm hurt you didn't recognize me." His tone was mocking. He narrowed his eyes and walked closer to Adina, showing no fear for the sword clutched in her hands. "And *you* are Adina."

"How do you know me?" Adina asked, eyeing the balcony and Utu-nah's position.

"The mists tell me," Utu-nah said. "I will take *that*!" He waved his hand suddenly, and Korsas's knife flew from his hand and into the satin cushion on the couch across the room. A swirl of green light glowed from Utu-nah's outstretched hand. Before the pair knew what was coming next, Utu-nah waved his hand once more and Korsas sailed through the air and was pinned against the stone wall, arms outstretched as if ready for crucifixion. Adina kept her gaze focused on the sorcerer.

"Now we have a fair fight, don't you think? A girl with a sword and an old man."

"You're more than an old man, Utu-nah."

He laughed. "So, you *do* know me, eh? Well, now I feel better. I had thought that my reputation might have preceded me. I shuddered to think you had no knowledge of my powers." Utu-nah feigned a shudder and looked at Korsas with a thin-lipped smile.

"Fight me or let us leave," Adina blurted.

Utu-nah snapped his head in her direction, raised his arm, sending her sliding backward, over the floor, up against the wall. A dancing girl sauntered into the chamber, and froze when she saw what was happening.

"Be gone!" Utu-nah shouted. The girl ran from the room.

"Interruptions! Always interruptions! Fight you or let you leave, you say?" Utu-nah laughed. "And, you believe you are in the position to make such demands? I wonder what it is that emboldens you so? Is it – *this*?" He waved his hand and Adina's sword flew through the air, bouncing off the stone very close to Korsas's head. A crimson dot showed on his earlobe, nicked by the flying blade.

Adina yelped, but couldn't move. A loud clatter sounded over the balcony, and Utu-nah lost his concentration. Adina fell to the floor with a dull thud.

The sorcerer ran to the archway. "Are there more of you out in the night? Where are the others? I should have known a lone woman would not be able to let loose a prisoner in Summu-ramat's prisons." He frantically looked over the railing, but saw nothing but darkness.

Adina picked herself from the floor as Utu-nah came back into the chamber. She watched as he raised his arms above his head, chanting: "*See-na-rah-manaha. Ah neij neij, ramaha. Seyana Seyana!*"

The dust in the corners of the room swirled, forming a spiral in the air. Soil from plant urns around the room joined the twisting clouds. Korsas stared at the twirling mass of dirt as more spirals took shape.

Adina counted the masses – four total. The spiraling dust soon took human form, but not of living men. Instead, the dust formed skeletons, animated, standing in a row ready to receive instructions.

"Dust to dust and dust to bone. Bones from the earth spring with life ever-lasting," Utu-nah shouted in a frenzied cry. The skeletons moved jerkily, but then with fluid motion as if alive. Utu-nah waved his hand once more and each skeleton held a gladius, ready to strike.

"Are you feeling so brave now, girl?" Utu-nah formed another ball of emerald light, rotating it, allowing it to hover over his palm. He let the ball fly and it exploded against the wall, narrowly missing Adina. Chunks of stone flew from the crater left behind.

Utu-nah let another ball fly. Adina ducked behind a marble urn. Korsas remained pinned to the wall, defenseless. The green ball exploded against a couch, splintering wood and spraying the floor with gilt and mother of pearl. The skeletons slowly moved toward Adina. Utu-nah didn't want his captives dead yet. He was obviously enjoying playing with them. He grew more agitated with each exploding ball of power.

"Now, I am tired of you, little girl. This one –" Utu-nah jerked his head in Korsas's direction, "I cannot kill. Queen Summu-ramat wishes to have his seed and then send his soul to Ishtar. But, you, *you*, I can purge from this earth." He drew back his hands, over his head, prepared to let loose a blast of magicks.

Adina watched his hands. The emerald glow pulsed from his flesh, and rose like a faint mist from his palm. The ball formed, growing larger, until it hovered over both hands. Then, when Utu-nah lunged forward, Adina ducked and rolled toward a table near the wall. She grabbed a large silver platter, throwing fruit into the air in every direction.

The green power ball burst against the surface of the silver tray, reflecting back toward the sorcerer – engulfing the evil man in a sphere of pulsating green light.

Utu-nah didn't even have time to scream. He evaporated into the air, and as he faded into nothingness the skeletons fell to dust, blowing through the chamber.

Korsas fell to the floor, cursing.

"Let's get out of here!" Adina ran to the balcony; Korsas on her heels. She climbed over, grasped the silk drapes and slithered down quickly, one hand over the other until she felt her feet touch the flagstones of the courtyard. Korsas followed, jumped to the ground and the two of them ran through the unmanned gate.

A narrow strip of land bordered a path winding along the cliffside. In the moonlight, they saw it followed outside the fortress walls and dead-ended. The cliffs on this side of the fortress ensured the walls were protected, eliminating the need for patrols. The only away from the fortress on this side, was straight down the cliffs.

(5)

They worked their way down the mountainside, fortunate that narrow ledges ran like steps close above each other. A few places were precarious, but they soon found themselves at the mid-way point and stopped to rest on a jutting rock formation.

"We should rest here until sunlight," Korsas said.

"The moon is full. There is plenty of light. I don't wish to stay near Nineveh any longer than I have to. We still may not be in the clear. For all we know, we'll get to the bottom of this cliff and Summu-ramat may be waiting for us with her army."

"I –" Korsas began, but was interrupted by a snorting sound. He dropped his voice to a whisper. "Did you hear that?"

Adina listened.

From the ledge above them, she heard a shuffle and sounds that reminded her of a rooting pig. A few rocks rained on them. Adina stared at Korsas. "I smell it." She withdrew her sword. Eyeing the ledge on which they sat, she prayed to Shar they didn't have to fight any of the queen's men in this tight space.

Snort. Snort.

"It's looking for us," Korsas whispered.

"Quickly, let's away down the cliff. Put some distance between whatever is there and us." Adina sheathed her sword and swung her leg over the rocky shelf, looking for safe footing. Korsas followed, retracing her path.

Something squealed and thudded onto the ledge they vacated.

Adina moved quicker now, looking for the fastest way down.

Looking upward, bright in the moonlight, she could see a hideous face with a glistening snout, peering down, sniffing for them. It grunted.

"What *is* that?" Korsas asked, clinging to the rocks.

"One of Utu-nah's ensorcelled creations, I'm sure. Keep moving!"

The beast above leapt to another rock formation, grunting louder. It jumped again. Rocks sprayed Korsas and fell onto Adina's head. She shook off the debris.

"Keep moving!" she hissed.

Bam! The creature bounded onto the jagged shelf protruding beside Korsas, and sprang for his arm, catching it between jutting tusks. Korsas screamed, but held firm to the cliff.

Adina threw a rock at the creature's head, narrowly missing. She scaled down beneath Korsas and tried to find a way to come up closer to the hog-like beast, but there were no protrusions or indentions to make the climb. Korsas tried unsuccessfully to shake off the beast.

The hog-thing shook Korsas's arm, sending blood coursing in thin streams where the teeth penetrated. The creature was toying with him.

"I'm slipping, Adina!" Korsas shouted.

Adina climbed below him, trying to give him a shoulder to put a foot upon, but her fingers were narrowly clinging to the rock.

The thing snorted and squealed, pulling Korsas. Adina could hear Korsas panting, trying to hold on. "I'm going to fall!"

"Hold on! Hold on!" Adina looked frantically for a way to get to the rocky ledge so she could fight the beast with her blade, but the shadows hid her path.

"I can't hold any more!" Korsas's voice was terrified.

Suddenly, a loud shriek like that of an eagle rent the night air. Adina looked toward the pearl of a moon, toward the sound.

"It's Ziz-nei! Hold on, Korsas!" she shouted.

Ziz-nei swooped below Korsas. "Let go, my friend!"

Korsas let go and fell onto the strong lion back of the gryphon. Adina made her way down the craggy cliff as fast as she could, with Ziz-nei hovering close.

"I will land with Korsas and return for you," Ziz-nei said to Adina. Adina continued her descent.

In a matter of minutes, the mighty gryphon returned, and carried Adina to the ground as well. The ensorcelled hog-like monstrosity slowly made its way down the cliffside by way of rocky ledges.

On the ground, Adina found they were not too far from where she had left her mount.

"We thought you were away for home," Adina said, wiping Korsas's blood from Ziz-nei's broad back with fabric from her tattered harem pants.

"I was, but something in my gut told me to return to make sure you cleared the cliff," Ziz-nei said.

"Thank the gods you returned," Korsas said, his tone grim. "It was certain death for me."

"Thank you, Ziz-nei," Adina said, as they found her horse and untied the reins from the tree she left him beside.

"My debt to you is paid. I go to my son, and I pray, your gods go with you," Ziz-nei said. He got a running start and sprang into the air; majestic wings spread wide, soaring through the black clouds.

They watched him for a moment, and then Adina swung up into the saddle. She extended her hand to Korsas, and gave him a yank up. "To Woldenstag!"

The horse bolted homeward, the rock-hewn fortress of Queen Summu-ramat silhouetted, black and sinister, against the illumination of the moon.

A Few Words with Fantasy Artist Boris Vallejo

By Aaron J. French

January 8th, 1941, saw the birth of artist Boris Vallejo in Lima, Peru. The talented boy grew up studying the Fine Arts, winning praise from all of his instructors. He went on to study medicine at university, but quickly became disillusioned with the medical field and left to take an artwork job for an advertising agency. Eventually this prompted him to leave his home country for New York City on September 13, 1964.

Soon after, Vallejo went freelance and started selling covers to Warren Publishing and Skywald Magazine. The Skywald gig introduced him to Sol Brodsky, who helped him secure a job with Marvel Comics, which had him doing covers for *The Savage Sword of Conan* and other professional fantasy magazines.

Vallejo began landing jobs with major publishers and thus began his career as one of the most renowned artists in the fantasy field. To date, he has illustrated hundreds of paperbacks and his cover art is perhaps the most widely known. His art has graced video game packaging, music CD covers, calendars, and even his own coffee table art books.

I recently chatted with Boris for this very special issue of *Dark Discoveries* magazine.

BORIS VALLEJO   PLATE TWO

AJF: Hello, Boris. Thanks for taking the time to sit down with *Dark Discoveries* for a moment. I would like to go back to the beginning, if we could. How did you get started with doing artwork?

BV: I always enjoyed drawing. My mother gave me my first lesson by teaching me how to draw Popeye the Sailor Man. As a child, I did all my drawings on the kitchen walls. Then as a teenager I won an interschool's contest and the prize was a scholarship to study art at the School of Fine Arts in my home country, Peru.

AJF: What were some of your early publications? How did they come about?

BV: While I was studying at the art school, I started doing advertising ads for local stores. Mostly for advertising in movie theaters before the movie would start. Later on, in the US, my first magazine cover was for a comic book, *Eerie*, published by Warren publishing

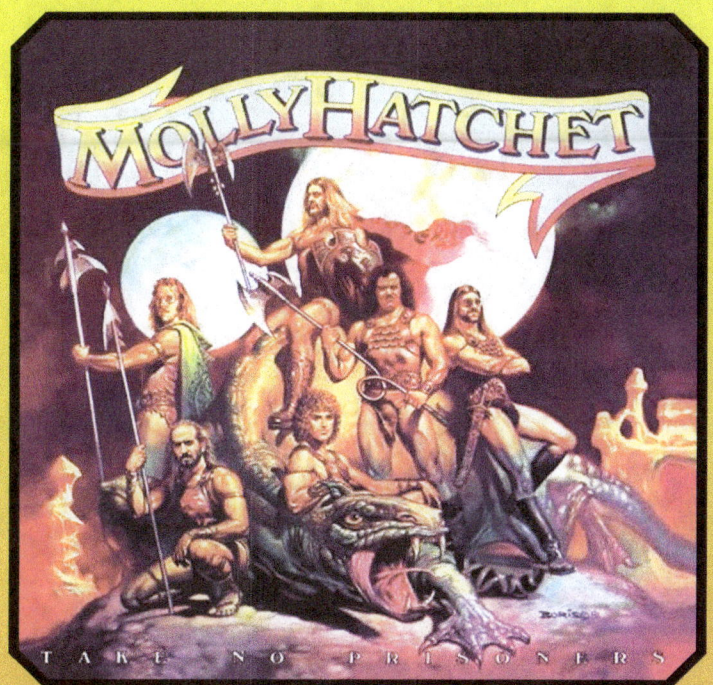

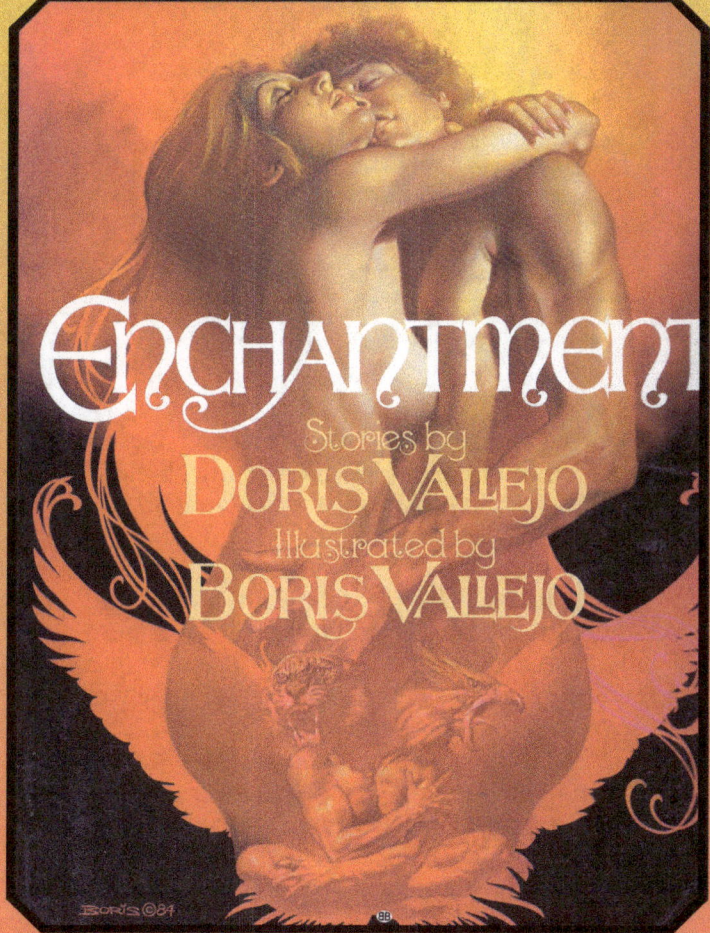

AJF: You've done a large number of book and magazine covers, movie posters, videogame covers and even album covers. I wanted to make sure to touch on how you got involved with doing the album covers for Ozzy Osbourne, Ted Nugent, Molly Hatchet, Flotsam and Jetsam, etc.?

BV: Well, the same way I get any other job. The people involved contacted me and we went from there.

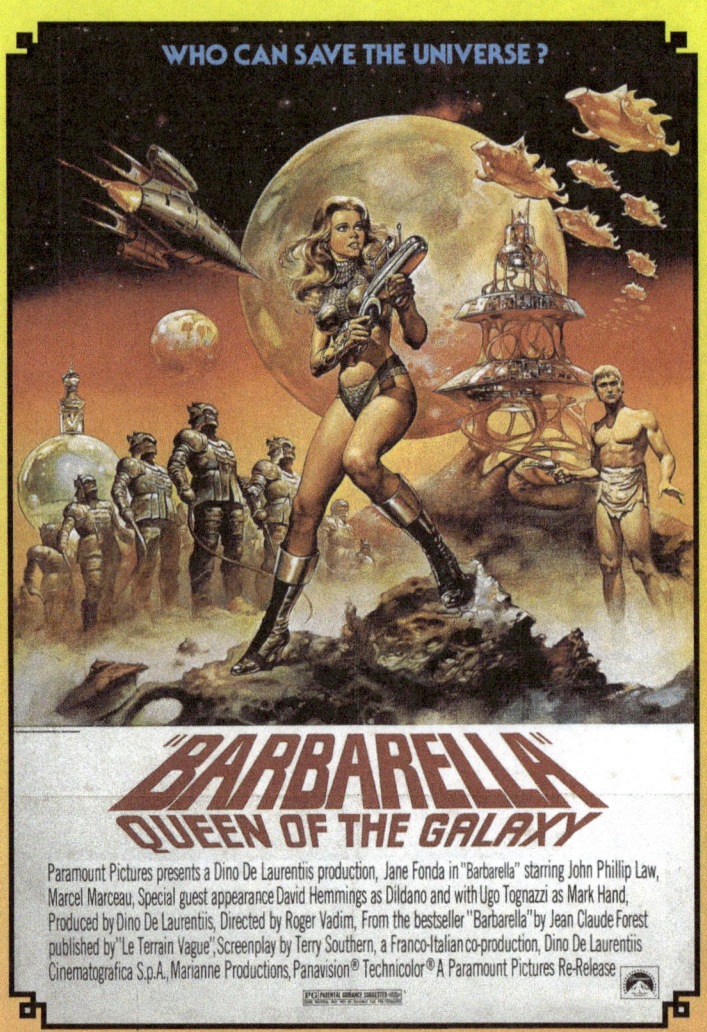

AJF: Was it a case of the record label just relaying what they wanted, or did you work with the musicians on the concepts?

BV: As I remember, Ozzy was the only one that personally talked to me about his concept for his album cover. All the others were done after talking to the art director of the recording company.

AJF: You've worked in all different genres and formats such as sword and sorcery/high fantasy, Gothic romance, horror, science fiction, erotica and more. What are some or your favorite types of fiction, movies, and music to illustrate for?

BV: I try not to play favorites. I like to think that once I get the job I put myself into each painting with the same love and dedication.

AJF: You work primarily with oil paint, right? Do you sketch out the pictures before painting them?

BV: Sure. No matter what media we work with a sketch is a very important way of defining the concept and composition.

AJF: Have you experimented with other mediums? Watercolor? Airbrush? Digital/Photoshop?

BV: Not really. Oil paint is my medium.

AJF: You've collaborated frequently with others—including your current wife Julie Bell, your previous wife Doris, and also your stepsons David and Tony Palumbo. Do you enjoy working with others and the spirit of finding common ground? As the aforementioned are, or have been, your family members, do you find it easier or more difficult because of that?

BV: I collaborate fairly frequently with Julie, and occasionally with Tony and/or David. We are a very tightly knitted family. Working together is very natural and enjoyable. We understand each other quite well.

AJF: I heard you often use yourself and your wife as models for your artwork. Is that true? If so, I have to ask: How did you go about it, as far as painting yourself?

BV: I work with photo reference. No problem at all.

AJF: What's coming up in the near future for you, Boris? Do you have any current projects you'd like to share with our readers?

BV: Hey, this is my life. More paintings!

AJF: Thank you for your time!

SWORD & SORCERY IN THE CINEMA: AN OVERVIEW AND FILMOGRAPHY

By Trever Nordgren

Prior to the highly successful Conan movies in the early 1980s starring Arnold Schwarzenegger (*Conan the Barbarian, Conan the Destroyer* and *Red Sonja*), there weren't many out and out Sword and Sorcery (or Heroic Fantasy as some call it) movies made (unlike Horror and Science Fiction, which established a foothold early on in the movie world). Most of what was produced was Fantasy-based with some swordplay and magic like the Sinbad films, The Thief of Baghdad/Ali Baba, Disney and Bakshi cartoons and Knights of the Roundtable features. It wasn't until the 1960s that Robert E. Howard's popular loincloth warrior really took hold of the publishing world and it was a few more years until it really started making a mark in films.

The 1980s were the high point of Sword and Sorcery movies produced in the US and other countries (a number of Italian, Spanish and other foreign directors also shifted from Horror and/or Science Fiction to dabble in the tales of High Fantasy with varying degrees of success), but a steady stream of S & S films continue to show up from time to time.

With the *Conan the Barbarian* remake starring Jason Momoa, and the recent announcement of Schwarzenegger's reprisal of Robert E. Howard's dark anti-hero in a new sequel, *The Legend of Conan*, (30 years after the first film made him a huge star) - it bears looking back on the history of Sword and Sorcery in the cinema.

Europe launched the first few shots with Hollywood soon to follow. Generally recognized as the first film in the "Sword and Sorcery" canon is German auteur Fritz Lang's *Die Nibelungen*, released in 1924. Based on Nordic Mythology, it is actually two films (totaling about 5 hours collectively) that tell of Siegfried, a son of a King who has mastered the art of sword making and goes on a journey to find a princess in the Kingdom of Burgundy, fights Dragons and other mythological creatures along the way and eventually becomes embroiled in battles over Kingdoms (that continue into the second movie and culminates in a huge battle finale). Italy actually started a bit earlier by producing a series of films based on the adventures of Hercules, the popular "Maciste" movies, that were the foundation of "Sword and Sandal" epics as they later became known. Most lack the "Sorcery" or magic elements of the films considered S & S, but they do serve as foundation of sorts to later Sword and Sorcery movies (more than 2 dozen films were produced between 1914 and 1926). They also weren't distributed much outside of Europe and many people didn't know about them until they were revived in the late 1950s after the popularity of Steve Reeves in the title role in the 1958 US film (and other Sword and Sandal historical epics like *Spartacus, Samson and Delilah*, and *The Ten Commandments*). For the next decade, those types of films dominated the Italian screens until Horror, Science Fiction and Giallo films replaced them.

1001 Arabian Nights also became the foundation for a number of films to come starting in 1924 with Douglas Fairbanks Sr. in the leading role. A few years later a British version co-directed by Michael Powell (*Peeping Tom, The Red Shoes*) hit the screens as well. Sinbad the Sailor was also a popular character and a number of films were made from the original sources with Douglas Fairbanks Jr. leading one, pioneering Russian director Aleksandr Ptushko helming one and of course a number with Ray Harryhausen's pioneering stop-motion animation in them (over 10 films and still being produced). Greek mythology was also mined in other films like Ulysses, Jason and the Argonauts, and others.

In the 1960s, there was a growing popularity for J.R.R. Tolkien's "Ring" books by the younger generation. With the "Hippie" community embracing Science Fiction and Fantasy books, there became a growing market for it. Science Fiction had a renaissance with landmark epics by Stanley Kubrick (*2001 A Space Odyssey* and *A Clockwork Orange*), Douglas Trumbill (*Silent Running*) and George Lucas (*THX1138* and *Star Wars*) and Fantasy was soon to follow. By the late 1970s, many adaptations were being done by Bass and Rankin and Ralph Bakshi. These and other offshoots became very successful and it opened up an interest in more Fantasy books and stories that hadn't been tapped. This I believe opened the way for Sword & Sorcery movies to start being made in the 1980s.

Producer Edward R. Pressman was the first to try. He tapped Edward Summer to adapt Robert E. Howard's Conan stories to the big screen. In 1976, Summer outlined six stories for film and hammered out a screenplay co-authored by Marvel Comics legend Roy Thomas. It was much more faithful to Howard's creation and writing. Oliver Stone was tapped to direct and also ended up doing some work on the screenplay, but Pressman couldn't get enough financing and after a few years he eventually sold it to Dino DeLaurantes, who finally brought it to the big screen after Oliver Stone dropped out and John Milus took the director's chair. This set the blueprint really for the Sword and Sorcery films (of the loincloth type) to follow.

Even though S & S is often defined in a lot of people's minds by Conan and his brethren, by definition any story that features both Swordsmanship and Magic fit the bill. Here's a list of movies that feature both (the * connotes the standout films in my opinion, but all have merit to make the list):

❋ ❋ ❋

Die Nibelungen (aka: *Siegfried, Siegfried's Death*) (1924) (Directed by Fritz Lang) (Germany)
The Thief of Baghdad (1924) (Directed by Raoul Walsh) (US)
The Thief of Baghdad (1940) (Directed by Ludwig Berger, Michael Powell, Tim Whelan) (UK)
The Iron Crown (1941) (Directed by Alessandro Blasetti) (Italy)
Sinbad the Sailor (1947) (Directed by Richard Wallace) (US)
Macbeth (1948) (Directed by Orson Welles) (US)
The Thief of Baghdad (1952) (Directed by Karel Larmac) (Germany)
The Magic Voyage of Sinbad (1953) (Directed by Aleksandr Ptushko) (Russia)
Knights of the Round Table (1953) (Directed by Richard Thorpe) (US)
Prince Valiant (1954) (Directed by Henry Hathaway) (US)
Son of Sinbad (1955) (Directed by Ted Tetzlaff) (US)
Ilya Muromets (aka: *The Sword and the Dragon*) (1956) (Directed by Aleksandr Ptushko) (Russia)
*The 7ᵗʰ Voyage of Sinbad (1958) (Directed by Nathan Juran) (US)

Sleeping Beauty (1959) (animated) (Directed by Clyde Geronimi) (US)
The Thief of Baghdad (aka: ll Ladrodi Baghdad) (1961) (Directed by Bruno Vailati) (Italy)
Jack the Giant Killer (1962) (Directed by Nathan Juran) (US)
The Magic Sword (1962) (Directed by Bert I. Gordon) (US)
Vulcan Son of Jupiter (aka: *Vulcan Son of Giove*) (1962) (Directed by Emimmo Salvi) (Italy)
Jason and the Argonauts (1963) (Directed by Don Chaffey) (US)
Captain Sinbad (1963) (Directed by Byron Haskin) (US)
Seven Tasks of Ali Baba (aka: *Lasette Fatiche di Ali Baba*) (1963) (Directed by Emimmo Salvi) (Italy)
The Sword in the Stone (1963) (animated) (Directed by – Wolfgang Reitherman) (US)
Sword of Lancelot (1963) (Directed by Cornel Wilde)
Sinbad and the Seven Saracens (aka: *Sinbad Contr I Sette Saracini*) (1964) (Directed by Emimmo Salvi) (Italy)
Hercules the Avenger (aka: *La Sfida Dei Giganti*) (1965) (Directed by Maurizio Lucidi) (Italy)
Treasure of the Petrified Forest (aka: *ll Tesoro Della Foresta Pietrificata*) (1965) (Dir. by Emimmo Salvi) (Italy)
Ruslan and Ludmila (1972) (Directed by Aleksandr Ptushko) (Russia)
*The Golden Voyage of Sinbad (1974) (Directed by Gordon Hessler) (UK)

Sinbad and the Eye of the Tiger (1977) (Directed by Sam Wanamaker) (UK)
Jabberwocky (1977) (Directed by Terry Gilliam) (UK)
Wizards (1977) (Directed by Ralph Bakshi) (US)
The Hobbit (1977) (Directed by Jules Bass, Arthur Rankin Jr.) (US)
The Lord of the Rings (1977) (Directed by Ralph Bakshi) (US)
* Return of the King (1980) (Directed by Jules Bass, Arthur Rankin Jr.) (US)
The Thief of Baghdad (1978) (Directed by Clive Donner) (UK)
Hawk the Slayer (1980) (Directed by Terry Marcel) (UK)
Clash of the Titans (1981) (Directed by Desmond Davis) (UK/US)
Dragonslayer (1981) (Directed by Matthew Robbins) (US)
Excalibur (1981) (Directed by John Boorman) (UK)
Conan the Barbarian (1982) (Directed by John Milius) (US)
Ator l'invincibile (aka: *Ator: The Fighting Eagle, Ator 1*) (1982) (Directed by Joe D'Amato) (Italy)
The Beastmaster (1982) (Directed by Don Coscarelli) (US)
The Flight of Dragons (1982) (animated) (Directed by Jules Bass, Arthur Rankin Jr.) (US)
The Last Unicorn (1982) (animated) (Directed by Jules Bass, Arthur Rankin Jr.) (US)
The Sword and the Sorcerer (1982) (Directed by Albert Pyun) (US)
The Sorceress (1982) (Directed by Brian Stuart (aka: Jack Hill)) (US)
Hundra (1982) (Directed by Matt Cimber) (Spain/Italy)
The Dark Crystal (1982) (Directed by Jim Henson & Frank Oz) (US)
Fire and Ice (1983) (Directed by Ralph Bakshi) (US)
Yor, Hunter From the Future (1983) (Directed by Antonio Margheriti) (Italy)

*Deathstalker (1983) (Directed by James Sbardellati) (US/Argentina)

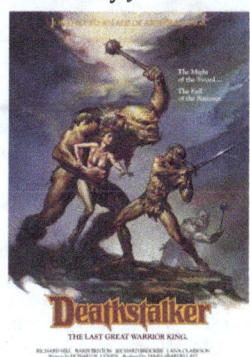

Hearts and Armour (1983) (Directed by Giacomo Battiato) (Italy)
Hercules (1983) (Directed by Luigi Cozzi) (Italy)
*Krull (1983) (Directed by Peter Yates) (UK/US)
*Fire and Ice (1983) (Animated) (Directed by Ralph Bakshi) (US)
Ator l'invincibile 2 (aka: *Ator 2: The Blade Master*) (1984) (Directed by Joe D'Amato) (Italy)
*Conan the Destroyer (1984) (Directed by Richard Fleischer) (US)
The Devil's Sword (1984) (Directed by Ratner Timoer) (Indonesia)
Sword of the Valiant: The Legend of Sir Gawain and the Green Knight (1984) (Directed by Stephen Weeks) (US)
The Warrior and the Sorceress (1984) (Directed by John Broderick) (US/Argentina)
*The Black Cauldron (1985) (Animated) (Directed by Ted Berman, Richard Rich) (US)
*Labyrinth (1986) (Directed by Jim Henson) (US/UK)
*Conquest (1985) (Directed by Lucio Fulci) (Italy)

* Red Sonja (1985) (Directed by Richard Fleischer) (US)
The Dungeon Master (aka: *Ragewar*) (1985) (Directed by Rosemarie Turko, John Buechler, David Allen, Stephen Ford, Peter Manoogian, Ted Nicolaou, Charles Band) (US)
Barbarian Queen (1985) (Directed by Hector Olivera) (Argentina)

She (1985) (Directed by Avi Nesher) (Italy)
*Ladyhawke (1985) (Directed by Richard Donner) (US)
Wizards of the Lost Kingdom (1985) (Directed by Hector Olivera) (Argentina/US)
Amazons (1986) (Directed by Alejandro Sessa) (US/Argentina)
*Highlander (1986) (Directed by Russell Mulcahy) (US/UK)
*Legend (1986) (Directed by Ridley Scott) (UK/US)
* Labyrinth (1986) (Directed by Jim Henson) (US)
The Barbarians (1987) (Directed by Ruggero Deodato) (Italy)
Deathstalker II (1987) (Directed by Jim Wynorski) (US/Argentina)
Iron Warrior (aka: *Ator 3*) (1987) (Directed by Alfonso Brescia) (Italy)
Masters of the Universe (1987) (Directed by Gary Goddard) (US)
*The Princess Bride (1987) (Directed by Rob Reiner) (US)
Gor (1988) (Directed by Fritz Kiersch) (US/South Africa)
Deathstalker and the Warriors from Hell (1988) (*Deathstalker 3*) (Directed by Alfonso Corona) (US)
*Willow (1988) (Directed by Ron Howard) (US)
Sinbad of the Seven Seas (1989) (Directed by Enzo Castellari) (Italy)
Barbarian Queen 2: The Empress Strikes Back (1989) (Directed by Joe Finley) (US/Mexico)
Wizards of the Lost Kingdom 2 (1989) (Directed by Charles B. Griffith) (US)
Quest for the Mighty Sword (aka: *Ator 4*) (1990) (Directed by Joe D'Amato) (Italy)
Beastmaster 2: Through the Portal of Time (1991) (Directed by Sylvio Tabet) (US)
Deathstalker IV: Match of Titans (1991) (Directed by Howard Cohen) (US)
Highlander II: The Quickening (1991) (Directed by Russell Mulcahy) (UK/France/Argentina)
Wizards of the Demon Sword (1991) (Directed by Fred Olen Ray) (US)

Aladdin (1992) (Directed by Ron Clements & John Musker) (US)
Army of Darkness (1993) (Directed by Sam Raimi) (US)
Quest of the Delta Knights (1993) (Directed by James Dodson) (US)
Eyes of the Serpent (1994) (Directed by Ricardo Jacques Gale) (US)
Guinevere (1994) (Directed by Jud Taylor) (US)
Highlander III: The Final Dimension (aka: *Sorcerer*) (1994) (Directed by Andrew Morahan) (US)
Yamato Takeru (1994) (Directed by Takao Okawara) (Japan)
Beastmaster III: The Eye of Braxus (1996) (Directed by Gabrielle Beaumont) (US)
Dragonheart (1996) (Directed by Rob Cohen) (US)
InuYasha (1996-2008) (manga) (Directed by Masashi Ikeda, Yasunao Aoki) (Japan)
The Lord Protector (aka: *The Dark Mist*) (1996) (Directed by Ryan Carroll)
Kull the Conqueror (1997) (Directed by John Nicolella) (US)
Prince Valiant (1997) (Directed by Anthony Hickox) (UK)
Merlin (1998) (Directed by Steve Barron) (US)
Arthur's Quest (1999) (Directed by Neil Mandt) (US)
The 13th Warrior (1999) (Directed by John McTiernan) (US)
Beowulf (1999) (Directed by Graham Baker) (US)
Sinbad: Beyond the Veil of Mists (2000) (animated) (Directed by Evan Ricks) (US)
Dungeons and Dragons (2000) (Directed by Courtney Solomon) (US)
Dragonheart: A New Beginning (2000) (Directed by Doug Lefler) (US)
Jason and the Argonauts (2000) (Directed by Nick Willing) (US)
Highlander 4: Endgame (2000) (Directed by Douglas Aarniokoski) (US)
*The Fellowship of the Ring (2001) (Directed by Peter Jackson) (US)

Voyage of the Unicorn (2001) (Directed by Philip Spink) (US)
Demonicus (2001) (Directed by Jay Woelfel) (US)
The Hexer (2001) (Directed by Marek Brodzki) (Poland)
The Monkey King (2001) (Directed by Cheang Pou-Soi) (Hong Kong)
The Scorpion King (2002) (Directed by Chuck Russell) (US)
The Two Towers (2002) (Directed by Peter Jackson) (US)
Crusade of Vengeance (2002) (Directed by Byron Thompson) (US)
The Return of the King (2003) (Directed by Peter Jackson) (US)
Barbarian (2003) (Directed by Chris Silvertson) (US/Russia)
Sinbad: Legend of the Seven Seas (2003) (animated) (Directed by Patrick Gilmore, Tim Johnson) (US)
The Red Knight (2003) (Directed by Helene Angel) (France)
Dark Kingdom: The Dragon King (aka: *Die Nibelungen, Ring of the Nibelungs, Curse of the Ring*) (2004) (Directed by Uli Edel) (Germany)
George and the Dragon (2004) (Directed by Tom Reeve) (US)
The Chronicles of Narnia: The Lion, the Witch and the Wardrobe (2005) (Directed by Andrew Adamson) (UK/US)
Beowulf and Grendel (2005) (Directed by Sturla Gunnarsson) (Canada/Iceland/UK)
Wrath of the Dragon God (2005) (Directed by Gerry Lively) (US)
Highlander: The Source (2006) (Directed by Brett Leonard) (US/UK)
Dragon (2006) (Directed by Leigh Scott) (US)
Eragon (2006) (Directed by Stefen Fangmeier) (US/UK/Hungary/Australia)
In the Name of the King: A Dungeon Siege Tale (2007) (Directed by Uwe Boll) (Germany/Canada/US)
Beowulf (2007) (Directed by Robert Zemeckis) (US)
Wolfhound (2007) (Directed by Nikolay Lebedev) (Russia)
Dragonlance (2007) (animated) (Directed by Will Meugniot) (US)
The Seeker: The Dark is Rising (2007) (Directed by David Cunningham) (US)
Scorpion King 2: Rise of a Warrior (2008) (Directed by Russell Mulcahy) (US)
Dragon Hunter (2008) (Directed by Steve Shimek) (US)
Djinn: An Ancient Fairy Tale (2008) (Directed by Shahin Sean Solimon) (India)
Outlander (2008) (Directed by Howard McCain) (US)
The Chronicles of Narnia: Prince Caspian (2008) (Directed by Andrew Adamson) (UK/US)
Merlin and the War of the Dragons (2008) (Directed by Mark Atkins) (US)
Odysseus: Voyage to the Underworld (2008) (Directed by Terry Ingram) (Canada)
Solomon Kane (2009) (Directed by Michael Basset) (France/Czech Republic/UK)
Kinights of Bloodsteel (2009) Directed by Philip Spink) (US)
Tales of an Ancient Empire (2010) (Directed by Albert Pyun) (US)
Sinbad and the Minotaur (2010) (Directed by Karl Zwicky) (Australia)
Journey to Promethia (2010) (Directed by Dan Garcia) (US)
The Chronicles of Narnia: The Voyage of the Dawn Treader (2010) (Directed by Andrew Adamson) (UK/US)
Prince of Persia: The Sands of Time (2010) (Directed by Mike Newell) (US)
Clash of the Titans (2010) (Directed by Louis Leterrier) (US)
Merlin and the Book of Beasts (2010) (Directed by Warren Sonoda)
Conan the Barbarian (2011) (Directed by Marcus Nispel) (US)
Season of the Witch (2011) (Directed Dominic Sena) (US)
Sinbad: The Fifth Voyage (2011) (Directed by Shahin Sean Solimon) (India)
In the Name of the King 2: Two Worlds (2011) (Directed by Uwe Boll) (Germany/Canada/US)
Ronal the Barbarian (2011) (animated) (Directed by Kresten Vestbjerg Anderson, Thorbjorn Christoffersen, Philip Einstein Lipski) (Denmark)
The Hobbit (2012) (Directed by Peter Jackson) (New Zealand/UK/US)
Jack the Giant Killer (2013) (Directed by Bryan Singer) (US)

Recommended Reading List:
Sword & Sorcery

As far back as 1200 BC, the Greek hero Hercules (or Heracles as he was first known) fought various demons, monsters, Sorcerers, and so on influencing what was later to become known as Sword and Sandal epics. These and other historical adventures like Ulysses, Beowulf, The Iliad and The Odyssey, and others set the foundation for later works to come. Lord Dunsany and T.H. White were also quite influential on the Arthurian Fantasy side – along with the legends of King Arthur and the Knights in the Roundtable of course.

With the rise of popularity of the pulps in the 1920s and 1930s, Weird Tales, the premier magazine of such material, loomed high above the rest. One of its more popular writers (besides H.P. Lovecraft and Seabury Quinn) was Robert E. Howard. Although Howard wrote horror and other fiction, he is most known for his popular stories featuring Conan the Barbarian. Influenced by Edgar Rice Burroughs, H. Rider Haggard and Talbot Mundy's exotic fantasy around the turn of the century, Howard soon created the blueprint that countless other writers have emulated. Other writers soon joined Howard like Clark Ashton Smith, C.L. Moore, Henry Kuttner and especially Fritz Leiber in the field of S & S (with Lieber coining the term eventually in 1961). The release of Howard's books in mass-market paperback during the 1960s by Glen Lord, L. Sprague de Camp and Lin Carter (including a large amount of pastiches and new stories featuring Howard's popular barbarian) secured the modern definition of S & S fantasy.

Here's a list of standout works in the genre:

Robert Adams –Coming of the Horseclans (1975), Swords of the Horseclans (1976), Revenge of the Horse Clans (1977), The Savage Mountains (1979), The Patrimony (1980), The Death of a Legend (1981).

Joe Abercrombie – The Blade Itself (2006), Before They Are Hanged (2007), The Last Argument of Kings (2008), Best Served Cold (2009).

Poul Anderson – The Broken Sword (1954), Hrolf Kraki's Saga (1973), Fantasy (1981), War of the Gods (1997).

Lin Carter - Wizard of Lemuria (1965),Thongor of Lemuria (1966), Conan (1967) (w/DeCamp & Howard), Thonger At the End of Time (1968), Warrior of the World's End (1974), Conan The Freebooter (19), Conan the Swordsman (1978) (w/de Camp and Nyberg).

Adrian Cole – The Dream Lords (1975), Lords of Nightmares (1975), Bane of Nightmares (1976).

Glen Cook – The Sword Bearer (1982), The Black Company (1984), Shadows Linger (1984), The Silver Spike (1989), Dreams of Steel (1990).

L. Sprague de Camp – The Goblin Tower (1968), The Clocks of Iraz (, Honorable Barbarian (, Fallable Fiend (1973), Conan (1967) (w/Carter & Howard), Conan and the Spider God (1978), Conan the Freebooter (19).

David Drake– The Dragon Lord (1979), Killer (1987) (w/Karl Edward Wagner).

Lord Dunsany – The King of Elfland's Daughter (1924)

Steven Erikson – Gardens of the Moon (1999), Dead Horse Gates (2000), Memories of Ice (2001), House of Chains (2002), Midnight Tides (2004).

Gardner F. Fox – Kothar (1969), Kothar of the Magic Sword (1969), Kothar and the Demon Queen (1969), Kothar and the Wizard Slayer (1970), Kyrik: Warlock Warrior (1975).

Terry Goodkind–Wizard's First Rule (1994), Stone of Tears (1995), Temple of the Winds (1997), Pillars of Creation (2002), Confessor (2007).

Robert E. Howard – Skull-Face and Others (1946), The Hour of the Dragon (aka: Conan the Conqueror) (1950), People of the Black Circle (1952), Red Nails (1952), The Dark Man and Others (1963), Almuric (1964), King Kull (1967), Red Shadows (1968), Bran Mak Morn(1969), Tigersof the Sea (1974), Skulls in the Stars (1978).

John Jakes – Brak the Barbarian (1968), Mark of Demons (1969), Versus the Sorceress (, When Idols Walked (.

Henry Kuttner – Elak of Atlantis (1985).

Tanith Lee – The Birthgrave (1975);Storm Lord (1976); Shadowfire (1978); Quest for the White Witch (1978).

Fritz Leiber–Swords Against Wizardry (1968), Swords in the Mist (1968), Swords of Lanhmar (1968), Swords Against Death (1970), Swords and Deviltry (1970), Swords & Ice Magic (1977), Knight & Knave of Swords (1991).

Brian Lumley – The Complete Khash (Volumes 1 & 2) (1991), Hero of Dreams (1986), Ship of Dreams (1986), Mad Moon of Dreams (1987), Iced on Aran (1992).

George R.R. Martin – A Game of Thrones (1996), A Clash of Kings (1998), A Storm of Swords (2000), A Feast for Crows (2005).

Michael Moorcock – Stormbringer (1965), Elric of Melbourne (1972), Bane of Black Sword (1967), Knight of Swords (1971), King of Swords (1971), The Vanishing Tower (1977), Elric at the End of Time (1984).

C.L. Moore–Jirel of Joiry (1969).

John Norman – Gor Series (1966 – Present).

Andre Norton – Witch World (1963), Warlock of Witch World (1967), Sorceress of Witch World (1968).

Andrew J. Offitt – Iron Lords (1979), Shadows out of Hell (1980), Lady of Snowmist (1983).

Norvell W. Page – Flame Winds (1969), Sons of the Bear-God (1969).

Alexi & Cory Panshin – Earthmagic (1978).

Joanna Russ – The Adventures of Alyx (1976).

Fred Saberhagen – The Broken Lands (1968), The Black Mountains (1971), Changeling Earth (1973), Empire of the East (1979), The Book of Swords series (1983 - 1994).

Jessica Amanda Salmonson – Tomoe Gozen (1981), The Swordswoman (1982), Thousand Shrine Warrior (1984).

Charles R. Saunders – Imaro (1981), Imaro II: Quest for Cush (1984), Imaro III: The Trail of Bohu (1985).

Darrell Schweitzer – The Shattered Goddess (1982), The White Isle (1989), Mask of the Sorcerer (1995).

Michael Shea – A Quest for Simbilis (1974), Nifft the Lean (1982).

Clark Ashton Smith – Out of Space & Time (1942), Lost Worlds (1944), Zothtique (1970), Xiccarph (1971).

Keith Taylor – Bard (1981), Bard II (1984), Bard III (1986), Bard IV (1987).

J.R.R. Tolkien – The Hobbit (1937), Lord of the Rings, The Two Towers (1954), The Return of the King (1955).

Jack Vance – The Dying Earth (1950), Eyes of the Overworld(1966), Cugel's Saga (1983).

Karl Edward Wagner – Darkness Weaves (1970), Death Angel's Shadow (1973),Bloodstone (1975), Dark Crusade (1976), Night Winds (1978), Legion from the Shadows (1976), The Road of Kings (1979), Midnight Sun.

T.H. White – The Once and Future King (1958)

Gene Wolfe –Shadow of the Torturer (1980),Claw of the Conciliator (1981), Sword of Lictor (1982).

ANTHOLOGIES

Amazons! (1979); Amazons II (1982) Edited by Jessica Amanda Salmonson.

Echoes of Valor(1987); Echoes of Valor II (1989); Echoes of Valor III (1991) Edited by Karl Edward Wagner.

Flashing Swords (Volumes #1 - #5) (1973 - 1981) Edited by Lin Carter.

Heroic Fantasy (1979) Edited by Gerald Page & Hank Reinhardt.

Kingdoms of Sorcery (1976) Edited by Lin Carter.

The Mighty Barbarians (1969) Edited by Hans Stefan Santesson.

The Mighty Swordsmen (1970) Edited by Hans Stefan Santesson.

Realms of Wizardry (1976) Edited by Lin Carter.

Savage Heroes (1977) Edited by Eric Pendragon (aka: Michael Parry).

The Spell of Seven (1965) Edited by L. Sprague de Camp.

Swords Against Darkness (Volumes #1 - #5) (1977 – 1979) Edited by Andrew J. Offutt.

Swords Against Tomorrow (1970) Edited by Robert Hoskins.

Swords & Sorcery (1963) Edited by L. Sprague de Camp.

Warlocks and Warriors (1971) Edited by L. Sprague de Camp

The Year's Best Fantasy (Volumes #1 - #6) (1975 – 1980) Edited by Lin Carter.

MAGAZINES

Adventures of Sword & Sorcery (1995 – 2000)

Avon Fantasy Reader (1946 – 1952)

Black Gate (2000 – Present)

Marion Zimmer Bradley's Fantasy (1988 – 2000)

The Dragon (1976 -2007)

The Fantasy Fan (1933 – 1955)

Fantasy & Science Fiction (1949 – Present)

Fantastic Stories (1952 – 1980)

Fantasy Tales (1977 – 1991)

Midnight Sun (1974 – 1979)

Realms of Fantasy (1994 – 2012)

Strange Tales (1931 – 1933)

Unknown (Worlds) (1939 – 1943)

Weirdbook (1968 – 1997)

Weird Tales (1923 – 1954; 1970 – 1971; 1984 – 1985; 1988 – Present)

Whispers (1973 – 1997)

A SHOW OF FIRE AND ICE: HBO's

GAME OF THRONES

By Trever Nordgren

With its third season ready to kick off in the spring of 2013, the television series adapted from George R.R. Martin's popular fantasy novel series, A Song of Fire and Ice, continues to gain fans and acclaim. With a huge ensemble cast, high production values, adult themes and interweaving plotlines, it's helped renew interest in the fantasy genre and is showing people that it's not just for kids.

Game of Thrones is set in the fictional continents of Westeros and Essos (which seem to be modeled somewhat on the early British Isles during the medieval period when feudalism was being developed). The series was initially conceived and developed in early 2007 after HBO acquired the rights from Martin. "When I began this series, I thought this could never be adapted for television or film. I was simply writing a book. I started it in 1991, right in the middle of 10 years that I spent in Hollywood," Martin said in an interview shortly before the first season.

The main cast members(the key players, so-to-speak) are a rich and diverse group.Sean Bean plays Lord Eddard "Ned" Stark, who is the head of the Stark family and one of the central characters. He and his wife Catelyn (played by Michelle Fairley) have five children: the eldest is Robb (Richard Madden), followed by his sister Sansa (Sophie Turner), tomboy Arya (Maisie Williams), adventurous Bran (Isaac Hempstead-Wright) and the youngest Stark child Rickon (Art Parkinson). On the fringe of the family is Ned's bastard son Jon Snow (Kit Harington) who faces the dangers in the frigid North in the company of the men of the Night's Watch, which includes his friend Samwell Tarly (John Bradley) and Lord Commander Jeor Mormont (James Cosmo). And lastly there is Ned's ward Theon Greyjoy (Alfie Allen).

 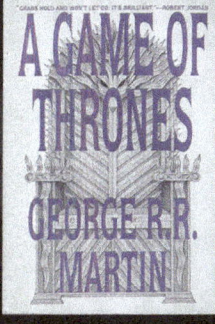

Next is King Robert Baratheon (Mark Addy), an old friend of Ned's who is married to Queen Cersei

Lannister (Lena Headey). In defiance of her father, the wealthy Lord Tywin Lannister (Charles Dance), Cersei has taken her twin, the "Kingslayer" Ser Jaime Lannister (Nikolaj Coster-Waldau), as her secret lover. She hates her younger brother, the clever dwarf Tyrion (Peter Dinklage), who is attended by his also-secret mistress Shae (Sibel Kekilli) and the swordsman-for-hire Bronn (Jerome Flynn). Cersei's oldest child is the spoiled Prince Joffrey Baratheon (Jack Gleeson), who is guarded by the scarred warrior Sandor "the Hound" Clegane (Rory McCann). The king's council of advisors includes the crafty brothel owner Lord Petyr "Littlefinger" Baelish (Aidan Gillen) and the eunuch spy Varys (Conleth Hill).After King Baratheon's death, Joffrey's throne is contested by Robert's two brothers: Stannis Baratheon (Stephen Dillane), who is advised by the foreign priestess Melisandre (Carice van Houten) and a former smuggler named Ser Davos Seaworth (Liam Cunningham); and Renly Baratheon (Gethin Anthony), who is married to the ambitious noblewoman Margaery Tyrell (Natalie Dormer), but secretly loves her brother Ser Loras (Finn Jones).

Lastly, across the Narrow Sea there are the siblings Viserys (Harry Lloyd) and Daenerys Targaryen (Emilia Clarke) – the exiled children of the king overthrown by Robert Baratheon – who are on the run for their lives and trying to win back their throne. Daenerys is married off like a slave (and initiated by rape

into the conjugal partnership) to Khal Drogo (Jason Momoa), the leader of the nomadic Dothraki, by her brother and she is guarded by the also-exiled knight Ser Jorah Mormont (Iain Glen).

And that's just the main characters! As of the filming of Season 3, there are no less than 257 cast members. There are multiple plot lines and unlike most series that use one book as the basis, Game of Thrones uses the first three of Martin's Song of Fire and Ice books. (The first follows the members of several noble houses in a civil war for the Iron Throne of the Seven Kingdoms; the second covers the rising threat of the impending winter and the mythical creatures of the North; and the third chronicles the attempts of the exiled last scion of the realm's deposed dynasty to reclaim the throne). Through its morally questionable characters, the Song of Fire and Ice books explore issues of social change and hierarchy, religion, civil wars, sexuality, crime and punishment and more.

"Well, the Starks are certainly the center of the story, at the start," Martin said. "It all begins at Winterfell, with occasional cuts to Daenerys across the ocean, because there was no way I could get her into Winterfell. But, we bring all the characters together at Winterfell, and they're all there for a while. By the time you're done with the first book, pretty much all of them have gone their separate ways."

Game of Thrones has been jokingly called "The Sopranos in Middle-earth" by one of the show's writers, David Benioff, who works with D.B. Weiss as the show's main writers and executive producers (along with Martin himself who is a co-producer and has also written a couple of the episodes as well). In the category of the scheming heirarchies, multi-character viewpoints, and plotlines with a dark edge/tone to it - and also the high quotient of violence and sex/nudity - it might qualify as this, but I'd put it more into the category of The Tudors as an adult costume drama with fantastic elements. The show's creators have specifically downplayed the fantasy and magic elements of the series to focus on the character development and melodramatic aspects, but it's not without its Fantasy elements though with a raven-haired sorceress who gives birth to creepy shadow babies and Daenarys becoming a mother-figure to three baby dragons.

The series has achieved a large amount of success and praise in just two years time. Peter Dinklage recently won both an Emmy and a Golden Globe for his work on the series as Tyrion Lannister, and a few other nominations have been received for the show and other cast members.Martin said this about Dinklage:"We never even auditioned for the part of Tyrion Lannister. Peter Dinklage was the only one we ever wanted. We knew he would be great for the role and, thankfully, we landed him. He's magnificent."

The critics' reviews have been mixed with Emily Nussbaum of the NY Times in favor of it saying, "Game of Thrones is an ideal show to binge-watch on DVD: with its cliffhangers and Grand Guignol dazzle, it rewards a bloody, committed immersion in its foreign world—and by this I mean not only the medieval-ish landscape of Westeros (the show's mythical realm) but the genre from which it derives. Fantasy—like television itself, really—has long been burdened with audience condescension: the assumption that it's trash, or juvenile, something intrinsically icky and low." On the other side of the fence, LA Times critics Ginia Bellafante said that the show was "boy fiction" and Neil Genzlinger called it "vileness for voyeurism's sake," directed at "Dungeons & Dragons types."

I, for one, am on the side of the former, in that I've enjoyed the series quite a lot. I've read the first three books in the Song of Fire and Ice Series (A Game of Thrones, A Clash of Kings and A Storm of Swords) and what the creators of the Game of Thrones series have done to work those into a cohesive physical narrative for television has been excellent. Having George Martin involved with the show is wonderful and has helped with keeping his vision intact. It's good to see the old Sword & Sorcery epics making a comeback with new Conan and Solomon Kane films and shows like Legend of the Seeker (based on Terry Goodkind's novel series) and Game of Thrones. Hopefully this will lead to other successful television series and movies of a similar nature.

Interview with Jonathan Maberry

By Joel B. Kirkpatrick

Every reader seems to have a preconceived notion of what horror fiction really is. Readers describe horror in wildly different terms. Publishing houses have struggled for years to make horror a functioning, marketable category. Often, they will market a book *away* from outright Horror, believing rightly or wrongly that audiences don't buy those themes. Jonathan Maberry has made a list, numbering at about four dozen different notions, of elements he believes truly define horror—and he includes the word *funny* on his list. He is not off the mark at all, and can readily point to any number of popular works to support all of his arguments. Listening to him, you don't doubt his long career has made him an expert consumer, and that when it puts his pen to paper to write…the result will be smashing, and horrible. Maberry has earned several Stoker Awards. He has also been writing professionally and teaching writing since the Carter Administration.

Jonathan Maberry

JBK: Many readers who know your work will be stunned to learn that, since graduating high school, you have written at least 34 feature magazine articles a year. *Twelve hundred by-line articles in thirty five years!* How do you find time to write anything else?

JM: The math is even screwier than that. In the span from 1978 through 1998 I wrote 1200 magazine features, 3000 columns, two plays, some goofy greeting cards, bad song lyrics (for a truly horrible heavy metal band), and a handful of college textbooks. Sleep, as I have been saying for years, is for the weak. From '99 through 2003 I wrote mainly how-to manuals on martial arts and one extremely large book on monster folklore under the pen name of Shane MacDougall. I switched to (mostly) fiction in 2005, and since then have fourteen novels, five more nonfiction books on monsters and lots of comics.

I really dig the fast lane.

JBK: Since you are also a founding member of the Liars Club, can you blame our skepticism of that previous statement? Classic authors—Tolkien, Lewis, Williams, et al—enormously enjoyed their informal and literary discussions as the Inklings in the '30s and '40s. Does the Liars Club serve the same purpose for you and your peers?

JM: The Liars Club is a kind of semi-sober, frequently useful think-tank and networking cooperative. It started out with just fantasist Gregory Frost and I sitting down over beers and sharing our individual knowledge/ insights on publicity and marketing for writers. He knew some, I knew some, but our collective knowledge exceeded the sum of the parts. We realized that if writers stopped acting like prima donnas (i.e., spending their time in moody isolation and lamenting the hard realities of the world of publishing) and worked together, they might get somewhere. We tried it and, sure enough, both of our careers moved forward. So, we invited a bunch of other writers to join us. Men and women of various genres (from writers of scholarly papers to thriller writers to playwrights) and various levels of skill. By working together, everyone seemed to get a career boost.

Then the economy went into the crapper, taking large chunks of publishing with it. We shifted

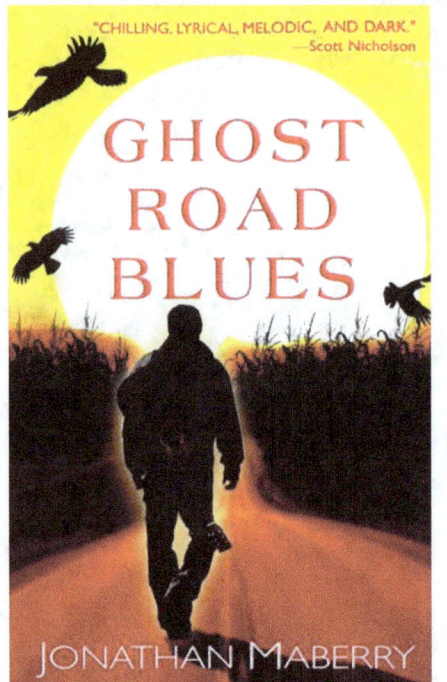

"CHILLING, LYRICAL, MELODIC, AND DARK."
—Scott Nicholson

GHOST ROAD BLUES

JONATHAN MABERRY

and expanded our focus so that instead of only helping each other, we worked to help independent bookstores, chain booksellers, libraries, literacy programs and more. The bottom line is that everyone in the publishing world pulls the oars on the same ship. In-fighting or hoarding useful information doesn't accomplish much.

JBK: In 1978 you began writing, but were fresh out of high school. What was your first professional sale, and when did it happen?

JM: I sold my first article during my second year of college. I pitched a piece to a martial arts magazine and eventually sold it. I never looked back. I think the longest stretch I've gone without publishing anything was 2003 to 2005. I was doing a ton of research while teaching myself how to write a novel. I finished that novel in early 2005, got an agent in April of that year, and a deal a month later.

JBK: It seems you waited almost twenty years to begin writing full length novels, and then your creative output exploded. You have produced multiple projects every year since 2002, but concentrated, at first, writing mostly non-fiction books. What sparked your interest to begin writing horror?

JM: I wrote *The Vampire Slayers' Field Guide to the Undead* in 2001 for a small press. Doing the research on vampires, werewolves and other monsters reignited a boyhood love of horror fiction. I began reading much more of it, but lamented the fact that most of the depictions of vampires and werewolves were retreads of the Hollywood version, and they in no way resembled the monsters in folklore. So, after complaining about that for a while, my wife suggested I stop grousing and try writing my own novel. I did, and that became *Ghost Road Blues.*

But my interest in horror goes way back. When I was in seventh grade, my middle school librarian— who was the secretary for a couple of clubs of professional writers—dragged me along to some meetings where I met authors such as Ray Bradbury, Richard Matheson, Harlan Ellison, Arthur C. Clarke, Robert Bloch, L. Sprage de Camp and so many others. Bradbury and Matheson both spent a lot of time with me, discussion the nature of horror (and fantasy), and encouraging me to write.

JBK: *Ghost Road Blues* (Pinnacle, 2006) won you the prestigious Stoker Award for First Novel in 2008. How long did you work on the ideas for *Ghost Road Blues*? Were you surprised that your first attempt at fiction horror would earn you such honors?

JM: I was totally floored. I was kind of knocked out that *Ghost Road Blues* had been on the recommendation list for the Bram Stoker Award. Even that would have been enough to validate my desire to keep writing horror. But then it was nominated twice—for Best First Novel and for Novel of the Year. When it won for Best First Novel my mind went numb. I have no recollection at all about what I said during the acceptance speech. I only hope that it was in English. That it didn't win Novel of the Year is totally fine…that year the Stoker went to some guy named Stephen King.

JBK: You once said, "*…I generally don't write anything simply to catch a trend.*" New authors may have difficulty avoiding all the trendy story ideas currently being published. How does a writer stay fresh and keep their stories original?

JM: It helps to read deeply into the genre if you want to avoid repeating or rehashing what others have done. I make a point of reading everything I can in a genre when I'm gearing up to write a book. For example, when I was working on *Patient Zero*, my first attempt at zombie fiction, I think I read every damn zombie book in print. The good, the bad, and the ugly. I already had strong ideas about what I wanted to do with the book, but having read so much other work, it allowed me to steer clear of clichés. On the other hand, it helped me identify some classic elements of zombie fiction and then deliberately spin them into something new.

Since a good chunk of my career over the last four years has been built around zombie fiction (the four books of the *Rot & Ruin* series, *Patient Zero*, *Dead of Night* and a forthcoming sequel, *Marvel Zombies Return*, and a slew of short stories),

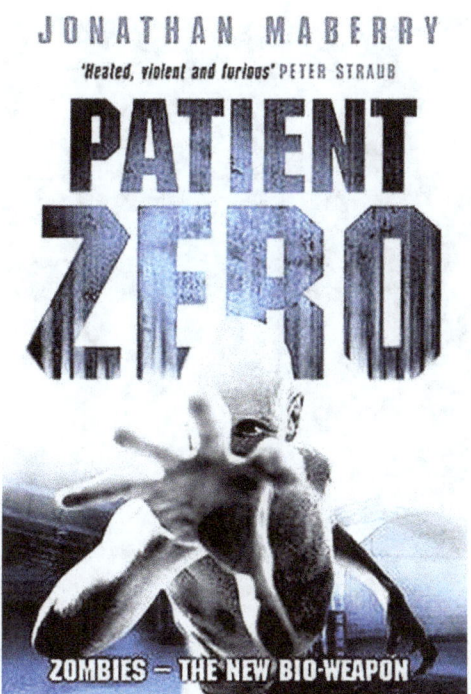

JONATHAN MABERRY

'Heated, violent and furious' PETER STRAUB

PATIENT ZERO

ZOMBIES — THE NEW BIO-WEAPON

I took it as a challenge to find something new, interesting, and fun with each new tale. Even *Dead of Night*, which is a deliberate homage to George Romero and *Night of the Living Dead*, I wanted to twist the model into my own shape. One thing that works for me is that I can separate myself my normal fanboy geek mode and step into the role of clinical observer. In that mode I look at the nuts and bolts of a situation, the day to day practicality of it. I imagine it in my life, in my world. How would I, as a reasonable, educated, practical person, react and respond to such a thing?

JBK: Horror fiction is constantly plagued by up and down trends in popularity, and reader confusion about what really fits the genre. Do you feel you were blessed by luck to earn your acclaim in the field, or is it only the product of very hard work by you and your agents?

JM: First off, I'll always admit that I've had great luck. No question. I've won awards and gotten deals that could just as easily have gone to another author. Case in point is the Best First Novel Stoker Award. I was up against Joe McKinney's *Dead City*. That book stands as my all-time favorite zombie novel. If Joe had won, it would have been absolutely just, and I would have applauded it. Why I won over him, I have no idea. Though, he came back and won Best Novel (for *Flesh Eaters*) in 2011 and my novel, *The King of Plagues*, wasn't even nominated.

When it comes to the relationship with my agent, the superb Sara Crowe at Harvey Klinger, Inc., she has done wonders with my career, always moving me to bigger houses, securing better deals and better rights packages. That said, I maintain a very open line of communication with her. We discuss and strategize what to do next, which project or pitch to present, what to dial back on, and so on. As a result of that partnership, Sara has so far sold nineteen novels (five of which are as yet unwritten), five nonfiction books, a TV development deal, a movie option, and she's negotiated very good page rates for my comic book work.

At the same time, I make it a point to know the business, the world of publishing, the markets, the realities of book marketing, the bookselling process, and so on. Every writer should know this stuff.

JBK: In a Moon Books Entertainment article you attempted to more clearly define the horror genre. Based on your 'rant', we could assume that most of the original *Twilight Zone* television series fits nicely into the horror casket. Do you agree?

JM: Yes, *Twilight Zone* was horror. Quite a lot of things are horror, but that word has gotten such a bad rap because of its unfair association with cheesy slasher movies and torture porn. Real horror comes in all sorts of delicious flavors. You have science gone wrong horror (*Frankenstein, The Andromeda Strain, 2001*), alien horror (*Aliens, Predator*), supernatural horror (vampires, demons, ghosts), comedy horror (*Buffy, Shaun of the Dead, Scream*), serial killer horror (*Silence of the Lambs*), existential horror (*Jacob's Ladder*), situational horror (*127 Hours*), gentle horror (*Frankenweenie*), musical horror (*Rocky Horror Show*), religious horror (*The Prophecy*), and on and on.

JBK: It sounds like you came into horror as a real fan, once likening re-reading favorite horror works to "*…buying another ticket for the same rickety, scary, wonderful roller-coaster every summer.*" Which horror classics do you return to?

JM: *The Haunting of Hill House*, both book and original film adaptation, is my gold standard. However I read Ray Bradbury's *Something Wicked This Way Comes* and Richard Matheson's *I Am Legend* every Halloween.

JBK: Marvel Comics tapped into your talents in 2009 for their *Black Panther* series in the 7th issue, but that is not the only comic book writing you have done. How does that process work? How much collaboration with the artists is required?

JM: I was scouted for Marvel by Editor-in-chief Axel Alonso after he read my novel, *Patient Zero*. They started me off with one-shot stories with Punisher and Wolverine. I did that brief stint on *Black Panther*, but for the most part I've concentrated on miniseries, which is a heckuva lot of fun. That's given me a chance to work with Marvel Zombies, Captain America, the Avengers and a lot of other heroes. The challenge in all this was the shift between writing novels to writing comic book scripts. The real learning curve was shifting my storytelling style to allow the story to be driven primarily by the art. Sure, the writer tells the artist what should go in each panel, but the artist brings soooo much to the project by interpreting that description and expanding on it. With novels it's such an isolated process—just you and your laptop. But with comics it's a collaborative effort. The editor's involved at every step, then there's a bit of back-and-forth with the artist, the inker, and even the letterer at times. It took a little while for me to get into that rhythm, but once I did I fell in love with it.

A 20 page comic script is usually about four or five thousand words. The format is very much like writing a script for an hour of television. And these days comics are told in four-to-six issue arcs, which allows for deep character development, lots of action, and plenty of room for the artist to shine.

JBK: *Patient Zero* (St. Martin's Griffin, 2009) was once adapted by Javier Grillo-Marxuach for ABC television and renamed 'Department Zero,' but unfortunately it never moved into production. We've heard that your book *Rot & Ruin* has been optioned for film. How is that going?

JM: *Department Zero* might have been a great show because Javi's script was outstanding. However the president of ABC decided to run with a remake of *Charlie's Angels*. That show lasted a couple of episodes and was cancelled.

As for *Rot & Ruin*, it's been optioned and is officially in development. We're at the very beginning of that process, so it'll be a couple of years before we're lining up at the ticket booth. Can't spill any details yet because they're planning a big announcement.

JBK: Your book *Rot & Ruin* (Simon & Schuster, 2011) the first in a four part series, takes place at a time fourteen years after a human-devastating zombie apocalypse. Do zombies just lie about, waiting, when living humans are hard to come by...or don't they decay away to dust?

JM: There's actually a solid scientific reason for the

zombies in the *Rot & Ruin* series to keep from rotting. I drop all that science in book four, *Fire & Ash*. But that's just part of the reveal in that last book. I tie up all of the loose ends in a way that I believe will be very satisfying for the readers.

JBK: Is it correct that *Rot & Ruin* was originally a novella, written for the adult horror market, and your agent made the suggestion that you expand and develop the story for a younger audience?

JM: *Rot & Ruin* began as a novella for the adult anthology, *The New Dead*, edited by Christopher Golden for St. Martin's Griffin. The antho also includes stories by Joe Hill, John Connolly, Max Brooks, Kelley Armstrong, Tad Williams, David Wellington, David Liss, Aimee Bender, and others. Chris asked each of us to write something that was outside of our normal comfort zone. I'd never written a story from a teenager's point of view before, nor had I tackled a post-apocalyptic story, so that's where I went. After it was done, my agent told me that she thought it read like the opening of a Young Adult novel. At that time I hadn't read much YA, so I told her she was nuts. I never win those arguments. She sent me a bunch of current YA novels that blew me away. So, I let her shop it as a teaser for a novel, and I gave her an expanded version of the story that really pleased me. We had several offers, but David Gale, the legendary senior editor of Simon & Schuster's Books for Young Readers made us an offer we couldn't refuse.

JBK: There is certainly a trend towards grittier subjects and darker themes in modern YA. Was that a surprise to you, and did it help you change your original vision for *Rot & Ruin*?

JM: Nowadays I read a ton of Young Adult fiction. It's amazing stuff. What I've found is that these books cross all kinds of genre lines. You can't get away with that in adult fiction. And the authors of YA are speaking frankly to their readers; they're starting conversations via their books about subjects that really matter. The audience—today's teens—don't need or want to be coddled. They want to have these conversations because these are subjects that

THEY ARE HUNTING US.

V WARS

JONATHAN MABERRY

matter. You have to respect that. God knows I do.

JBK: The August 2012 release, *V Wars*, a collection of threaded stories by various authors, was conceived and edited by you. What do you enjoy more, editing or creative writing?

JM: I'll always be a writer first. That's my defining quality. Editing is fun, though, because I get to read some new material that no one else has seen. I'm editing a wacky anthology right now called *Redneck Zombies from Outer Space*. Crazy stuff.

V-Wars had been cooking in my head for some time. A bit of science and some what-if elements. When I pitched it to IDW, I knew that I wanted it to be a shared-world project. The other writers I was able to bring in were all friends, folks whose work I love and whose temperament I trusted. We had Scott Nicholson, Nancy Holder, Yvonne Navarro, Keith R.A. DeCandido, Gregory Frost, John Everson and James A. Moore on that. Terrific fun, and they each brought their A-game.

JBK: In a Renew Theaters interview with Chris Collier, you said: *"There is a golden rule in writing horror: If you focus on the monster it is bad horror. If you deal with the people, you are writing good horror."* Is that a personal observation, or something you can attribute to a source?

JM: It's a personal observation and it's mostly—but not always—true. Some folks focus on the monster, but in doing so they explore those elements of humanity present in the creature, as with *Frankenstein*, or they explore what a being is like whose essential humanity has been stripped away, as with *Silence of the Lambs.* But overall, stories are about people. Not monsters, not events, not things…people. After all it's people who are reading these stories, and writers are always looking for that tether that connects their words to real hearts and minds.

JBK: Please define the differences between *fast* and *slow* zombies, and why you prefer the latter in fiction.

JM: I prefer whichever kind of zombie best suits

the story. I've used both fast and slow zoms in different books, often in the same story. In the *Rot & Ruin* books I use slow zombies at first because that book is an homage to George Romero's *Night of the Living Dead.* I mean, after all, the backstory openly borrows from that wonderful film; and even the main character—Benny Imura—is named after Ben, the lead character from *Night.* As the series goes on the characters encounter fast zombies, and I even cooked up a good reason why slow zombies could speed up. In *Dead of Night*, the zombies are faster when they're fresh and slower as rigor sets in. In *Patient Zero*, they come in all speeds.

JBK: JournalStone's Anne Petty is editing your latest project, *LIMBUS*, a shared anthology of works by five accomplished horror/dark fiction authors. Have you read the works yet from your peers in that project? Do projects of this sort require close collaboration from the authors?

JM: I've read all of the stories in the first *LIMBUS* anthology and I was dazzled by them. It's proof of something I've been saying for years, that you can take any basic idea and if you give it to a bunch of good writers they'll come up with entirely different stories.

We had no collaboration on the project, as least not as far as I was concerned. I read the other stories first only because a previous deadline made me be the last to submit. And, I wanted to make sure I wasn't covering any of the same ground, but I needn't have worried. Everyone was way off in an interesting corner of their own warped imaginations.

JBK: Author Petty conceived the idea of LIMBUS, a secretive organization that selectively recruits *specially* talented individuals for jobs that entail otherworldly adventures. How did you learn of the project?

JM: They reached out to me about *LIMBUS* and at first I didn't think I'd have the time. But they kept teasing me about the project and finally they made it sound so appealing that I jumped aboard. I'm glad I did, too, because the format allowed me to take some creative risks with the story I wrote.

JBK: The character in your LIMBUS story, Sam

Hunter, is savvy but jaded, yet realistic about how dark the fight against evil can be. He is uniquely suited to join the shadowy organization, Limbus Inc. Is Sam a character your readers will recognize?

JM: Sam Hunter was introduced in the short story, *"Like Part of the Family,"* first published in *Best New Vampire Tales*, even though Sam isn't a vampire. He's a former cop from the Twin Cities who was thrown off the force because of some unusually excessive bits of police brutality. Sam takes a rather strong dislike to anyone who preys on the innocent and he, in turn, preys on them. He's a good guy, but not a very nice guy.

JBK: After writing close to a dozen novels, you finally penned one that "…*creeped (you) out while writing it.*" Why did *Dead of Night* affect you more thoroughly than all your other spooky creations?

JM: About the time I started writing *Dead of Night*, my father-in-law began suffering from dementia. He was a great guy, a top professional musician who had a first-class intellect. I saw that intellect begin to fracture. Tragic as that was it wouldn't have been as bad if he was so far gone that he was unaware he was losing it. But dementia is insidious. He did know, and that both horrified me and broke my heart.

I explore that, in my own way, in *Dead of Night.* In that novel the people who are transformed into flesh-eating zombies don't completely die. Their consciousness is trapped inside their bodies, but they are no longer able to control anything. Not a single function, not even the twitch of a finger is left in their control. They are helpless passengers as their zombie bodies commit murder and devour family and friends. That concept, that degree of helpless horror, scares me more than any vampire or werewolf. The thought of being trapped inside your own body, unable to communicate, unable to control even the simplest function, and yet to still be aware…jeez, that creeps me out.

JBK: You like returning to characters in series works; Joe Ledger and Benny Imura are familiar names to your fans. Currently another character Dylan Quinn is being developed for 2014 and 2015 release. Do these projects materialize because of fan pressure, or do the characters themselves pester you to write about them?

JM: I never write to satisfy fan pressure. That would feel weird. I write to satisfy the reader in my own head. I write the books I would want to read.

Dylan Quinn reflects some characteristics and aspects of me when I was a teenager. By the time I got to high school I was well over six feet tall and very muscular, I was a black belt, and I was also a straight-A student. I read a lot. And I wasn't a jackass. It was interesting being one of the smarter (though not the smartest) kid in school, and also being one of the toughest. And I had a strong moral code because of martial arts. So…Dylan is a bit like that. His own intellect makes him an outsider in a tough inner city school in Detroit; but his ethics and strength nudge him toward helping other kids who are being bullied.

Watch Over Me will be the first book in a series. No zombies, no aliens, no gunplay. It's a straight myster-thriller.

JBK: A lot of your non-fiction work has been derived from your Martial Arts skill as an 8th degree Black Belt of the Shinowara-ryu Jujutsu discipline. Yet right in the middle of your non-fiction bibliography are some works about monsters, vampires, zombies, and supernatural predators. How did those delightful projects come about?

JM: It's funny, but since I had exposure to so much information on monsters growing up, thanks to my grandmother, one of the things I used to think about when practicing martial arts was how jujutsu and kenjutsu would work against them. I started martial arts when I was six, so all through my boyhood, when I was training with weapons, or working out on the bags, or doing kata, instead of imagining that I was fighting ninjas or thugs, I imagined I was fighting vampires, werewolves, mummies and other critters.

I even did a couple of projects (for belt tests) where I demonstrated techniques that would work against monsters. My teachers, though amused, grilled me pretty hard on the logic, physics, physiology, psychology and tactics of those kinds of fights. They made me take it seriously, and in no small way did that influence my writing.

JBK: About what percent of your current output is hired, verses being a work you conceived and then developed?

JM: All of my short story work is hired, in that I have never pitched a short story or novella—all of it has been written in response to invitations from editors of magazines or anthologies. As for my novels, only one of those was a hire job. Universal Pictures reached out to me a few years ago and asked if I'd like to novelize the remake of *The Wolfman.* I thought it would be fun, so I did it. The movie, sadly, tanked; but the novel went on to become my first New York Times bestseller, and then went on to win the Scribe Award for best movie adaptation.

JBK: In an earlier interview, you advised writers to write daily without exception. You cautioned that it was the only true way to develop skill and success, and admitted that you don't even understand writer's block, because it doesn't happen to you. Some new authors might hear all that advice, believing they should work on a single book until it is complete. That is not your meaning at all, is it?

JM: Yes and no. I'm a big believer in finishing what you start. Too many writers have partially written manuscripts cluttering up their lives, and while I understand that they might drop a stale project in favor of something new and exciting, there are problems with that. First, it doesn't teach discipline, and a professional writer needs discipline. It also doesn't challenge the creative mind. If you drop something because it's become stale, that doesn't encourage you to find a way to rekindle the story into something that catches fire in your heart.

That said, there are times when a writer can work successfully on more than one project at a time. For example, while writing a novel you can take time out to write a short story, or a new blog entry, or something like that.

I start every day with a fifteen minute writing exercise specifically designed to make me stretch as a writer. One day I might challenge myself to write the opening to a Harlequin-style romance; the next I might have to write a scene of political satire, or an action scene in a western involving ferrets. The idea is to never hit a point where you say: I can't write that.

JBK: Self-published authors have a very skeptical view of the modern publishing industry. There are so many ways to find readers currently, that even traditionally published authors are exploring the more intimate means of reaching readers. Is that style of authorship attractive to you?

JM: I have friends who self-publish, and I know a few who have made some serious cash that way; but overall I advocate that any writer who thinks they have a good book should try and find an agent. Traditional publishing will, of need, change as digital publishing and the prevalence of eReaders become more common, but publishing as an industry will never go away.

JBK: We've learned that you tour a lot, speaking at schools, libraries, and conferences. Many budding authors dream of the day they can tour and speak about their books. They may have misconceptions, however, how book touring really works. Is it merely one of the marketing tools employed by your publisher, or is the whole process of public appearance and speaking the natural result of being invited by fans and organizations?

JM: Simon & Schuster sets up my tour for each new YA novel, but those tours last a few weeks or a month. After that I'm on my own, which is fine. Most of my appearances are the result of invitations from conferences, library chains, schools, and bookstores. Since I write in several genres and for several publishers, I usually have a new product out every few weeks.

JBK: You credit your grandmother with instilling in you a love of folklore and supernatural legend. What sort of stories did she tell you? Were those same stories part of her childhood?

JM: My grandmother was a walking encyclopedia of European folklore. She was born on the border of France and Germany, but was of Scottish and Irish heritage. So she had four cultures upon which to draw. She read voraciously and her house was filled with books and curios from all over the world. She taught me to read tarot cards when I was a kid, and always had books for me to read–everything from Hans Holzer to Alistair Crowley to Bullfinch.

Her personal belief system was odd. She called herself a druid, but she didn't belong to any particular group. I suspect she called herself that because it sounded spooky and intriguing.

JBK: We can tell that you will be busy into the next several years. What other ventures on your plate would you like to mention?

JM: Well, I'm currently writing the sixth Joe Ledger thriller, *Code Zero*; and after that I'll be writing *Fall of Night*, the sequel to *Dead of Night*. Then I write *Watch Over Me*. All of those are due this year. Next year I have to write Joe Ledger #7 (which doesn't have a title yet), and the second in the Dylan Quinn series, tentatively titled *Cold, Cold Heart*.

I have some comic book pitches out there and we're having some very interesting discussions; but nothing I can talk about yet.

I'm having a lot of fun with short stories… because so many of them are in wildly different genres. I have a charming tale about a little girl Flying Monkey for *Oz Reimagined*, due out at the end of February. I recently wrote a western ghost story, a steampunk story, a contemporary monster story set in Pine Deep (the town from *Ghost Road Blues*), a vampires and mixed martial arts story, a Cthulhu story, a techno-thriller, and a story for an anthology of Auguste Dupin stories (Poe's character from *Murders in the Rue Morgue)*. This is why I dig the short story market…it's always different and I never know what they'll ask me to do next!

✸✸✸

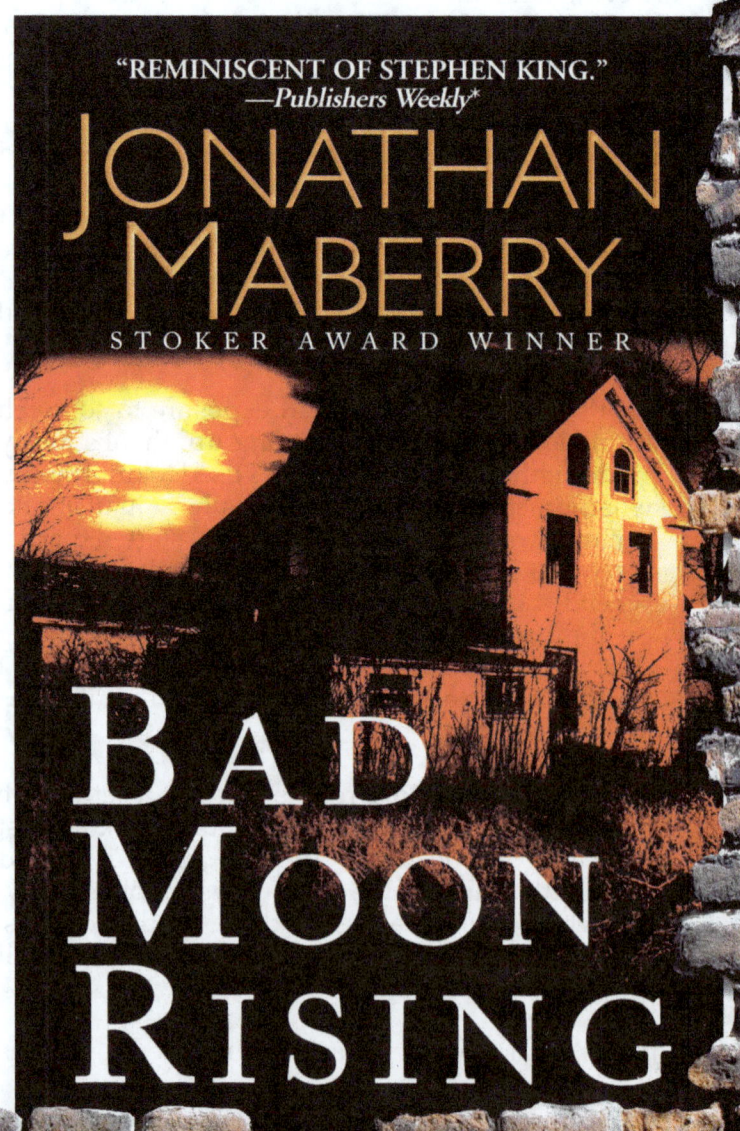

"REMINISCENT OF STEPHEN KING."
—*Publishers Weekly**

JONATHAN
MABERRY

STOKER AWARD WINNER

BAD
MOON
RISING

LIKE PART OF THE FAMILY

By Jonathan Maberry

"My ex-husband is trying to kill me," she said.

She was one of those cookie-cutter East Coast blondes. Pale skin, pale hair, pale eyes. Lots of New Age jewelry. Not a lot of curves, and too much perfume. Kind of pretty if you dig the modeling-scene heroin chic look. Or if you troll the anorexia twelve-steps or crack houses looking for easy ass that's so desperate for affection they'll boff you blind for a smile. Not my kind. I like a little more meat on the bone, and a bit more sanity in the eyes. This one came to me on a referral from another client.

"He actually try?"

"I can tell, Mr. Hunter."

Yeah, I thought and tried not to sigh. What I figured.

"You call the cops?"

She shrugged.

"What's that mean? You call them or not?"

"I called," she said. "They said that there wasn't anything they could do unless he did something first."

"Yeah," I said. "Can't arrest someone for thinking about something."

"He threatened me."

"Anyone hear him make the threat?"

"No."

"Then it's your word."

"That's what the police said." She crossed her legs. Her legs were on the thin side of being nice. Probably were nice before drugs or stress or a fractured self-image wasted her down to Sally Stick-figure.

Skirt was short, shoes looked expensive. I have three ex-wives and I pay alimony bigger than India's national debt. I know how expensive women's shoes are. I was wearing black sneakers from Payless. Glad I had a desk between me and her.

"Your husband ever hurt you?" I asked. "Or try to?"

"*Ex*," she corrected. "And…yes. That's why I left him. He hit me a few times. Mostly when he was drunk and out of control."

I held up a hand. "Don't make excuses for him. He hit you. Being drunk doesn't change the rules. Might even make it worse, especially if he did it once while drunk and then let himself come home drunk again."

She digested that. She'd probably heard that rap before but it might have come from a female caseworker or a shrink. From the way her eyes shifted to me and away and back again I guessed she'd never heard that from a man before. I guess for her, men were the Big Bad. Too many of them are.

It was ten to five, but it was already dark outside. December snow swirled past the window. It wasn't accumulating, so the snow still looked pretty. Once it started piling up I hated the shit. My secretary, Mrs. Gilligan, fled at the first flake. Typical Philadelphian—they think the world will come to a screeching halt if there's half an inch on the ground. She's probably at Wegmans stocking up on milk, bread and toilet paper. The staples of the apocalypse. Me, I grew up in Minneapolis, and out in the Cities we think twenty inches is getting off light. Doesn't mean I don't hate the shit, though. A low annual snowfall is one of the reasons I moved to Philly after I got my PI license. Easier to hunt if you don't have to slog through snow.

"When he hit you," I said, "you report it?"

"No."

"Not to the cops?"

"No."

"Women's shelter?

"No."

"Anyone? A friend?"

She shook her head. "I was…embarrassed, Mr. Hunter. A black eye and all. Didn't want to be seen."

Which means there's no record. Nothing to support her case about ex-hubby wanting to kill her.

I drummed my fingers on the desk blotter. I get these kinds of cases every once in a while, though I stayed well clear of domestic disputes and spousal abuse cases when I was with Minneapolis PD. I have a temper, and by the time they asked for my shield back I had six reprimands in my jacket for excessive force. At one of my IA hearings the captain said he was disappointed that I showed no remorse for the last 'incident'. I busted a child molester and somehow while the guy was, um, resisting arrest he managed to get mauled and mangled a bit. The pedophile tried to spin some crazy shit that I sicced a dog on him, but I don't *have* a dog. I said that he got mauled by a stray during a foot pursuit. Even at my own hearing I couldn't keep a smile off my face to save my job. Squeaked by on that one, but next time something like it happened—

this time with a guy who whipped his wife half to death with an extension cord because she wasn't 'willing enough' in the bedroom—I was out on my ass. He ran into the same stray dog. Weird how that happens, huh? Long story short, I already didn't have the warm fuzzies for her husband. We all have our buttons, and when the strong prey on the weak, all of mine get pushed.

"Did you go to the E.R.?"

"No," she said. "It was never that bad. More humiliating than anything."

I nodded. "What about after the divorce? He lay a hand on you since?"

She hesitated.

"Mrs. Skye?" I prompted.

"He tried. He chased me. Twice."

"*Chased* you? Tell me about it."

She licked her lips. She wore a very nice rose-pink lipstick that was the only splash of color. Even her clothes and shoes were white. Pale horse, pale rider.

"Well," she said, "that's where the story gets really…strange."

"Strange how?"

"He—David, my ex-husband—*changed* after I filed for divorce. He's like a different person. Before, when I first met him, he was a very fastidious man. Always dressed nicely, always very clean and well-groomed."

"What's he do for a living?"

"He owns a nightclub. *The Crypt*, just off South Street."

"I know it, but that's a Goth club, right? Is he Goth?"

"No. Not at all. He bought the club from the former owner, but he remodeled it after *The Batcave*."

"As in Batman?"

"As in the London club that was kind of the prototype of pretty much the whole Goth club scene. David's a businessman. There's a strong Goth crowd downtown, and they hang together, but the clubs in Philly aren't big enough to turn a big profit, and not near big enough to attract the better bands. So, he bought the two adjoining buildings and expanded out. He made a small-time club into a very successful main stage club, and he keeps the music current. A lot of post-punk stuff, but also the newer styles. Dark cabaret, deathrock, Gothabilly. That sort of thing. Low lights, black-tile bathrooms, bartenders who look like ghouls."

"Okay," I said.

"But this was all business to David. He didn't dress Goth. I mean, he wore black suits or black silk shirts to work, but he didn't dye his hair, didn't wear eyeliner. Funny thing is, even though he was clearly not buying into the lifestyle, the patrons loved him. They called him the Prince. As in Prince of—?"

"Darkness, yeah, got it. Go on."

"David was more fussy getting ready to go out than I ever was. Spent forever in the bathroom shaving, fixing his hair. Always took him longer to pick out his clothes than me or any of my girlfriends."

"He gay?"

"No." And she shot me a 'wow, what a stereotypically homophobic thing to say' sort of look.

I smiled. "I'm just trying to get a read on him. Fastidious guy having trouble with a relationship with his wife. Drinking problem, flashes of violence. Not a gay thing, but I've seen it before in guys who are sexually conflicted and at war with themselves and the world because of it."

She studied me for a moment. "You used to be a cop, Mr. Hunter?"

"Call me Sam," I said. "And, yeah, I was a cop. Minneapolis PD."

"A detective?"

"Yep."

"Okay." That seemed to mollify her. I gestured to her to continue. She took a breath. "Well… toward the end of our relationship, David stopped being so fastidious. He would go two or three days without shaving. I know that doesn't sound like the end of the world, but I never saw David without a fresh shave. Never. He carried an electric razor in his briefcase, had another at home and one in the office at the club. Clothes, too. Before, he'd sometimes change clothes twice or even three times a day if it was humid. He always wanted to look fresh. Showered at home morning and night, and had a shower installed in his office."

"I get the picture. Mr. Clean. But you say that changed while you were still together?"

"It started when he fell off the wagon."

"Ah."

"When I met him he said that he hadn't taken a drink for over two years. He was proud of it. He thought that his thirst—he always called it that—was evil, and being on the wagon made him feel like a real person. Then, after we started having problems, he started drinking again. Never in front of me, and he always washed his mouth out before he came home. I never smelled alcohol on him, but he was a different person from then on. And he started yelling at me all the time. He called me horrible names and made threats. He said that I didn't love him, that I was just trying to use him."

"I have to ask," I said, being as delicate as I could, "but was there someone else?"

"For me? God, no!"

"What set him off? From his perspective, I mean. Did he say that there was something that made him angry or paranoid?"

"Well…I think it was his health."

"Tell me."

"He started losing weight. He was never fat, not even stocky. David was very muscular. He lifted a lot of weights, drank that protein powder twice a day. He had big arms, a huge chest. I asked him if he was taking steroids. He denied it, but I think he was trying to turn into one of those muscle freaks. Then, about a year and a half ago, he started losing weight. When he taped his arms and found that his biceps were only twenty-two inches, he got really angry."

"David has twenty-two inch biceps?" Christ. Back in his Mr. Universe days, Arnold the Terminator had twenty-four inch arms, fully pumped. I think mine are somewhere shy of fifteen, and that's after three sets on the Bowflex.

"Not anymore," said Mrs. Skye. "He lost a lot of muscle mass. Really fast, too. I was scared; I told him to go to a doctor. I thought he might have cancer."

"Did he go to the doctor?"

"He said so…but I don't think he did. He kept losing weight. After six months, he didn't even have much definition. He was kind of ordinary sized."

"Was he drinking by this point?"

"I'm sure of it."

"That when he started putting his hands on you?"

"Yes. And he became paranoid. Kept trying to make it all my fault."

"How long did this go on?"

"Well…after the first time he, um, *hurt* me, I gave him a second chance. After all, he was my husband. I figured he was just scared because of his health. But then it happened again. The second time he knocked me around pretty good. I couldn't go out of the house for a few days."

"Was that when you left?"

It took her so long to answer that I knew what her answer would be. I've done too many interviews of this kind. If self-esteem is low enough then victimization can become an addiction.

"I stayed for two more months."

"How many times did he hurt you during that time?" I asked.

"A few."

"A few is how many?"

Another long pause. "Six."

"Six," I said, trying to put no judgment in my tone. "What was the last straw?"

She looked at her hands, at the clock, at the snow falling outside. If there'd been a magazine on my desk she would have picked it up and leafed through it. Anything to keep from meeting my eyes. "He choked me."

"I see."

"It was in the middle of the night. We were… we were…"

I almost sighed. "Let me guess. Make-up sex?"

She nodded, but she didn't blush. I'll give her that. "He'd been sweet to me for two weeks straight without getting mad or yelling, or anything. He acted like his old self. Charming." She finally met my eyes. "David has enormous charisma. He makes everyone like him, and he always seems so genuine."

"Uh huh," I said, wondering how that charm would work on a blackjack across his teeth.

"We sat up talking until late, then we went to bed. And in the middle of the night...things just started happening. You know how it is."

I didn't, but I said nothing.

"I was, um...on top. And we were pretty far into things, and then all of a sudden David reaches up and grabs me around the throat. I thought for one crazy moment that he was doing that auto-whatever it's called."

"Autoerotic asphyxiation," I supplied.

"Yeah, that. I thought he was doing that. He talked about it once before, but we'd never tried it. He's really strong and I'm pretty small. But...I guess I thought he was trying to change things, you know? Create a new pattern for us. A fresh start."

Naivety can be a terrible thing. Jesus wept.

"But it wasn't sex play," I prompted.

"No. He started squeezing his hands. Suddenly I couldn't breathe. It was weird because we were so close to...you know...and David kept staring at me, his eyes wide like he was in some kind of trance. I tried to pull his hands apart, but it just made him squeeze tighter. That's when he started calling me names again, making wild accusations, accusing me of destroying his life."

"How did you get away?"

Her eyes cut away again. This was obviously very hard for her.

"I threw myself sideways and when I landed I kicked him in the, um...you know."

I smiled.

"Good for you," I said, but she shook her head.

"I grabbed my clothes and ran out. Next day I drove past the house and saw that his car was gone. I had a locksmith come out and change the locks and change the security code on the alarm. I hired a messenger company to take a couple of suitcases of his clothes to the club. Next day I rented a storage unit and had a moving company take all of his stuff there. I used the same messenger service to send him the key."

"I'm impressed. That was quick thinking."

"I...I'd already looked into that stuff before. Until that last stretch where he was nice I was planning to leave him. I'd already talked to my lawyer, and I filed for divorce by the end of that week."

"What did David do?"

"At first? Nothing, except for some hysterical messages on my voicemail. He didn't try to break in, nothing like that. But after a while I started seeing his car behind mine when I was going to work."

"Where do you work?"

"I'm a nurse supervisor at Sunset Grove, the assisted living facility in Jenkintown. Right now I'm on the four to midnight shift. I've spotted David's car a lot, sometimes every night for weeks on end. I've seen him drive by when I'm going into the staff entrance, and his car is there sometimes when I get back home, cruising down the street or parked a block up."

"What makes you think he's planning to do more than just harass you?"

"He's said so."

"But—"

"He didn't say or do anything at first...but over the last couple of weeks it's gotten worse. About three weeks ago I came out of work and stopped at a 7-11 for some gum, and when I came out he was leaning against my car. I told him to get away, but he pushed himself off the car and came up to me, smiling his charming smile. He told me that he knew who I was and what I was and that he was going to end me. His words. *'I'm going to end you'*. Then he left, still smiling."

"Did anyone see this?"

"At one in the morning? No."

Convenience stores have security cameras, I thought. If this thing got messy I could have her lawyer subpoena those tapes. I had her write down the address of the 7-11.

"That's how it went for a couple of weeks," she said. "But last night he really scared me."

"What happened?"

"He was in my bedroom."

"How?"

"That's it...I don't know. The alarms didn't go off and none of the windows were broken. I heard a sound and I woke up and there he was, standing by the side of my bed. He's really thin now and as pale as those Goth kids at his club. He stood there, smiling. I started to scream and he put a finger to his lips and made a weird shushing sound. It was so strange that I actually did shut up. Don't ask me why. The whole thing was like a nightmare."

"Are you sure it wasn't?"

She hesitated, but she said, "I'm positive. He pointed at me and said that he knew everything about me. Then he started praying."

"Praying?"

"At least I think that's what he was doing. It was Latin, I think. He was saying a long string of things in Latin and then he left."

"How'd he get out?"

"The same way he got in, I guess...but I don't know how. I was so scared that I almost peed myself and I just lay there in bed for a long time. I don't know how long. When I finally worked up the nerve, I ran downstairs and got a knife from the kitchen and went through the whole house."

"You didn't call the cops?"

"I was going to...but the alarm never went off. I checked the system...it was still set. I began wondering if I *was* dreaming."

"But you don't think so?"

"No."

"Why are you so sure?"

She fished in her purse and produced a pink cell phone. She flipped it open and pressed a few buttons to call up her text messages. She pointed to the number and then handed me the phone.

"That's David's cell number."

The text read: *Tonight.*

"Okay," I said. "Let me see what I can do."

"What *can* you do?" she asked.

"Well, the best first thing to do is go have a talk with him. See if I can convince him to back off."

"And if he won't?"

"I can be pretty convincing."

"But what if he won't? What if he's...I don't know...too crazy to listen to reason?"

I smiled. "Then we'll explore other options."

The Crypt is a big ugly building on the corner of South and Fourth in Philadelphia. Once upon a time it was a coffin factory—which I think would have been a cooler name. Less trendy and obvious. The light snow did nothing to make it look less ugly. When we pulled to the corner, Mrs. Skye pointed to a sleek silver Lexus parked on the side street.

"That's his."

I jotted down the license plate and used my digital camera to take photos of it and the exterior of the building. You never know.

"Okay," I said, "I want you to wait here. I'll go have a talk with David and see if we can sort this out."

"What if something happens? What if you don't come out?"

"Just sit tight. You have a cell phone and I'll give her the keys. If I'm not out of there in fifteen minutes, drive somewhere safe and call the name on the back of my card." I gave her my business card. She turned it over and saw a name and number. Before she could ask, I said, "Ray's a friend. One of my pack."

"Another private investigator?"

"A bodyguard. I use him for certain jobs, but I don't think we'll need to bring him in on this. From what you've told me I have a pretty good sense of what to expect in there."

As I got out my jacket flap opened and she spotted the handle of my Glock.

"You're not...going to *hurt* him," she asked, wide eyed.

I shook my head. "I've been doing this for a lot of years, Mrs. Skye. I haven't had to pull my gun

once. I don't expect I'll break that streak tonight."

* * *

The breeze was coming from the west and the snow was just about done. I squinted up past the streetlights. The cloud cover was thin and I could already see the white outline of the moon. Nope, no accumulation. Typical Philly winter.

I crossed the street and tried the front door. Place didn't do much business before late evening, but the doors were unlocked. The doors opened with an exhalation of cigarette smoke and alcohol fumes. There was probably an anti-smoking violation in that. Something else to use later if I needed to go the route of making life difficult for him.

It was too early for a doorman, and I walked a short hallway that was empty and painted black. Heavy black velvet curtains at the end. Cute. I pushed them aside and entered the club. Place was huge. David Skye must have taken out the second floor and knocked out everything but the retaining walls of the adjoining properties. The red and white maximum occupancy sign said that it shouldn't exceed four hundred, but the place looked capable of taking twice that number. Bandstand was empty, so someone had put quarters in to play the tuneless junk that was beating the shit out of the woofers and tweeters. Whoever the group was on the record they subscribed to the philosophy that if you can't play well, you should play real goddamn loud.

There were maybe twenty people in the place, scattered around at tables. A few at the bar. Everyone looked like extras from a direct-to-video vampire flick. The motif was black on black with occasional splashes of blood red. White skin that probably never saw the sun. Eyeliner and black lipstick, even on the guys. I was in jeans and a Vikings warm-up jacket. At least my sneakers and my leather porkpie hat were black. Handle of my gun was black, too, but they couldn't see that. Better for everyone if nobody did.

The bartender was giving me *the look*, so I strolled over to him. He knew I wasn't there for a beer and didn't waste either of our time by asking.

"David Skye," I said, having to bend forward and shout over the music.

"Badge me," he said.

I flipped open my PI license. "Private."

"Fuck off," he suggested.

"Not a chance."

"I can call the cops."

"Bet I can have L and I here before they show. Smoking in a public restaurant?"

Another smartass remark was on his lips, but he didn't have the energy for it. He was paid by the hour and this had to be a slow shift for tips. I took a twenty from my wallet and put it on the bar.

"This isn't your shit, kid," I said. "Call your boss."

He didn't like it, but he took the twenty and made the call.

"He says come up." The bartender pointed to another curtained doorway beside the bar. I gave him a sunny day smile and went inside.

There was a long hallway with bathrooms on both sides and a set of stairs at the end. I took the stairs two at a time. The stairs went straight up to his office and the door was open. I knocked anyway.

"It's open," he yelled. I went inside; and as I looked around I hoped like hell that the office décor was not modeled after the interior landscape of David Skye's mind. The walls were painted a dark red, the trim was gloss black. Instead of the band posters and framed *'look at who I'm shaking hands with'* eight-by-tens, the walls were hung with torture devices and S and M clothes. Spiked harnesses, leather zippered masks, thumbscrews, photos from Abu Graib, diagrams of dissected bodies. A full-sized rack occupied one corner of the room and an iron maiden stood in the other, one door open to reveal rows of tarnished metal spikes. The only other furniture was a big desk made from some dark wood, a black file cabinet, and the leather swivel chair in which David Skye sat. He wore a black poet's shirt, leather wristbands, and a smile that was already belligerent.

"The fuck are you and the fuck you want?"

The man was a charmer. I could just taste the charisma his wife had mentioned flowing like sweetness from his pores.

I flipped my ID case open. "We need to have a chat. It can be friendly or not. Your call."

"Go fuck yourself."

So much for *friendly.*

"That whore send you?" he demanded.

I smiled but didn't answer.

He had a handsome face, but his wife was right when she said that he'd lost weight. His skin looked thin and loose, and he had the complexion of a mushroom. More gray than white.

"Did my wife send you?" he said, pronouncing the words slowly as if I'd come here on the short bus.

"Why would your ex-wife send me?"

His eyes flickered for a second at *'ex*-wife'. I strolled across the room and stood in front of his desk. He didn't get up; neither of us offered a hand to the other.

"She makes up stories," he said.

"What kind of stories?"

"Bullshit. Lies. Says I slapped her around."

"Who'd she say that to?"

He didn't answer. He did, however, give me the ninja secret death stare, but I manned my way through it.

"What are you supposed to be?" he said.

"Just what the license says."

"Private investigator. Private *dick.*"

"Yes, and that was funny back in the 1950s. Why do *you* think I'm here?"

"She's probably trying some kind of squeeze play. The club's doing okay, so she wants a bigger slice."

"Try again," I said, though he might have been right about that.

"Oh, I get it….you're supposed to scare me into leaving her alone."

"Do I look scary?"

He smiled. He had very red lips and very white teeth. "No," he said, "you don't."

"Right…so let's pretend that I'm here to have a reasonable discussion. Man to man."

Skye leaned back in his chair and stared at me with his dark eyes. It was a calculating look, and I'm sure he took in everything from my slightly threadbare Vikings jacket to my cheap black sneakers. Put everything I was wearing together and it would equal the cost of his shirt. I was okay with that. I don't dress to impress. Skye, on the other hand, smiled as if our mutual understanding of my material net worth clearly made him the alpha.

I smiled back.

"What does she want?" he asked.

"For you to leave her alone."

"What is she afraid of?"

"She thinks you're trying to kill her."

"What do *you* think?"

"What I think doesn't matter. I'm not a psychic, so I don't know whether you're trying to kill her or if you're playing some kind of mindgame on her. Whatever it is, I'm here to ask you to lay off."

"Why should I?"

"Because I asked real nice."

He smiled at that.

"Because it's illegal and I could build a harassment case against you and you could lose your club and sink a quarter mil into legal fees. Because I know inspectors who can slap you with fifteen kinds of violations that will hurt your business. I can have your car booted by *accident* three or four times a week, every week."

"And I could have you killed," he said, the smile unwavering.

"Maybe," I said. "You could try, and I might fuck up anyone you send and then come back here and fuck you up."

"Think you could?"

"You really want to find out?" When he didn't answer, I took a glass paperweight off his desk and turned it over in my hands. A spider was trapped inside, frozen into a moment of time for the amusement of the trinket crowd. I knew he was watching me play with the paperweight, wondering what I was going to do with it.

I put it back down on the desk.

"Really, though," I said, "how long do we need to circle and sniff each other? We don't run in the same pack and I don't give a rat's ass what you do, who you are, or how tough you think you are. We both know that you're either going to stop bothering your ex-wife and go on with your life, or you're going to make a run at her—either because you have some loose wiring or because I'm pushing your buttons by being here. If you back off, we're all friends. I'll advise my client not to file a restraining order and you two can let the divorce lawyers earn their paychecks by kicking each other in the nuts."

"Or...?" he asked. Still smiling.

"Or, you don't back off and then this is about you and me."

"Nonsense. You're no part of this. This is about me and—"

I cut him off. "I'm *making* this about you and me. Maybe I have a wire loose, too, but once I tell a client that I'm going to keep her safe, I take it amiss if anything happens to her."

"'Amiss'," he repeated, enjoying the word.

"But that's a minute from now. We're still on the other side of it until you give me an answer. What's it going to be? You leave her alone? Or this gets complicated."

"What were you before you started doing this PI bullshit?"

"A cop."

He grunted. "You sound like a thug. An asshole leg-breaker from South Philly."

"Thin line sometimes."

He steepled his fingers. It was one of those moves that looked good when Doctor Doom did it in a comic book. Maybe in a boardroom. Looked silly right now, but he had enough intensity in his eyes to almost pull it off. He gave me ten seconds of *the stare*.

I stood my ground.

His cell phone rang and he flipped it open, listened.

"I'm in a meeting," he said, and closed the phone.

His smile returned.

I heard the footsteps on the stairs even though they were quiet.

I sighed and turned. There were four of them. All as pale as Skye, but much bigger. "Really? You want to play that card?"

"It's one of the classics. Though, to be fair, it'll be more than a typical beating. I...hm, am I wrong in presuming you *have* had your ass kicked?"

"That cherry was popped a long time ago."

The four men entered the room and fanned out behind me.

"So, our challenge, then," Skye said, "is to put a new spin on this. Something surprising and fresh so that you'll be entertained."

"Mind if I take my jacket off first?"

"Go right ahead."

I heard a hammer-cock behind me.

Skye said, "You can put your jacket on my desk here, and take off your shoulder holster and put that—and your piece—on top of it."

"Sure, whatever," I said. I shrugged out of the jacket. I bought it the year the Vikings took their eighteenth division title. I'll buy a new one if they ever win the Super Bowl. Or when pigs sprout wings and learn to fly, whichever comes first. I folded it and set it down, unclipped my shoulder rig, set that down. If I was going to ruin my clothes, then at least nothing I was currently wearing had sentimental value.

I leaned on the desk. "Let's agree on a couple of things first, okay?"

"Sure," he said with a grin.

"When I'm done handing these clowns their asses, then you and I dance a round or two."

"That would be fun," he said, "but I doubt I'll have the pleasure."

"Second, if I walk out of here on my own steam, then it's with the understanding that you will leave the lady alone."

"If you walk out of here? Sure. But, tell me something," he said, and he looked genuinely interested, "Why do you care? What is she to you?"

"Maybe I'm the possessive type, too. Maybe now that she's asked for my help, it's like she's part of the family. So to speak."

"Part of the family? You fucking kidding me here?"

"Nope."

"You Italian? This some kind of dago thing?"

"I said it's *like* she's part of the family. My family," I said, "and I protect what's mine."

"That's it? It's just a macho thing with you?"

"No, it's more than that," I admitted. I gestured to the torture and pain motif in which his office was decorated. "But, seriously, I doubt you would understand."

"Mmm, probably not. I'm not into sentimentality and that bullshit. Not anymore."

"What happened? What changed you?"

His smiled faded to a remote coldness. "I learned that there was something better. Better than family, better than blood ties. Better than any of this ordinary shit."

"You found religion?" I said.

"It's a 'higher order' sort of thing that I really don't want to explain and I doubt *you'd* understand."

"I might surprise you."

"I don't think that's possible. But *we* might surprise you. In fact I can pretty fucking well guarantee it."

"Rock and roll," I said.

I straightened and turned toward the four goons. They took up positions like compass points. The office was big, but not big enough to give me room to maneuver. They were going to fall on me like a wall, and they knew it. The guy with the gun even snugged it back into his shoulder rig. They were *that* confident, and they were smiling like kids at a carnival.

"You shouldn't have bothered Mr. Skye," said the guy in front of me. He was the gun who'd holstered his gun. He stood on the East point of the compass. "You should have—"

I kicked him in the nuts. I really didn't need to hear the speech.

I'm not that big, but I can kick like a Rockette. I *felt* bones break and he screamed like a nine-year-old girl. Dumbass should have kept his gun out.

I stepped backward off of him and put an elbow into West's face. It had all of my mass in motion behind it. I heard more bones break. Cartilage, too. And he went down so fast that I wondered if I'd snapped his neck.

That left South and North. South spent a half second too long looking shocked, so I jumped at him with a leaping knee—the only Muay Thai kick I know—and drove him all the way to the wall. By the time North closed in I'd grabbed South by the ears and slammed him skull-first into a replica of a torture rack. Blood splattered in a Jackson Pollack pattern.

I pivoted and rushed to intercept North, who was barreling at me with a lot of furious speed; so I veered left and clothes-lined him with my stiff right forearm. He did a pretty impressive back flip and landed face down on the black-painted hardwood floor.

If this was an action movie everything would switch to slow motion as the four thugs toppled to the ground and I turned slowly, looking badass, to face the now startled and unprotected villain.

The real world is a lot less accommodating.

I caught movement behind me, figuring it for Skye going after my gun, so I whirled and made ready to launch into a diving tackle.

Only it wasn't Skye.

It was East and West getting to their feet. West's face was smeared with blood from his broken nose, but he was smiling. As I watched he took his nose between thumb and forefinger and *snapped* it into place, then spit a hocker of blood and snot onto the floor.

North was chuckling as he rose; and behind me I could hear South shifting to stand behind me again. I turned in a slow circle. They were all smiling. They shouldn't have been *able* to. They should have been sprawled on the floor and I should have been giving some kind of smart-ass

speech as I closed in to lay a beating on Skye. That was the script I'd written in my head.

What the hell was this shit?

"Surprise!" said Skye dryly.

"What the hell are these fuckers *taking*?"

"You wouldn't believe me if I told you?"

"Try me."

"Blood," he said.

"What the—"

And I looked more closely at the smiles. Lots of white teeth. Lots of long, pointy white teeth.

"Oh, balls," I said.

"Yeah, kind of cool, huh?"

"Vampires?" I said.

"Yeah."

"Actual vampires."

Skye laughed. The four—well, let's call a spade a spade—*vampires* laughed with him.

Even I laughed.

"Geez. When shit goes wrong it goes all the way wrong, doesn't it," I said.

"On the up side," said Skye, "you did win the first round. Nice moves."

"Thanks."

The four of them circled me. My pulse jumped from 'uh-oh' to 'oh shit'. It was cold in his office, but I was starting to sweat pretty heavily.

"I guess I shouldn't be surprised," I said. "You're one, too? Am I right?"

"A recent convert," he admitted.

"So...that whole weight loss, going all weird on the missus, that was—?"

"A transition process. It's not like they show in the movies, you know. Takes weeks. The whole metabolism changes."

"No kidding."

One of the vampires faked a lunge to psyche me out and I jumped a foot in the air. I'm pretty sure I didn't yelp like a Chihuahua, but I wouldn't swear to that in court. They all laughed at that, too. I didn't.

"Which explains why you lost all that weight."

"Who needs steroids and free-weights," he agreed and spread his hands. "This package comes with honest to God super strength. I'm like Spider-Man and Wolverine rolled into one. Super strong and I heal from damn near anything."

"Could you be more specific on that last point?"

"Cute."

"Worth a try." I looked at them, at their grinning, evil faces. My nuts were trying to crawl up inside of my chest cavity. I mean...*fucking vampires?*

"Weird thing was," I said, "I was starting to build a case in my head about your wife. You losing weight and getting pale, blaming her for it all, and you saying you *know* what she is. Is she a vampire, too? Is she the one who bit you?"

Skye laughed. "Christ, no. And she's not a succubus, either. She's just a nagging, soul-draining, passive-aggressive, codependent bitch."

"Wow. You're really a chauvinistic prick, aren't you?"

"Better than being pussy whipped."

I dropped it. I had bigger fish to fry than trying to bring this macho jackass into the twenty-first century. Namely the fact that I was in a roomful of vampires.

I know I keep harping on that, but really…it's not the sort of shit that happens all the time to me. Or, like…*ever.*

"Say, man," I said to Skye, "any chance we can roll back this tape to the point where we were still friends? I just walk out of here and we all call it a day?"

Skye made a face as if pretending to consider it. "Mmm…no, I don't see that happening."

"You want to make a deal of some kind?"

"Nah," he said. "You got nothing I want. Except the O-positive."

"AB-neg," I corrected.

"Never tried that."

"You wouldn't like it. Goes right to your hips."

The wattage on his smile was dimmer. Jaunty banter can buy only so many seconds and then it's back to business.

I tried to keep my face neutral, but my pulse was like a jazz drum solo.

"I'm going to throw something out here," I said. I could hear a tremor in my voice. Fuck.

"Oh, please." He gestured to the four killers and they started forward.

"Wait! Just hear me out. What have you got to lose?"

The thugs looked at Skye. West gave a 'why not?' kind of shrug.

Skye sighed. "Okay, what is it? Last words? A little begging?" he suggested.

"Mm, more like last threat."

"This I got to hear."

The five of them looked genuinely interested.

"Okay, so here you are, five vampires. That's some really scary shit, am I right? I mean creatures of the night and all that."

He nodded, nothing to disagree with.

"To most people that's enough to make them go apeshit crazy. I mean…vampires. Not your everyday thing. It opens up all kinds of metaphysical questions. If vampires exist, what *else* does? If there are supernatural monsters, does that mean God and the Devil are real? You follow me?"

"Sure. We get that a lot."

"And I'm outnumbered here. Five to one. Tough odds even without you fellows being the undead. So…why am I not I scared?"

His eyes narrowed.

"I mean, yeah, my pulse is racing and I'm sweating. But do I look as scared as I *should* be? I

don't, do I? Now…why is that?"

"So you put up a good front. It'll be a good anecdote later," he said. "For us."

"Maybe he's got a hammer and stake," suggested West.

That got a laugh.

"Nope."

My heart rate had to be close to two hundred. It was machinegun fire in my chest.

"Coupla garlic bulbs in your pocket?" asked East.

"Nah. I don't even like it on my pizza."

"You don't have any backup," said North. "And you don't got your gun."

My blood pressure could have scalded paint off a battleship. I wiped sweat off my brow with my thumb.

"Okay, jokes over," snapped Skye. "What's the punch line here? Why aren't you as scared as you should be?"

I smiled.

"I'll show you."

The first time it happened, way back when I was thirteen, it took almost half an hour. I screamed and cried and rolled around on the floor. First time's always the hardest. Each time since, it was easier. My grandmother and her sister could do it in the time it took you to snap your fingers. My best time was during a foot chase back when I was with Minneapolis PD. I was running down the guy who'd beaten his wife with the extension cord. He saw me coming and ducked into his apartment. I kicked the door and he came out of the bedroom with a gun and opened up. I went through the change in the time it took me to leap through the doorway. Like the snap of my fingers. One minute me, next minute *different* me.

I tore the shit out of him. I lost my badge and pension and had to make up all sorts of excuses. On the plus side, I didn't die, which *would* have happened if I hadn't managed the change so fast. I'm only mortal when I look like one.

That night in Skye's office wasn't my best time. Maybe third or fourth best. Say, two, three seconds. It felt like an explosion. It hurts. Feels like my heart is bursting, like cherry bombs are detonating inside my muscles. It starts in the chest, then ripples out from there as muscle mass changes and is reassigned in new ways. Bones warp, crack and re-form. Nails tear through the flesh of my fingers and toes, my jaw shifts and the longer teeth spike through the gums. It's bloody and it's ugly and it hurts like a motherfucker.

But the end result is a stunner. A real kick-ass dramatic moment that wows the audience.

I think all four of the thugs screamed. They jerked back from me, looks of shock and horror on their faces. If I wasn't so deeply into the moment, I would have smiled at the irony. Monsters being scared by a monster.

I crouched in the center of the room, hands flexing, claws streaked with blood, hot saliva dripping from my mouth onto my chest.

It would have been cool and dramatic to have said "Surprise!" to them, the way Skye had said it to me, but my mouth was no longer constructed for human speech. All I could do was roar.

I did.

And then I launched at them.

Vampires are strong. Four or five times stronger than an ordinary human.

Werewolves?

Hell, we're a whole different class.

I slammed into West with both sets of front claws. He flew apart like he was made of paper and watery red glue. North and East tried to take me high and low, but they'd have done better to try and run. I brought my knee up into East's jaw as he went for the low tackle and his head burst like a casaba melon. I caught North by the throat and squeezed. Red geysered up from the stump of his neck as his head fell away. South backed away, putting himself between me and Skye, arms spread, making a more heroic stand than I'd have thought. I tore the heart from his chest. Turns out, vampires *need* their hearts.

Skye had my gun in his hands. He racked the slide and buried the barrel against me as I leaped over the desk. He got off four shots. They hurt.

Like wasp stings.

Maybe a little less.

I don't load my piece with silver bullets. I'm not an idiot.

He looked into my eyes and I would like to think that he saw the error of his ways. Don't fuck with the innocent. Don't fuck with my clients. My clients are *mine*, like members of my pack. Mess with them and the pack leader has to put you down. Has to.

So I did.

* * *

She saw me coming from across the street, her face concerned and confused. I was wearing a different pair of pants and different shoes. My own had been torn to rags during the change. Stuff I was wearing used to belong to the bartender. He didn't need them anymore. He'd been on the same team as Skye and the four goons.

I opened the door and climbed in behind the wheel.

"Are you all right, Sam?" she asked, studying my face. "Are you hurt? Is that blood?"

I dabbed at a dot on my cheek. Missed a spot. I pulled a tissue out of my jacket pocket and wiped my cheek.

"Just ketchup," I said.

"You stopped for *food*?" she demanded, eyes wide.

"It was on the house. I was hungry. No biggie."

She stared at me and then looked at the club across the street. The snow was getting heavier, the ground was white and it was starting to coat the street.

"What happened in there?"

I put the key into the ignition.

"I had a long talk with your ex. I told him that you were feeling threatened and uncomfortable with his actions, and I asked him to back off."

"What did he say?"

"He won't be bothering you anymore."

"Just like that? He agreed to leave me alone just like that?" She snapped her fingers.

"More or less. I told him that I had some friends on the force and in L & I. Guess I made it clear that I could make his life *more* uncomfortable than he was making yours. He didn't like it, but..." I let the rest hang.

"And he *agreed*?"

"Take my word for it. He's out of your life."

She continued to study me for several long seconds. I waited her out and I saw the moment when she shifted from doubt and fear to belief and acceptance. She closed her eyes, sagged back against the seat, put her face in her hands, and began to cry.

I gripped the wheel and looked out at the falling snow, hiding the smile that kept trying to creep onto my mouth. I was digging the P.I. business. Fewer rules than when I was a cop. It allowed me to be closer to the street, to go hunting deeper into the forest.

Even so—and despite what I'd said to Skye—I *was* pretty rattled that he'd been a vampire. I mean, being who and what I am, I always suspected other things were out there in the dark, but until now I'd never met them. Now I knew. How many vampires were there? *Where* were they? Would they be coming for me?

I didn't have any of those answers. Not yet.

I also wondered what *else* was out there. I could feel the excitement racing through me. I wanted to find out. Good or bad.

I reached out a hand and patted Mrs. Skye's trembling shoulder. It felt good to know that one of the pack was safe now. It felt right. It made me feel powerful and satisfied on a lot of different levels. I knew that I was going to want to feel this way again. And again.

The snow swirled inside the thickening shadows.

Inside my head the wolf howled.

THE END

BRAM STOKER
AWARD WINNERS

Each year since 1987 the Horror Writers Association has presented The Bram Stoker Awards during a ceremony either held at the World Horror Convention (since those started in 1991) in alternating years, or separately on its own. In 2012, HWA and the Stokers both celebrated 25 years in a banquet at the WHC in Salt Lake City, Utah. This year HWA and the World Horror Convention join forces again to hold both functions in New Orleans, LA. Since Dark Discoveries magazine's new publisher JournalStone is one of the sponsors (and since we've also got a couple of the Guests of Honor and former award-winners in this issue), we thought it would be nice to do a special appreciation section for the Horror Writers Association and the World Horror Conventions. Here is an overview of the current nominees for the Bram Stoker Awards, past winners, current and past Guests of Honor for World Horror Convention, and even a number of appreciations and reminiscences from past HWA officers and Stoker award-winners and WHC Guests of Honor.

2012 BRAM STOKER AWARD FINAL BALLOT

(To Be Presented In 2013)

SUPERIOR ACHIEVEMENT IN A NOVEL

Ethridge, Benjamin Kane – *Bottled Abyss* (Redrum Horror)
Everson, John – *NightWhere* (Samhain Publishing)
Kiernan, Caitlin R. – *The Drowning Girl* (Roc)
Little, Bentley – *The Haunted* (Signet)
McKinney, Joe – *Inheritance* (Evil Jester Press)

SUPERIOR ACHIEVEMENT IN A FIRST NOVEL

Boccacino, Michael – *Charlotte Markham and the House of Darkling* (William Morrow)
Coates, Deborah – *Wide Open* (Tor Books)
Day, Charles – *The Legend of the Pumpkin Thief* (Noble YA Publishers LLC)
Dudar, Peter – *A Requiem for Dead Flies* (Nightscape Press)
Gropp, Richard – *Bad Glass* (Ballantine/Del Rey)
Soares, L.L. – *Life Rage* (Nightscape Press)

SUPERIOR ACHIEVEMENT IN A YOUNG ADULT NOVEL

Bray, Libba – *The Diviners* (Little Brown)
Lyga, Barry – *I Hunt Killers* (Little Brown)
Maberry, Jonathan – *Flesh & Bone* (Simon & Schuster)
McCarty, Michael – *I Kissed A Ghoul* (Noble Romance Publishing)
Stiefvater, Maggie – *The Raven Boys* (Scholastic Press)
Strand, Jeff – *A Bad Day for Voodoo* (Sourcebooks)

SUPERIOR ACHIEVEMENT IN A GRAPHIC NOVEL

Bunn, Cullen – *The Sixth Gun Volume 3: Bound* (Oni Press)
Moore, Terry – *Rachel Rising Vol. 1: The Shadow of Death* (Abstract Studio)
Thornton, Ravi – *The Tale of Brin and Bent and Minno Marylebone* (Jonathan Cape)
Wacks, Peter J., and Guy Anthony De Marco – *Behind These Eyes* (Villainous Press)
Wood, Rocky, and Lisa Morton – *Witch Hunts: A Graphic History of the Burning Times* (McFarland)

SUPERIOR ACHIEVEMENT IN LONG FICTION

Burke, Kealan Patrick – *Thirty Miles South of Dry County* (Delirium Books)
Ketchum, Jack, and Lucky McKee – *I'm Not Sam* (Sinister Grin Press)
McKinney, Joe, and Michael McCarty – *Lost Girl of the Lake* (Bad Moon Books)
O'Neill, Gene – *The Blue Heron* (Dark Regions Press)
Prentiss, Norman – *The Fleshless Man* (Delirium Books)

SUPERIOR ACHIEVEMENT IN SHORT FICTION

Boston, Bruce – *Surrounded by the Mutant Rain Forest* (Daily Science Fiction)
McKinney, Joe – *Bury My Heart at Marvin Gardens* (Best of Dark Moon Digest, Dark Moon Books)
Ochse, Weston – "Righteous" (*Psychos*, Black Dog and Leventhall Publication)
Palisano, John – Available Light (Lovecraft eZine, March 2012)
Snyder, Lucy – Magdala Amygdala (Dark Faith: Invocations, Apex Book Company)

SUPERIOR ACHIEVEMENT IN SCREENPLAY

Goldman, Jane – *The Woman in Black* (Cross Creek Pictures)
Kim, Sang Kyu – *The Walking Dead*, "Killer Within" (AMC TV)
Minear, Tim – *American Horror Story: Asylum*, "Dark Cousin" (Brad Falchuk Teley-Vision, Ryan Murphy Productions)
Ross, Gary, Suzanne Collins, and Billy Ray – *The Hunger Games* (Lionsgate, Color Force)
Whedon, Joss, and Drew Goddard – *The Cabin in the Woods* (Mutant Enemy Productions, Lionsgate)

SUPERIOR ACHIEVEMENT IN ANTHOLOGY

Castle, Mort, and Sam Weller – *Shadow Show* (HarperCollins)
Guignard, Eric J. – *Dark Tales of Lost Civilizations* (Dark Moon Books)
Miller, Eric – *Hell Comes to Hollywood* (Big Time Books)
Scioneaux, Mark C., R.J. Cavender, and Robert S. Wilson – *Horror for Good: A Charitable Anthology* (Cutting Block Press)
Swanson, Stan – *Slices of Flesh* (Dark Moon Books)

SUPERIOR ACHIEVEMENT IN FICTION COLLECTION

Carroll, Jonathan – *Woman Who Married a Cloud*: Collected Stories (Subterranean Press)
Castle, Mort – *New Moon on the Water* (Dark Regions)
Hand, Elizabeth – *Errantry: Strange Stories* (Small Beer Press)
Hirshberg, Glen – *The Janus Tree* (Subterranean Press)
Oates, Joyce Carol – *Black Dahlia and White Rose: Stories* (Ecco)

SUPERIOR ACHIEVEMENT IN NON-FICTION

Collings, Michael – *Writing Darkness* (CreateSpace)
Klinger, Les – *The Annotated Sandman, Volume 1* (Vertigo)
Morton, Lisa – *Trick or Treat: A History of Halloween* (Reaktion Books)
Paffenroth, Kim, and John W. Morehead – *The Undead and Theology* (Pickwick Publications)
Phillips, Kendall R. – *Dark Directions: Romero, Craven, Carpenter, and the Modern Horror Film* (Southern Illinois University Press)

SUPERIOR ACHIEVEMENT IN POETRY

Addison, Linda, and Stephen M. Wilson – *Dark Duet* (NECON eBooks)
Boston, Bruce, and Gary William Crawford – Notes from the Shadow City (Dark Regions Press)
Collings, Michael – *A Verse to Horrors* (Amazon Digital Services)
Simon, Marge – *Vampires, Zombies & Wanton Souls* (Elektrik Milk Bath Press)
Turzillo, Mary A. – *Lovers & Killers* (Dark Regions)

NOTE: In two categories there are six nominees because two works tied for fifth place.
LIFETIME ACHIEVEMENT: Clive Barker & Robert McCammon

2011 Bram Stoker Award Nominees & Winners
[presented in 2012]

Novel: *Flesh Eaters* by Joe McKinney
First Novel: *Isis Unbound* by Allyson Bird
Young Adult Novel: *The Screaming Season* by Nancy Holder (tie)
Dust and Decay by Jonathan Maberry (tie)
Graphic Novel: *Neonomicon* by Alan Moore
Long Fiction: "The Ballad of Ballard and Sandrine" by Peter Straub (*Conjunctions: 56*)
Short Fiction: "Herman Wouk Is Still Alive" by Stephen King (*The Atlantic Magazine*, May 2011)
Screenplay: *American Horror Story*, episode #12: "Afterbirth" by Jessica Sharzer
Anthology: *Demons: Encounters with the Devil and his Minions, Fallen Angels and the Possessed* edited by John Skipp
Collection: *The Corn Maiden and Other Nightmares* by Joyce Carol Oates,
Nonfiction: Stephen King: *A Literary Companion* by Rocky Wood
Poetry: *How to Recognize a Demon Has Become Your Friend* by Linda Addison
Specialty Press Award: Bad Moon Books and Hippocampus Press (tie)
Lifetime Achievement: Rick Hautala, Joe Lansdale
Richard Laymon:
President's Award Karen Lansdale
Silver Hammer: Guy Anthony DeMarco

2010 Bram Stoker Award Nominees & Winners
[presented in 2011]

Novel: *A Dark Matter* by Peter Straub
First Novel: *Black and Orange* by Benjamin Kane Ethridge (tie)
Castle of Los Angeles by Lisa Morton (tie)
Long Fiction: *Invisible Fences* by Norman Prentiss
Short Fiction: "The Folding Man" by Joe R. Lansdale (*Haunted Legends*)
Anthology: *Haunted Legends* edited by Ellen Datlow and Nick Mamatas
Collection: *Full Dark, No Stars* by Stephen King
Nonfiction: *To Each Their Darkness* by Gary A. Braunbeck
Poetry: *Dark Matters* by Bruce Boston
Specialty Press Award: Dark Regions Press
Lifetime Achievement: Ellen Datlow, Al Feldstein

Richard Laymon:
President's Award Michael Colangelo
Silver Hammer: Angel Leigh McCoy

2009 Bram Stoker Award Nominees & Winners
[presented in 2010]

Novel: *Audrey's Door* by Sarah Langan
First Novel: *Damnable* by Hank Schwaeble
Long Fiction: *The Lucid Dreaming* by Lisa Morton
Short Fiction: *In the Porches of My Ears* by Norman Prentiss
Anthology: *He Is Legend: An Anthology Celebrating Richard Matheson* edited by Christopher Conlon
Collection: *A Taste of Tenderloin* by Gene O'Neill
Nonfiction: *Writers Workshop of Horror* by Michael Knost
Poetry: *Chimeric Machines* by Lucy A. Snyder
Specialty Press Award: Tartarus Press
Lifetime Achievement: Brian Lumley, William F. Nolan.
Richard Laymon:
President's Award Vince A. Liaguno
Silver Hammer: Kathryn Ptacek

2008 Bram Stoker Award Nominees & Winners
[presented in 2009]

Novel: *Duma Key* by Stephen King
First Novel: *The Gentling Box* by Lisa Mannetti
Long Fiction: *Miranda* by John R. Little
Short Fiction: "The Lost" by Sarah Langan
Anthology: *Unspeakable Horror* edited by Vince A. Liaguno and Chad Helder
Collection: *Just after Sunset* by Stephen King
Nonfiction: *A Hallowe'en Anthology* by Lisa Morton
Poetry: *The Nightmare Collection* by Bruce Boston
Specialty Press Award: Bloodletting Press
Lifetime Achievement: F. Paul Wilson, Chelsea Quinn Yarbro
Richard Laymon:
President's Award John Little
Silver Hammer: Sephera Giron

2007 Bram Stoker Award Nominees & Winners
[presented in 2008]

Novel: *The Missing* by Sarah Langan
First Novel: *Heart-Shaped Box* by Joe Hill
Long Fiction: *Afterward, There Will Be a Hallway* by Gary Braunbeck
Short Fiction: "The Gentle Brush of Wings" by David Niall Wilson
Anthology: *Five Strokes to Midnight* edited by Gary Braunbeck and Hank Schwaeble
Collection: *Proverbs for Monsters* by Michael A. Arnzen
Nonfiction: *The Cryptopedia: A Dictionary of the Weird, Strange & Downright Bizarre* by Jonathan Maberry & David F. Kramer
Poetry: *Being Full of Light, Insubstantial* by Linda Addison (Tie)
Vectors: *A Week in the Death of a Planet* by Charlee Jacob & Marge Simon (Tie)
Specialty Press Award: none awarded this year
Lifetime Achievement: John Carpenter, Robert Weinberg
Richard Laymon:
President's Award Stephen Dorato, Christopher Fulbright, Mark Worthen
Silver Hammer Award: none awarded this year

2006 Bram Stoker Award Nominees & Winners
[presented in 2007]

Novel: *Lisey's Story* by Stephen King
First Novel: *Ghost Road Blues* by Jonathan Maberry
Long Fiction: *Dark Harvest* by Norman Partridge
Short Story: "Tested" by Lisa Morton
Anthology: *Retro Pulp Tales* edited by Joe Lansdale (Tie)
Mondo Zombie edited by John Skipp (Tie)
Collection: *Destinations Unknown* by Gary Braunbeck
Nonfiction: *Final Exits: The Illustrated Encyclopedia of How We Die* by Michael Largo (Tie)
Gospel of the Living Dead: George Romero's Visions of Hell on Earth by Kim Paffenroth (Tie)
Poetry: *Shades Fantastic* by Bruce Boston
Specialty Press Award: PS Publishing
Lifetime Achievement: Thomas Harris
Richard Laymon:
President's Award Lisa Morton
Silver Hammer Award: Donna K. Fitch

2005 Bram Stoker Award Nominees & Winners
[presented in 2006]

Novel: *Creepers* by David Morrell (Tie)
Dread in the Beast by Charlee Jacob (Tie)
First Novel: *Scarecrow Gods* by Weston Ochse
Long Fiction: "Best New Horror" by Joe Hill
Short Fiction: *We Now Pause for Station Identification* by Gary Braunbeck
Fiction Collection: *20th Century Ghosts* by Joe Hill
Anthology: *Dark Delicacies: Original Tales of Terror and the Macabre* edited by Del Howison & Jeff Gelb
Nonfiction: *Horror: Another 100 Best Books* by Stephen Jones & Kim Newman
Poetry Collection: *Freakcidents* by Michael A. Arnzen (Tie)
Sineater by Charlee Jacob (Tie)
Specialty Press Award: Necessary Evil Press
Lifetime Achievement: Peter Straub
Richard Laymon:
President's Award Lisa Morton

2004 Bram Stoker Award Nominees & Winners
[presented in 2005]

Novel: *In the Night Room* by Peter Straub
First Novel: *Covenant* by John Everson (Tie)
Stained by Lee Thomas (Tie)
Long Fiction: *The Turtle Boy* by Kealan-Patrick Burke
Short Fiction: "Nimitseahpah" by Nancy Etchemendy
Fiction Collection: *Fearful Symmetries* by Thomas F. Monteleone
Anthology: *The Year's Best Fantasy and Horror, 17th Annual* edited by Ellen Datlow, Kelly Link and Gavin Grant
Nonfiction: *Hellnotes* edited by Judi Rohrig
Illustrated Narrative: *Heaven's Devils* by Jai Nitz
Screenplay: *Eternal Sunshine of the Spotless Mind* by Charlie Kaufman, Michel Gondry and Pierre Bismuth (Tie)
Shaun of the Dead by Simon Pegg and Edgar Wright (Tie)
Work for Young Readers: *Abarat: Days of Magic, Nights of War* by Clive

Barker (Tie)
Oddest Yet by Steve Burt (Tie)
Poetry Collection: *The Women at the Funeral* by Corrine De Winter
Alternative Forms: *The Devil's Wine* edited by Tom Piccirilli
Lifetime Achievement: Michael Moorcock

2003 Bram Stoker Award Nominees & Winners
[presented in 2004]

Novel: *lost boy lost girl* by Peter Straub
First Novel: *The Rising* by Brian Keene
Long Fiction: "Closing Time" by Jack Ketchum
Short Fiction: "Duty" by Gary A. Braunbeck
Fiction Collection: *Peaceable Kingdom* by Jack Ketchum
Anthology: *Borderlands 5* edited by Elizabeth and Thomas Monteleone
Nonfiction: *The Mothers and Fathers Italian Association* by Thomas F. Monteleone
Illustrated Narrative: *The Sandman: Endless Nights* (collection) by Neil Gaiman
Screenplay: *Bubba Ho-Tep* by Don Coscarelli
Work for Young Readers: *Harry Potter and the Order of the Phoenix* by J. K Rowling
Poetry Collection: *Pitchblende* by Bruce Boston
Alternative Forms: *The Goreletter* (email newsletter) by Michael Arnzen
Lifetime Achievement: Martin H. Greenberg
Anne Rice

2002 Bram Stoker Award Nominees & Winners
[presented in 2003]

Novel: *The Night Class* by Tom Piccirilli
First Novel: *The Lovely Bones* by Alice Sebold
Long Fiction: *El Dia De Los Muertos* by Brian A. Hopkins (Tie)
"My Work Is Not Yet Done" by Thomas Ligotti (Tie)
Short Fiction: "The Misfit Child Grows Fat on Despair" by Tom Piccirilli
Fiction Collection: *One More for the Road* by Ray Bradbury
Anthology: *The Darker Side* edited by John Pelan
Nonfiction: *Ramsey Campbell, Probably* by Ramsey Campbell
Illustrated Narrative: *Nightside* (Issues 1-4) by Robert Weinberg
Screenplay: *Frailty* by Brent Hanley
Work for Young Readers: *Coraline* by Neil Gaiman
Poetry Collection: *The Gossamer Eye* by Mark McLaughlin, Rain Graves, and David Niall Wilson
Alternative Forms: *Imagination Box* (multimedia CD) by Steve and Melanie Tem
Lifetime Achievement: Stephen King
J.N. Williamson

2001 Bram Stoker Award Nominees & Winners
[presented in 2002]

Novel: *American Gods* by Neil Gaiman
First Novel: *Deadliest of the Species* by Michael Oliveri
Long Fiction: *In These Final Days of Sales* by Steve Rasnic Tem
Short Fiction: "Reconstructing Amy" by Tim Lebbon
Fiction Collection: *The Man with the Barbed-Wire Fists* by Norman Partridge
Anthology: *Extremes 2: Fantasy and Horror from the Ends of the Earth* edited by Brian A. Hopkins
Nonfiction: *Jobs in Hell* edited by Brian Keene
Illustrated Narrative: "Freezes Over" (Hellblazer 158-161) by Brian Azzarello
Screenplay: *Memento* by Christopher & Jonathan Nolan

Work for Young Readers: *The Willow Files 2* by Yvonne Navarro
Poetry Collection: *Consumed, Reduced to Beautiful Grey Ashes* by Linda Addison
Alternative Forms: *Dark Dreamers: Facing the Masters of Fear* by Beth Gwinn &
Stanley Wiater
Lifetime Achievement John Farris

2000 Bram Stoker Award Nominees & Winners
[presented in 2001]

Novel: *The Traveling Vampire Show* by Richard Laymon
First Novel: *The Licking Valley Coon Hunters Club* by Brian A. Hopkins
Long Fiction: *The Man on the Ceiling* by Melanie and Steve Rasnic Tem
Short Fiction: "Gone" by Jack Ketchum
Fiction Collection: *Magic Terror* by Peter Straub
Anthology: *The Year's Best Fantasy & Horror, 13th Annual Collection* edited by Ellen
Datlow and Terri Windling
Nonfiction: *On Writing* by Stephen King
Illustrated Narrative: *The League of Extraordinary Gentlemen* (miniseries) by Alan
Moore
Screenplay: *Shadow of the Vampire* by Steven Katz
Work for Young Readers: *The Power of Un* by Nancy Etchemendy
Poetry Collection: *A Student of Hell* by Tom Piccirilli
Other Media: *Chiaroscuro* (web site) edited by Steve Eller, Sandra Kasturi, Patricia
Lee Macomber and Brett A. Savory
Lifetime Achievement: Nigel Kneale

1999 Bram Stoker Award Nominees & Winners
[presented in 2000]

Novel: *Mr. X* by Peter Straub
First Novel: *Wither* by J.G. Passarella
Long Fiction: "Five Days in April" by Brian A. Hopkins (Tie)
"Mad Dog Summer" by Joe R. Lansdale (Tie)
Short Fiction: "Aftershock" by F. Paul Wilson
Fiction Collection: *The Nightmare Chronicles* by Douglas Clegg
Anthology: *999: New Stories of Horror and Suspense* edited by Al Sarrantonio
Nonfiction: *DarkEcho* edited by Paula Guran
Illustrated Narrative: *Sandman: The Dream Hunters* by Neil Gaiman
Screenplay: *Sixth Sense* by M. Night Shyamalan
Work for Young Readers: *Harry Potter and the Prisoner of Azkaban* by J.K. Rowling
Other Media: *I Have No Mouth and I Must Scream* (Audio) by Harlan Ellison
Lifetime Achievement: Edward Gorey
Charles L. Grant

1998 Bram Stoker Award Nominees & Winners
[presented in 1999]

Novel: *Bag of Bones*, by Stephen King
First Novel: *Dawn Song* by Michael Marano
Long Fiction: "Mr. Clubb and Mr. Cuff" by Peter Straub
Short Fiction: "The Dead Boy at Your Window" by Bruce Holland Rogers
Fiction Collection: *Black Butterflies* by John Shirley
Anthology: Horrors!: *365 Scary Stories* by Stefan Dziemianowicz, ed., Martin H.
Greenberg, ed. & Robert Weinberg, ed.
Nonfiction: *DarkEcho Newsletter, Vol. 5, #1-50* by Paula Guran, ed.
Illustrated Narrative: *The Dreaming: Trial and Error* by Len Wein
Screenplay *Gods and Monsters* by Bill Condon (Tie)
Dark City by Alex Proyas, David Goyer, & Lem Dobbs

Work for Young Readers: "Bigger than Death" by Nancy Etchemendy
Other Media: No Award
Lifetime Achievement Ramsey Campbell
Roger Corman

1997 Bram Stoker Award Nominees & Winners
[presented in 1998]

Novel: *Children of the Dusk* by Janet Berliner & George Guthridge
First Novel: *Lives of the Monster Dogs* by Kirsten Bakis
Long Fiction: "The Big Blow" by Joe R. Lansdale
Short Fiction: "Rat Food" by Edo van Belkom & David Nickle
Fiction Collection: *Exorcisms and Ecstasies* by Karl Edward Wagner
Nonfiction: *Dark Thoughts: On Writing* by Stanley Wiater
Lifetime Achievement William Peter Blatty
Jack Williamson

1996 Bram Stoker Award Nominees & Winners
[presented in 1997]

Novel: *The Green Mile* by Stephen King
First Novel: *Crota* by Owl Goingback
Long Fiction: "The Red Tower" by Thomas Ligotti
Short Fiction: "Metalica" by P.D. Cacek
Fiction Collection: *The Nightmare Factory* by Thomas Ligotti
Nonfiction: *H.P. Lovecraft: A Life* by S.T. Joshi
Lifetime Achievement Ira Levin
Forrest J. Ackerman

1995 Bram Stoker Award Nominees & Winners
[presented in 1996]

Novel: *Zombie* by Joyce Carol Oates
First Novel: *The Safety of Unknown Cities* by Lucy Taylor
Long Fiction: "Lunch at the Gotham Cafe" by Stephen King
Short Fiction: "Chatting With Anubis" by Harlan Ellison
Fiction Collection: *The Panic Hand* by Jonathan Carroll
Nonfiction: *The Supernatural Index* by Michael Ashley & William Contento
Lifetime Achievement Harlan Ellison

1994 Bram Stoker Award Nominees & Winners
[presented in 1995]

Novel: *Dead in the Water* by Nancy Holder
First Novel: *Grave Markings* by Michael A. Arnzen
Long Fiction: "The Scent of Vinegar," by Robert Bloch
Short Fiction: "Cafe Endless: Spring Rain" by Nancy Holder (Tie)
"The Box" by Jack Ketchum (Tie)
Fiction Collection: *The Early Fears* by Robert Bloch
Lifetime Achievement Christopher Lee

1993 Bram Stoker Award Nominees & Winners
[presented in 1994]

Novel: *The Throat* by Peter Straub

First Novel: *The Thread that Binds the Bones* by Nina Kiriki Hoffman
Novella: "Mefisto in Onyx" by Harlan Ellison (Tie)
"The Night We Buried Road Dog" by Jack Cady (Tie)
Novelet: "Death in Bangkok" by Dan Simmons
Short Fiction: "I Hear the Mermaids Singing" by Nancy Holder
Fiction Collection: *Alone with the Horrors* by Ramsey Campbell
Nonfiction: *Once Around the Bloch* by Robert Bloch
Other Media: *Jonah Hex: Two-Gun Mojo* by Joe R. Lansdale
Lifetime Achievement: Joyce Carol Oates
Special Trustees Award: Vincent Price

1992 Bram Stoker Award Nominees & Winners
[presented in 1993]

Novel: *Blood of the Lamb* by Thomas F. Monteleone
First Novel: *Sineater* by Elizabeth Massie
Long Fiction: "Aliens: Tribes" by Stephen Bissette (Tie)
"The Events Concerning a Nude Fold-Out Found in a Harlequin Romance" by Joe R. Lansdale (Tie)
Short Fiction: "This Year's Class Picture" by Dan Simmons
Fiction Collection: *Mr. Fox and Other Feral Tales* by Norman Partridge
Nonfiction: *Cut! Horror Writers on Horror Film* by Christopher Golden
Lifetime Achievement Ray Russell

1991 Bram Stoker Award Nominees & Winners
[presented in 1992]

Novel: *Boy's Life* by Robert R. McCammon
First Novel: *The Cipher* by Kathe Koja (Tie)
Prodigal by Melanie Tem (Tie)
Long Fiction: "The Beautiful Uncut Hair of Graves" by David Morrell
Short Fiction: "Lady Madonna" by Nancy Holder
Fiction Collection: *Prayers to Broken Stones* by Dan Simmons
Nonfiction: *Clive Barker's Shadows of Eden* by Stephen Jones
Lifetime Achievement Gahan Wilson

1990 Bram Stoker Award Nominees & Winners
[presented in 1991]

Novel: *Mine* by Robert R. McCammon
First Novel: *The Revelation* by Bentley Little
Long Fiction: "Stephen" by Elizabeth Massie
Short Fiction: "The Calling" by David B. Silva
Fiction Collection: *Four Past Midnight* by Stephen King
Nonfiction: *Dark Dreamers* by Stanley Wiater
Lifetime Achievement: Hugh B. Cave
Richard Matheson

1989 Bram Stoker Award Nominees & Winners
[presented in 1990]

Novel: *Carrion Comfort* by Dan Simmons
First Novel: *Sunglasses After Dark* by Nancy A. Collins
Long Fiction: "On the Far Side of the Cadillac Desert With Dead Folks" by Joe R. Lansdale
Short Fiction: "Eat Me" by Robert R. McCammon

Fiction Collection: Collected Stories by Richard Matheson
Nonfiction: Harlan Ellison's Watching by Harlan Ellison (Tie)
Horror: The 100 Best Books by Stephen Jones & Kim Newman (Tie)
Lifetime Achievement Robert Bloch

1988 Bram Stoker Award Nominees & Winners
[presented in 1989]

Novel: *The Silence of the Lambs* by Thomas Harris
First Novel: *The Suiting* by Kelley Wilde
Long Fiction: "Orange is for Anguish, Blue for Insanity" by David Morrell
Short Fiction: "The Night They Missed the Horror Show" by Joe R. Lansdale
Fiction Collection: *Charles Beaumont: Selected Stories* by Charles Beaumont
Lifetime Achievement: Ray Bradbury
Ronald Chetwynd-Hayes

1987 Bram Stoker Award Nominees & Winners
[presented in 1988]

Novel: *Misery* by Stephen King (Tie)
Swan Song by Robert R. McCammon (Tie)
First Novel: *The Manse* by Lisa Cantrell
Long Fiction: "The Pear-Shaped Man" by George R.R. Martin (Tie)
"The Boy Who Came Back from the Dead" by Alan Rodgers (Tie)
Short Fiction: "The Deep End" by Robert R. McCammon
Fiction Collection: *The Essential Ellison* by Harlan Ellison
Nonfiction: *Mary Shelley* by Muriel Spark
Lifetime Achievement: Fritz Leiber
Frank Belknap Long
Clifford D. Simak

Disclaimer

"This focus on the Horror Writers Association's Bram Stoker Awards and the World Horror Convention is not affiliated with, endorsed by, or sponsored by either association/organization. Information and/or images from both are used by permission."

WHC & HWA QOUTES

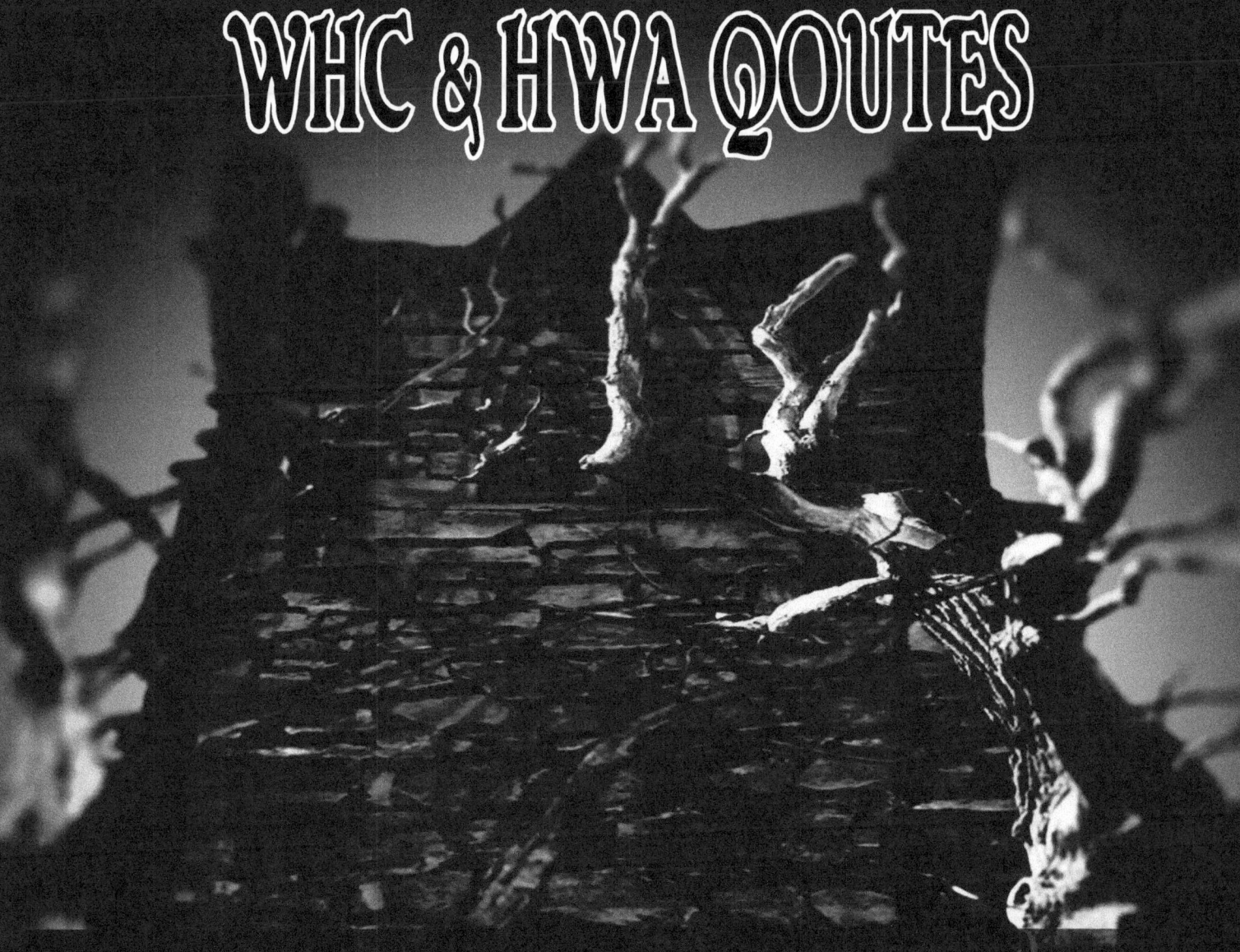

"The HWA encourages new writers and subsequently I received the award for superior achievement in the first novel category, for Isis Unbound, in 2012. It meant a great deal to me. I had just moved to New Zealand and needed to find the right place to live, get a house built, and settle down. I felt displaced. The HWA supports fledgling writers, celebrates the work of our most experienced, and has honored our great authors such as Ray Bradbury, Joyce Carol Oates, Joe Lansdale, Robert Bloch, Richard Matheson, Harlan Ellison, Ramsey Campbell, Alice Sebold, Peter Straub, Stephen King, Fritz Leiber...and many more." – Allyson Bird (Bram Stoker award-winning author of the novel *Isis Unbound*)

"Winning the Bram Stoker Award for my first novel was a big deal to me. I know that awards don't prove anything (there are far too many great artists who don't receive them), but I've been a lifelong horror fan and knowing that my name would be included on a list of my favorite authors blew my mind. Despite naysayers or the perpetual chorus of award critics, I'm thankful the stars aligned for me. This little castle is the coolest trophy I'll ever receive." - Benjamin Kane Ethridge (Bram Stoker award-winning author of the novel *Black and Orange*)

"You can never have too many Bram Stoker Awards." – Stephen King (12-time Bram Stoker award-winning author and current record holder)

"What I remember most was how hard my wife worked to put the first HWA newsletters together. In fact, she created the current organization based on an idea by Robert McCammon, supported by a number of writers, me, Dean Koontz, McCammon, Melissa Mia Hall, and so many others. I saw the organization created on our kitchen table. It was photocopied downtown, stapled together, stuffed in envelopes, and went out in bundles of mail. It was like a fanzine at first, a club formed by kids on the block. Except it grew and grew, until Dean Koontz offered to take it over, put some money in it and make it professional. We wanted an organization for writers who had the unique interest of horror fiction, and by golly, we got it. My suggestion is think less about the awards, and think about why the organization was created in the first place. It was originally a mail-connected collection of writers and would-be writers who just wanted to interact with each other, find out about markets, writing tips, and make new friends. That was its main purpose, and still should be." – Joe R. Lansdale (9-time Bram Stoker award-winning author and co-founder of HWA)

"The fact that HWA is still around, shows there was interest for the organization. I know writing is a solitary business and I felt this would help Joe have contact with others with the same interest. I am glad it worked for him and all that have been involved." – Karen Lansdale (Co-founder of HWA)

"The HWA has been a constant supporter of my writing for many years. It's a wonderful organization with many hard-working volunteers who only want to help other writers. I was absolutely thrilled to accept a Stoker Award in 2009 in large part because it showed the recognition of the HWA's membership. I continue to feel a strong bond to the organization and encourage all horror authors to join and see if they can benefit as much as I have." – John R. Little (Bram Stoker award-winning author of the novella *Miranda* and recipient of the Richard Laymon President's Award)

"It's almost impossible to understate the positive impact that winning a Stoker Award has had on me and my career. Being able to say that I'm a Stoker winner gets attention –from readers, booksellers, librarians, fellow-authors, and pretty much everyone else. It's also a conversation starter because it opens the door to discuss what makes good horror in today's literary climate. On a more personal note, having won a Stoker for my first novel, *Ghost Road Blues*, it validated my belief that I could –and probably should—keep going with fiction. It's a constant reminder that this is a path worth walking. It's also helped forge bonds with so many other writers of horror that I might otherwise not have met, read or become friends with…and that's a priceless thing. There is no more supportive crowd than the horror writers." – Jonathan Maberry (New York Times bestselling author of *Extinction Machine* and *Flesh & Bone* and proud member of the HWA)

"Winning the Stoker was huge for me. I remember walking up to the podium after they called my name. I felt like my legs were going to turn to water. And then I got handed the award by Joe R. Lansdale and Robert McCammon, two of my literary heroes, and it suddenly brought all those long, frustrating hours spent staring at the ceiling of my office into focus. I felt like all the time spent developing and sharpening my craft was justified. All the dead ends and false starts were worth the effort. That's a mighty good feeling, but it's also a trap. It's a trap because every award worth winning has to come as a promise to yourself. There's never time to rest on past laurels. I have to challenge myself with every new book, every new story or poem. Every word has to be crafted, every sentence squeezed and squeezed until every drop of truth has been wrung from it. That's the real meaning of the Stoker - a promise to yourself to never quit, never look back, never settle for what's merely good enough." – Joe McKinney (Bram Stoker award-winning author of *Flesh Eaters*)

"I've been a member of HWA since it began. The collegiality and stimulating exchange of ideas have been invaluable to me as a writer. Plus, the conferences are a blast." – David Morrell (3-time Stoker recipient and New York Times bestselling author of *Creepers*)

"Around 1992 I reconnected with a friend, the writer Dennis Etchison. He had just been elected president of something called the Horror Writers Association, and he urged me to join. I was just starting to pursue prose, but my screenplay credits qualified me for active membership. I followed his advice and joined… and it was probably the smartest business move I ever made. Over the years, connections and information gleaned via HWA have led to sales, promotional tips, agents, awards and lifelong friends. It's safe to say I owe a significant part of my writing career to HWA and I'm betting that a few of you reading this do as well. I've done my best to give back to HWA, and have served the organization in a variety of capacities, including trustee, treasurer and vice president." – Lisa Morton (Bram Stoker award-winning author of the books *Castle of Los Angeles* and *The Lucid Dreaming* and the current Vice President of the HWA)

"How did I feel about being awarded a Stoker for Lifetime Achievement? I was honored – and totally delighted. Made me feel that all the years of hard work had paid off, that my writing had touched the lives of many others. Writing is often a lonely business. The Stoker Award told me I was not alone, that I'd achieved something of value. I have heard other writers "put down" awards, declaring them worthless. Not so with me. Awards are badges of recognition; they are proof of excellence. I am grateful for each award I've been given over the years. Keep 'em coming!" – William F. Nolan (Award-winning author of *Logan's Run, Seven for Space, Dark Universe* and many others)

"I've been a member of HWA off and on (mostly on) since they were H.O.W.L. A lot has happened in those years, good and bad, but the one thing HWA has always meant to me is connections, and people. It's hard to be a writer, sometimes, because you are working in a vacuum. It's harder still to work in an ill-defined and critically shunned genre like horror. Having had the chance to meet, mingle with and eventually befriend so many talented people, covering such an incredible span of years, styles, and temperament, has been a blessing. The world of publishing is changing rapidly, and I think the HWA is evolving along with it. I'll be curious, intrigued, and I'm sure enriched by the process." – David Niall Wilson (2-time Bram Stoker award-winning author and former President of HWA)

"I am proud to give back to the HWA through serving as President. When my first book was published in 2006 I knew literally no-one. But I flew from Australia to Toronto for the Bram Stoker Awards Banquet in Toronto in 2007 anyway and made lifelong friends over just a few days. The HWA has massively expanded my network and allowed further support for my newer works - for instance I met my second publisher at the Bram Stoker Awards Weekend in Burbank. So, career development and friendships - what more could one ask for?" – Rocky Wood (Bram Stoker award-winning author of the book *Stephen King: A Literary Companion* and current President of HWA)

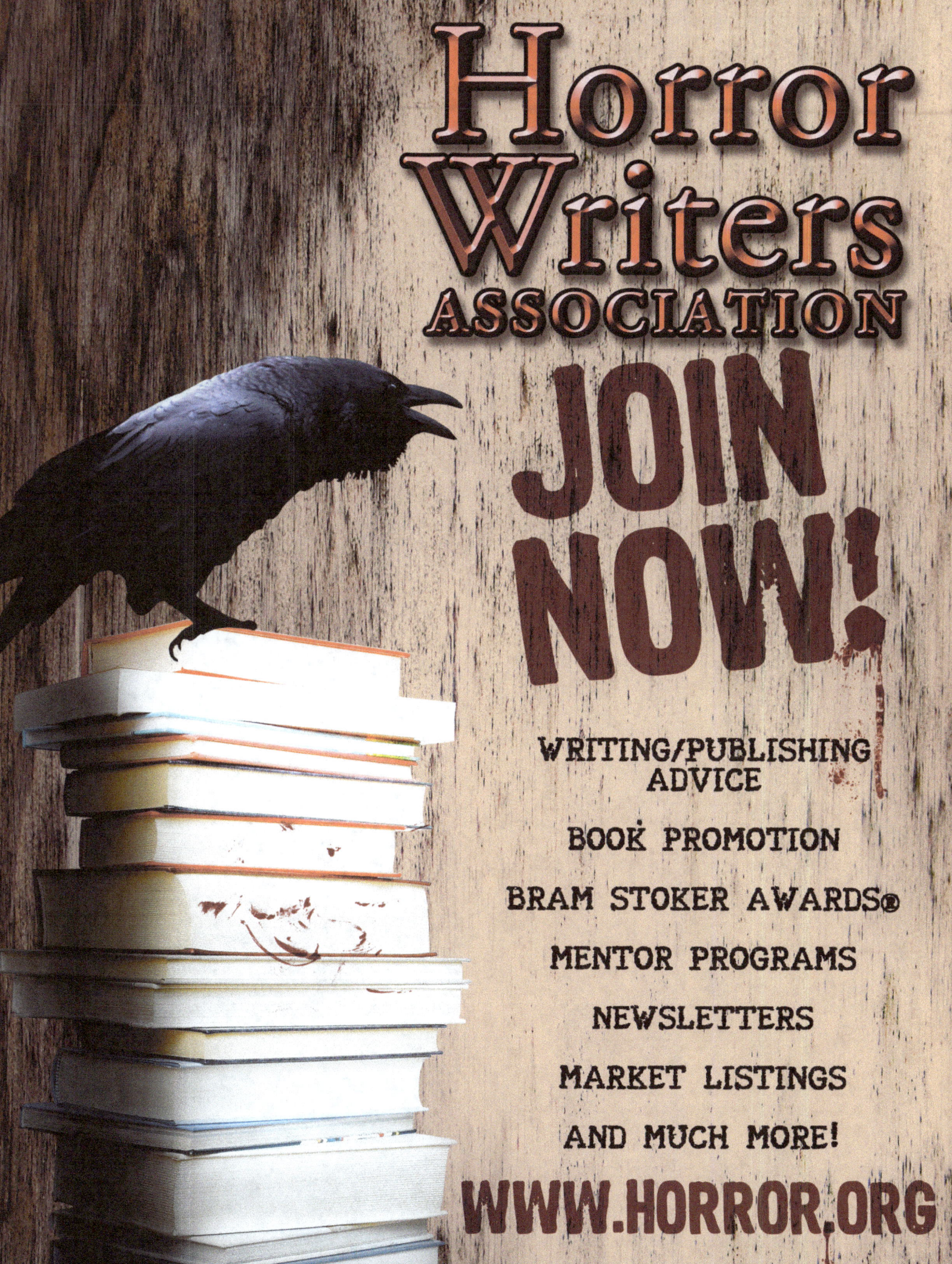

WORLD HORROR CONVENTIONS:
Guest Lists 1991-2013

World Horror Convention, 2013, New Orleans, LA. http://www.whc2013.org
Author Guest of Honor: Ramsey Campbell
Author Guest of Honor: Catlin Kiernan
Artist Guest of Honor: Glenn Chadbourne
Editor Guest of Honor: John Joseph Adams
Media Guest of Honor: Amber Benson
Other Special Guests: Robert McCammon, Jonathan Mayberry, Bruce Boston
Toastmaster: Jeff Strand

World Horror Convention 2012, Salt Lake City UT, http://www.whc2012.org
Author Guest of Honor: Simon R. Green
Author Guest of Honor: Sherrilyn Kenyon
Artist Guest of Honor: Mike Mignola
Editor Guest of Honor: Scott Allie
Other Special Guests: John Picacio, Mort Castle, Michael R. Collings, Michaelbrent Collings, Rocky Wood & David Farland
Grand Master: T. E. D. Klein
Toastmistress: P. N. Elrod

World Horror Convention 2011, Austin, TX, http://whc2011.org
Author Guest of Honor: Sarah Langan
Author Guest of Honor: Joe Hill
Media Guest of Honor: Steve Niles
Editor Guests of Honor: Brett Alexander Savory & Sandra Kasturi
Artist Guest of Honor: Vincent Chong
Toastmaster: Joe R. Lansdale
Special Guests: Brian Keene & Del Howison
Grand Master: Jack Ketchum
Co-Chairs: Nate Southard & Lee Thomas

World Horror Convention 2010, Brighton, UK, www.whc2010.org
Author Guest of Honor: Tanith Lee
Author Guest of Honor: David Case
Artist Guest of Honor: Les Edwards
Artist Guest of Honor: Dave Carson
Editor Guest of Honor: Hugh Lamb
Special Guest of Honor: James Herbert
Mistress of Ceremonies: Jo Fletcher
Special Media Guest: Ingrid Pitt
Grand Master: James Herbert
World Horror Society Lifetime Achievement Award: Basil Copper
Chair: Amanda Foubister

World Horror Convention 2009, Winnipeg, Manitoba, Canada, www.whc2009.org
Guest of Honor: Conrad Williams
Guest of Honor: Edo van Belkom
Guest of Honor: F. Paul Wilson
Guest of Honor: Joshua Gee
Artist Guest of Honor: Tommy Castillo
Grand Master: Tanith Lee
Chair: Linda Ross-Mansfield

World Horror Convention 2008, Salt Lake City, Utah, www.whc2008.org
Author Guest of Honor: Dennis Etchison
Artist Guest of Honor: John Jude Palencar
Academic Guest of Honor: Michael R. Collings
Special Guest: Jeff Strand
Special Guest: Dave Dinsmore, Biting Dog Press
Special Guest: Mort Castle
Toastmaster: Simon Clark
Special HWA Guest: Gary A. Braunbeck
Special Academic Guest, Dr. A. L. Carlisle
Ghost of Honor: Edgar Allen Poe
Grand Master: Robert McCammon
Chair: Charlene Harmon

World Horror Convention 2007, Toronto, Ontario, www.whc2007.org
Author Guests of Honor: Michael Marshall Smith, Nancy Kilpatrick
Artist Guest of Honor: John Picacio
Publisher Guest of Honor: Peter Crowther
Editor Guest of Honor: Don Hutchison
Media Guest of Honor: Peter Atkins
Mistress of Ceremonies: Sèphera Girón
Grand Master: Joe R. Lansdale
Special HWA Guest: Gahan Wilson
Chair: Amanda Foubister

World Horror 2006 – San Francisco, CA, USA, www.whc2006.org
Author Guests of Honor: Kim Newman, Koji Suzuki
Artist Guest of Honor: Brom
Media Guest of Honor: Bill Moseley
Editor Guest of Honor: John Pelan
Writer's Workshop: Mort Castle
Editor's WOrkshop: Nancy Kilpatrick
Toastmaster: Peter Straub
Grand Master: Ray Garton
Chairs: Jeremy Lassen, Darren McKeeman and Chad Savage

World Horror 2005 – New York, NY, USA, www.whc2005.org
Author Guests of Honor: Harlan Ellison, Joe R. Lansdale, Tim Lebbon, Tom Piccirilli, Jack Ketchum, Mort Castle and Amber Benson
Filmmaker Guest of Honor: Mick Garris
Artist Guest of Honor: Allen K (Koszowski),
Editor Guests of Honor: Tom and Elizabeth Monteleone
Writer's Workshop: Mort Castle
Masters of Ceremonies: Stan Wiater and Poet Linda Addison
Grand Master: F Paul Wilson
Chair: Monica O'Rourke

World Horror 2004 – Phoenix, Arizona, USA, www.leprecon.org/whc2004/
Author Guest of Honor: Douglas Clegg
Artist Guest of Honor: Caniglia
Editor Guest of Honor: Stephen Jones
Media Guest of Honor: Dee Snider
Special Guest of Honor: Adam Niswander
Writer's Workshop: Mort Castle
Editor's WOrkshop: Nancy Kilpatrick
Toastmaster: David Morrell
Grand Master: Jack Williamson
Chair: Mike Willmoth

World Horror 2003 – Kansas City, Missouri, USA, www.whc2003.org
Author Guest of Honor: Brian A. Hopkins
Publisher Guest of Honor: Don D'Auria
Artist Guest of Honor: Nick Smith
Special Guest of Honor: Forrest J. Ackerman
Writer's Workshop: Mort Castle
Mistress of Ceremonies: Laurell K. Hamilton
Grand Master: Chelsea Quinn Yarbro
Chair: Dee Willis

World Horror 2002 – Chicago, Illinois, USA
Author Guests of Honor: Gene Wolfe, Neil Gaiman
Editor Guests of Honor: Melissa Ann Singer
Artist Guest of Honor: Randy Broecker
Poetry Guest of Honor: Jo Fletcher
Photography Guest of Honor: Beth Gwinn
Music Guest of Honor: Liz Mandville Greeson
Comics and Young Adult Guest of Honor: Jill Thompson
Media Guests: Rich "Svengoolie" Koz, Patricia Tallman, Robert Z'dar
Special Guests: Karen Taylor, Yvonne Navarro, Brian A. Hopkins
Toastmaster: Gahan Wilson
Grand Master: Charles L. Grant
Chairs: Rich Lukes & Tina L. Jens

World Horror 2001 – Seattle, Washington, USA
Guest of Honor in Memorium: Richard Laymon
Writer Guests of Honor: Simon Clark, Michael Slade, Jessica Amanda Salmonson
Publisher Guests of Honor: Barbara Roden, Christopher Roden
Artist Guest of Honor: Charles Vess
Toastmaster: Jack Ketchum
Grand Master: Ray Bradbury
Chair: Paul M. Carpenter

World Horror 2000 – Denver, Colorado, USA, www.whc2000.org
Writer Guests of Honor: Peter Straub, Melanie Tem, Steve Rasnic Tem, J. Michael Straczynski, Graham Joyce
Artist Guest of Honor: Rick Lieder
Editor Guest of Honor: Ellen Datlow
Master of Ceremonies: Dan Simmons
Grand Master: Harlan Ellison
Chair: Edward Bryant

World Horror 1999 – Atlanta, Georgia, USA
Writer Guests of Honor: Michael Bishop, John Shirley
Artist Guest of Honor: Lisa Snellings
Master of Ceremonies: Neil Gaiman
Grand Master: Ramsey Campbell
Chair: Ed Kramer

World Horror 1998 – Phoenix, Arizona, USA, www.otsp.com/otsp/whc98
Author – Brian Lumley
Artist – Bernie Wrightson
Publisher – Tom Doherty
Toastmaster – John Steakley
Media – Tom Savini
Chairs: Doreen Webbert & Jean Goddin

World Horror 1997 – Niagara Falls, New York, USA
Writer Guests of Honor: Ramsey Campbell, Poppy Z. Brite, Joe R. Lansdale
Artist Guest of Honor: Rick Berry
Media Guest of Honor: Gunnar Hansen
Editor Guest of Honor: Darrel Schweitzer
Master of Ceremonies: Edo van Belkom
Grand Master: Peter Straub
Chairs: Lisa & Shawn Passero

World Horror 1996 – Eugene, Oregon, USA
Writer Guests of Honor: Clive Barker, Charles de Lint, Nina Kiriki Hoffman, Don Maitz, Janny Wurtz
Special Guests: Tim Powers, Edward Bryant
Grand Master: Dean Koontz
Chair: Christine F. York

World Horror 1995 – Atlanta, Georgia, USA
Writer Guests of Honor: John Farris, Neil Gaiman, R. L. Stine
Artist Guest of Honor: Alan M. Clark
Special Media Guest: Alice Cooper
Master of Ceremonies: Brian Lumley
Grand Master: Clive Barker
Chair: Edward E. Kramer

World Horror 1994 – Phoenix, Arizona, USA
Writer Guests of Honor: Charles L. Grant, Dan Simmons
Artist Guest of Honor: Gahan Wilson
Master of Ceremonies: Edward Bryant
Grand Master: Anne Rice
Chairs: Doreen Webbert & Jean Goddin

World Horror 1993 – Stamford, Connecticut, USA
Writer Guests of Honor: Peter Straub, Les Daniels
Artist Guest of Honor: Stephen Gervais
Special Media Guest: Paul Clemens
Master of Ceremonies: Stanley Wiater
Grand Master: Richard Matheson
Chair: Harold Kinney

World Horror 1992 – Nashville, Tennessee, USA
Writer Guest of Honor: Richard Matheson
Artist Guest of Honor: Harry O. Morris
Special Media Guest: Richard Christian Matheson
Master of Ceremonies: Brian Lumley
Grand Master: Stephen King
Chair: Maureen Dorris

World Horror 1991 – Nashville, Tennessee, USA
Artist Guest of Honor: Jill Bauman
Masters of Ceremonies: David J. Schow, John Skipp, Craig Spector, Richard Christian Matheson
Grand Master: Robert Bloch
Chair: Maureen Dorris

☙ ☙ ☙

The Catastrophist

by Weston Ochse

A drunk man looks at his thistle.

I examine the line on the screen, both not knowing why I wrote it, and knowing exactly why I wrote it. It's the calling card of the Catastrophist. What else could an obscure MacDiarmid reference be? It's my muse cluing me in that he's about to erupt center stage with all the fanfare and festoonery of Lady Gaga riding a Wildebeest juggling spiked purple dildos.

I ignore it as best I can. I'm attempting to write a story about New Orleans, trying to find the city's soul, a potential rediscovery since many of those not in the know have believed it fled during the horrible event created by Hurricane Katrina. My normal tool to divine such things is stream of consciousness and without looking back, I let if off the leash.

City as Character: What if the levies break? What if the water back-flows into the streets? What if it all happens again and the city dies? I can't go outside. I can't stay inside. I can't even think about the black mold that huddles in the walls of all the buildings. The fact is that the Big Easy ain't so easy anymore and I don't know what to do about it. A song by Poco. In the heart of the night in the cool southern rain there's a full moon in sight shining down on the Pontchartrain.

Domo Arigato, Mister Roboto.
You've blown, burned, and kicked me up.
You've shot me full of holes.
You've exploded the fuck out of me.

Most times I don't care what you do. I exist to serve. Some people don't even care about me. I'm a throw away. I'm what you do to pass the time when you're copping a squat. I'm what you refer to when you don't have the dedication to give to my hated cousin the novel. I'm a thought, carried only so far, brought home, then ended in media res.

But I can be better. We can be better. We can destroy things. We can blow shit up. There's a reason every Japanese movie either has a samurai or a monster. Come on, dude. You gotta trust your Catastrophist.

I try not to sigh too loudly or too dramatically. That the Catastrophist has taken ownership of New Orleans is nothing new. It knows my mind and does such things all the time. It once wanted me to attack San Francisco with Godzilla, and all I wanted to do was write a love story of two men in a VA hospital. It begged me to rain down meteors onto Anchorage while I was trying to write a bleak tale of the old Yukon. Once, when I was drunk as three people on two buck Chuck, it fooled me into believing that a volcano in Omaha was a good idea, so instead of the used car salesman with a heart of gold adopting a passle of mentally-handicapped kids, I killed everyone and everything, leaving them in a city-sized lava carpet. And of course everyone laughed at that story, just as they'd laughed at my tale of Denver falling into a sink hole. One thing about the Catastrophist is that it wants things destroyed. Unlike its counterparts who love happy endings, solid relationships, and the reaffirmation of ideals, the Catastrophist desires nothing more than unmitigated mayhem, murder, and unrelenting destruction.

So I was ready for it when I sat down to write a story about New Orleans. Or so I thought.

Poppy's going to get you. Poppy's going to get you.

It knows that I'm intimidated by the legend of Poppy Z. Brite. I know she's off doing her own thing, but she sort of owns New Orleans. Not the bright green glossy NOLA, but the part after midnight, where the fun happens and tourists stagger down Bourbon Street and B reel runs for the porn sites.

My intent with this New Orleans story is to write a narrative about one man's awakening and how he discovers himself just when he thinks there's nothing else to live for. Isn't New Orleans the perfect setting for such a tale? NOLA is palimpsest for disregard and the ability to overcome itself in the face of a universe of obstacles.

I really ought to get a little comfortably numb otherwise I might just fuck it up? Will Poppy rear up from the hedges like a miniature Godzilla and tackle me, force thirty-seven Kamikazes down my throat, then make me sit and listen to her talking about being a gay man trapped in a woman's body? I don't know what I don't know but what I do know is that she scares me and I don't want to do anything to piss her off. Nice Poppy. Easy Poppy.

Aw hell. That last bit was the Catostrophist pretending it was me. Bastard snuck into my thinking. Usually it announces itself. It has a fondness for Old Dennis DeYoung Styx tunes and the poetry of Pink Floyd, hence the *Domo Arigato* welcome earlier, and the *Comfortably Numb* bit it snuck in there.

The trick to discovering a city is to get into the flow. It can't be done anywhere else but the location, because above all, I believe in a sense of place. There's a DNA to the air, which once breathed, changes a person. So I opened a new screen as I sat in Lafayette Park and cast NOLA as a person. Once again, I cast it *in media res* and let it have its own voice.

City as Character: Then again I don't want you to act like a sissy about it. Sure we've been bruised. Sure we've been hurt. Fuck it. We've been rolled hard and put away wet by that hard bitch Katrina. Bodies floating down the street, people forgotten in their homes, gunmen killing to protect other people's capitalistic ideals, and a domed stadium where people were raped, burned, beaten and buried beneath old plastic tarps. You want the romance of New Orleans? You want Spanish moss hanging from trees bullshit and above ground cemeteries to spook you? Before you get that you gotta have a taste of the other. No Yin without the Yang. No beauty without the ugly. No saint without the sinner.

The headlines read these are the worst of times. Remember the BP spill? Wasn't that a boot up the ass after everything else that happened in the last decade? Forget a man finding himself. What about a man who wants to find himself but goes to New Orleans, only to discover that he's as hopeless as the city? Remember what the public sentiment was after Katrina? Maybe we should let it sink into the swamp, everyone was saying? Maybe it'll cost too much. You and your fucking palimpsests. Abandon all hope ye who enter here is palimpsested throughout your protagonist. So let's figure out what we're going to do. Your precious city has experienced and survived wars, Ann Rice, epidemics, hurricanes, tornadoes and ecological crises. Do you know what I think? I think she deserves a Krakon!

I rein in the Catastrophist and try to stop laughing. Ever since we saw the new Wrath of the Titans it's been Krakon crazy. Every time I have a city setting even near the water it wants to *UNLEASH THE KRAKON*. I almost feel sorry for it, although such thinking is dangerous. No. Don't feel sorry for it. And don't ignore it either, because as rampantly murderous as it is, it occasionally has a good idea.

Now back to the city as character: It ain't easy being the Big Easy.It ain't easy being the Big Easy.It ain't queezy drinking in the Big Easy. You and your mass-murdering sidekick notwithstanding, Mr. Author, you really need to get down and talk to the people. Get away from Bourbon Street if Ms. Poppy will let you go. Leave behind memories of Mardi Gras, Fat Tuesday, Ash Wednesday, and the parade spirit. Leave behind the brass bands and the funerals and the dancing and idea that nothing can keep me down and go into the neighborhoods. Go to the Garden District. Slip on down to the Lower Ninth. If a man is the sum of his parts, then a city is the sum of her people. Talk to them. Listen to them.

Come sail away, come sail away, come sail away with me. Go ahead and talk to her people. You'll find them as down on their luck as your main character.

You'll discover that they have an acceptance for whatever befalls them, calling it an easy way of living, but it really is them just saying, fuck it, ain't nothing I can do about it. Like your character who discovers himself. He's going to discover how badly screwed he is, just like the people of this city.

City as character: You need to take your Catastrophist and shove it where the sun don't shine, Mon Cher. We have the easy way of life because we don't want to get caught up in all the hatred everyone else seems to have. We're easy on the eye. We're easy on your pocket. Hell, we're even easy if you want us to be, know what I mean? But that's only because at the end of the day, when every other city is trying to get an identity, we already have one of a place where it doesn't matter where you come from, you're welcome into our big old easy arms just as you are.

I save the document and shut it down, the equivalent of silencing the voice of New Orleans. I am pretty sure I know what I want with the story now. I have a good understanding of my character, an Iraqi war vet moving to New Orleans to start a new life. I have a great feeling about the setting. I plan on using third person present tense to establish a pace and energy much faster than the sometimes laconic past tense. There's only one thing I need to do before I can actually start writing the story.

All in all it's just another brick in the wall. It ain't easy being the Big Easy. Did you hear that nonsense?

I heard.

She's a fool if she thinks her city doesn't need a good Krakon.

Is that what you really think New Orleans deserves? A Krakon?

You're going to do it, aren't you?

Yes, I'm going to do it.

About damn time!

But only because of all the cities, I think New Orleans can handle it.

How's it going to start?

Private First Class Nathan Hill steps off the bus on his new legs into a new life. He's practiced balancing at Walter Reed Medical Center for the last six months, and if you didn't know otherwise, you wouldn't recognize that he is a double amputee, courtesy of a roadside bomb near Haditha Dam. He inhales the thick sweet air. He looks around at the lush green, so much different from the somnolent brown of the desert. This is the start he's been looking for.

Where the hell is the Krakon?

Wait for it.

Hurry up.

As he walks down Loyola Avenue towards the canal, he has no idea that the idyllic day will soon be destroyed by a Krakon that has been awoken by the underwater furies of British Petroleum. He has no idea that the fate of the citizens of New Orleans will rest in his hands, and that by the end of the day, he'll save the city, kill the Krakon, and win the heart of a girl.

There had to be a girl. Please tell me a lot of the city will be destroyed.

Yes. A lot of the city will be destroyed.

Will there be an appearance of Poppy?

Yes. She'll appear as a Krakon killer.

Cool. Will she be wearing spandex?

And a cape too.

For the first time my catastrophist stopped interrupting and let me write the story; one about a city and a girl and a soldier and a Krakon and the most unlikely superhero.

THE BEGINNING.

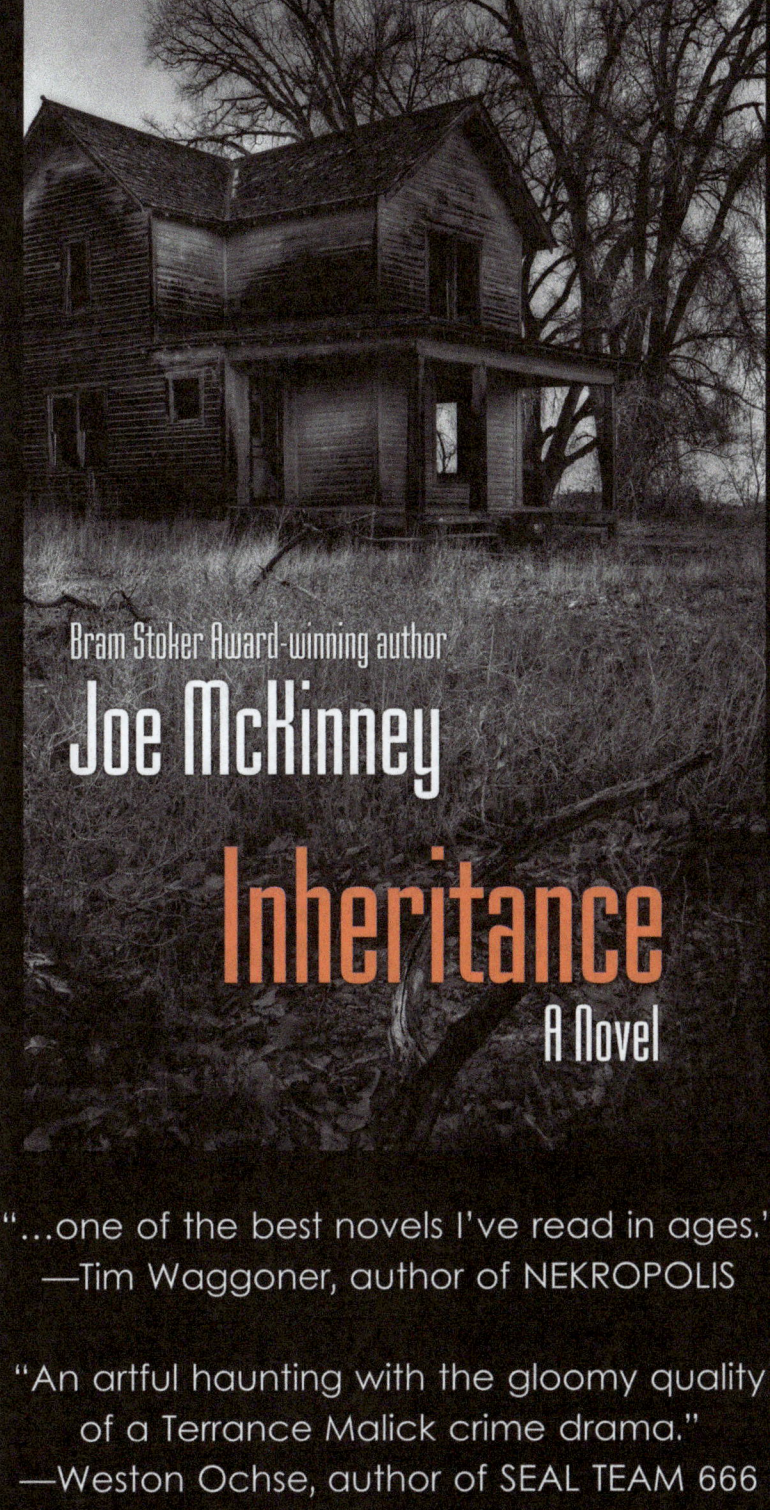

The Woman Who Collected McCammon

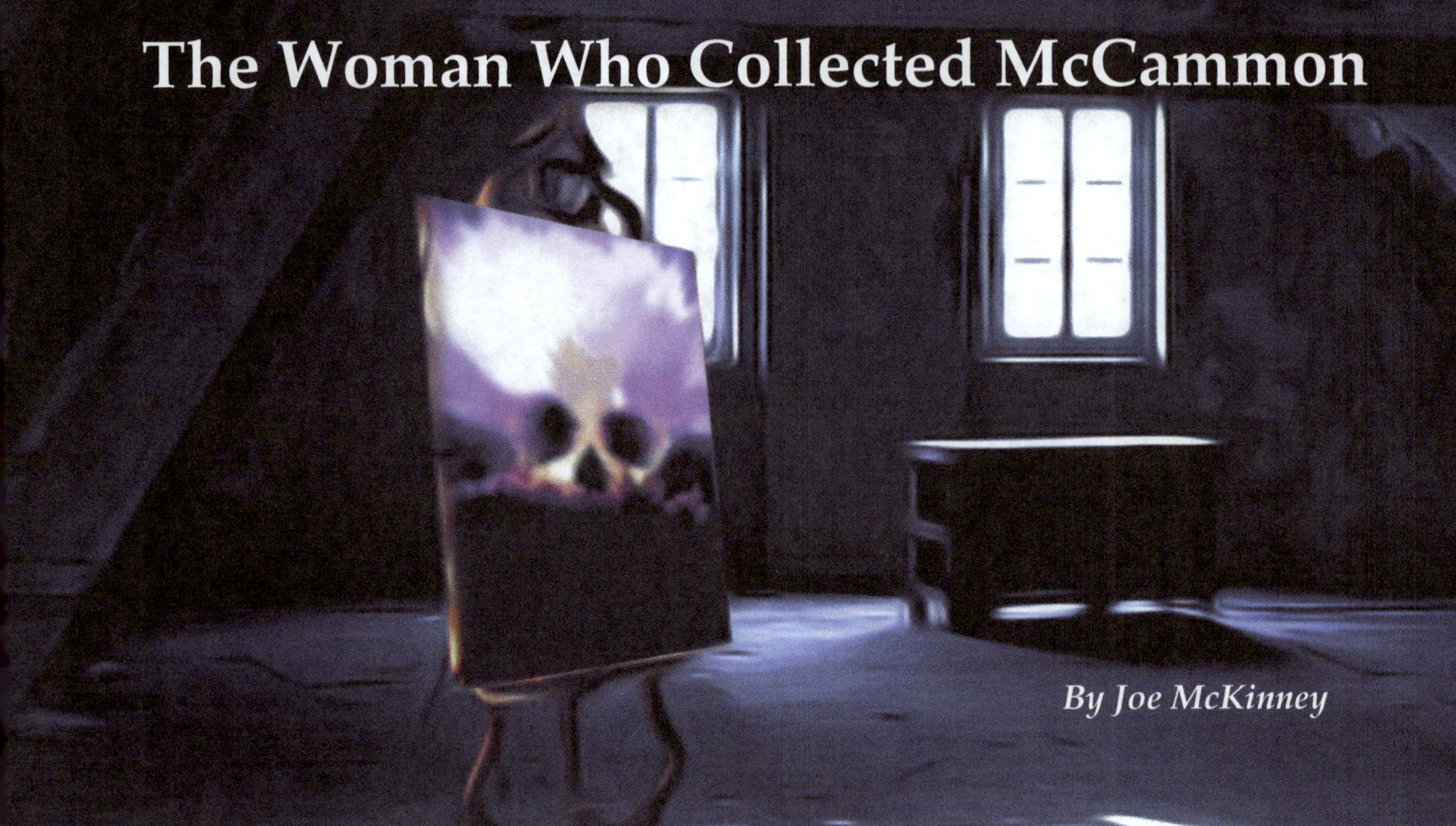

By Joe McKinney

True! She made me nervous. Very, very nervous I had been, and am still. But did I think her mad? No, of course not. I'm a cop, in addition to being a writer, and I've been through all the mental health courses they offer to peace officers. While out on patrol I've dealt with just about every kind of crazy there is. I know a lunatic when I see one, and Lucy Parkes was no lunatic. She was an artist, and with her the beauty of art was like a disease. Nay, it *was* the disease, for she suffered for it, and because of it. Her quest for perfection made her senses sharp, honed them like a knife, so that everything about her was acutely focused. Too acutely focused, I think, for most people's taste. Perhaps that was why some thought her crazy.

From our very first meeting I was aware of the two passions that dominated her life. The first, as I've mentioned, was her art. We met at World Horror when it was at Brighton, back in 2010. That was where I learned of her paintings. I was wandering the meeting rooms of the Royal Albion Hotel, shaking hands with the few people I knew and trying to work up the courage to introduce myself to some of the writers I'd been reading since grade school. Rumor had it Neil Gaiman would be making an appearance, and I didn't want to miss that for the world. I got a drink and wandered through the Dealer's Room, eventually finding myself in front of a table staring at a spread of some dozen hand-painted pictures. I am a great lover of images of abandoned buildings and other hallmarks of the apocalypse, and the images I saw displayed out on that table that day were the work of a kindred spirit. I was startled by her use of red, like a latter day Carpaccio, but without the heavy religious overtones. Instead, I found the common day realities of my world suddenly made strange. For the first time in a long time I found myself alarmed by what I saw.

"May I?" I said, pointing at one of the pictures. They were all matted on heavy bond mounting paper and encased in clear plastic envelopes. The woman behind the table, wild haired and dressed like a gypsy, had been staring about the room as though searching for somebody, but she now turned her full attention on me. The intensity of her stare was nearly enough to cause me to take a step back.

"What?" she asked.

"May I pick this one up?" I asked. "Have a closer look?"

She looked at the painting, and then at me. "Why?" she said.

I was expecting yes or no, not an injunction to defend my request. I felt flustered. "Well," I said, "it looks familiar."

A pause.

"Familiar how?"

The painting closest to me was of a gas station in the middle of a burning cornfield, missiles rising from the ground at the edge of the frame. Another showed a young girl with her hand on the trunk of an apple tree in the middle of a blasted field. Still another showed a homeless woman huddled in fear in a subway. The last in the row was of a man shrouded in smoke, one ghastly red eye glaring back at me.

A title card behind the paintings read *The Angel of the Apocalypse Series*, which offered absolutely no help whatsoever.

"I…don't know," I said. "But I've seen these images before, I think. Not from a movie, though. Maybe, from a book?"

I hadn't interested her until then, but now it seemed I was the only person in the room.

"Go on," she said.

And then it hit me. The girl in the blasted field. The Man with the Scarlet Eye. I pointed at the picture closest to me. "That's the gas station scene from *Swan Song*! The corn fields on fire. The missiles climbing out of the ground."

She didn't answer. Instead, she pointed at another picture, the old homeless woman in the subway. "And that?" she said.

"Sister Creep realizes the world has gone to hell," I said.

She bounced in her chair. She clapped her hands and giggled with a sudden enthusiasm I found a little weird, but strangely charming.

"You're a Robert McCammon fan," she said.

"Well, duh," I said. "What horror fan wouldn't be? The guy's amazing."

Here then, was her second passion. She was in love with Robert McCammon. Not the man himself, mind you, but the public image that was Robert McCammon. This woman, who was so obviously talented, was nonetheless debilitated by her crush. The cop in me picked up on that right away. Here was a woman willing to hide in the shadows, refusing to demand recognition from the world for her talent, for the simple reason that she was in love with the public face of a man she had never met. Even her greatest gift, her greatest passion, was made subservient, was held slave to that passion.

I thought of my own desire to shake hands with Neil Gaiman and I understood.

Or, sort of. I wasn't half as crazy about Gaiman as she so obviously was for McCammon.

Still, I got it. I understood the whole fan thing.

Though I found that part of her a little unnerving, I stayed to talk with her because she was mighty talented. She certainly didn't need to apologize for the artwork she had on display. I thought it was fantastic. All that red really popped.

And because there was a bag of black licorice from the candy shop I'd found in town earlier that morning. She had an open bottle of the hotel's house merlot open as well, and I had an empty glass.

I asked, she filled.

I sat, we talked.

For the next six hours.

And nearly every word of it was how much we both loved the writing of Robert McCammon. From *Baal* to the absolutely transcendent *Boy's Life* and *Gone South* to the amazing *Speaks the Nightbird*, we both loved reading Robert McCammon.

In Lucy Parkes, I had found a kindred spirit.

# # #

That was in March, 2010.

The next year, World Horror was in Austin…and so was I. In fact, I was on the planning committee. I was the Dealer's Room coordinator, working pretty much nonstop to get the convention off the ground. I've been told that the Austin convention was one of the smoothest ever. I wish I could claim some responsibility for that, but I can't. The real credit goes to Lee Thomas and Nate Southard for running such a tight ship. What I can claim credit for is bringing Lucy Parkes to the States. She had such a fun time in Austin (my god, you should have seen the look in that woman's eyes when she ate barbequed pork ribs for the first time!) that she relocated from London to Texas. She fell in love with the live music and the food and the literary culture of Austin, and settled there.

It was a good year for both of us. She was starting to get commissions for book covers, and even did a cover for *The Magazine of Fantasy & Science Fiction* that made the short list for the Hugos. My Dead World Series was picking up as well. Sales for *Dead City* had never really slacked off the way my publisher was expecting them to, and so they came looking for more. I gave them *Apocalypse of the Dead*, which my editor loved, and on the strength of those sales I got another two book deal.

On the last day of the convention my wife and I took Lucy out for more barbeque, and though we were both artists on the rise, on the cusp of commercial success, and should have been content to enjoy the meal and each other's company, our conversation was almost entirely on Robert McCammon, and not very pleasant.

Lucy was upset, you see, because Jack Ketchum was getting the World Horror Convention Grand Master Award.

"Personally," my wife said, "I think Dallas Mayr is a great choice to receive the award. *The Girl Next Door* actually made me shake with emotion. I haven't read many books capable of doing that. And the stories in *Peaceable Kingdom* were amazing. I like just about everything I've read from him."

"Yeah, that's the point," Lucy said, suddenly angry, taking my wife and I by surprise. "You *like* his stuff, but I *love* McCammon's stuff. There's so much heart in it. You can see it on every page. The man puts his *heart* into it. His *heart*. People should recognize that. They should stand up and take notice. When a man writes like he does, attention should be paid."

Those final words were punctuated by her fist hitting the table. And hard enough to make the folks at the next table over turn around and frown at us.

Lucy was almost crying.

Her lips were trembling.

My wife and I traded a quick, worried glance.

"I agree McCammon deserves the recognition," I said, trying to play the peacemaker. "And you're right, his heart is there on every page. There's no question about that. He just keeps getting better and better. As much as I hate to admit it, I enjoyed *Mister Slaughter* even more than *Boy's Life*, and you know how in love I am with that book. But you won't ever hear me say a bad word about Dallas Mayr. In my opinion, he's long overdue for the Grand Master Award. As is Neil Gaiman."

She huffed. She sipped her sweet tea and watched the traffic go by on I-35. "You and Gaiman," she said.

I shrugged.

She smiled.

We were friends again.

But afterward, after Lucy was on a plane back to England and my wife and I were in the car and headed home to San Antonio, my wife said, "That woman gives me the creeps."

"She's not so bad," I said.

"Are you kidding? She's a lunatic. You heard the way she talks about Robert McCammon. It's like…I don't know, it's creepy. It's like listening to your cousin Jessielynn talk about Jesus."

"Lucy Parkes is nothing like Jessielynn," I said, trying to keep it light. "And besides, Lucy's doing that cover for *Night of the Fire Hag* for me. I can't wait to see what she does with all that red."

My wife turned and looked out her window. "She gives me the creeps," she said.

\# \# \#

Needless to say, Lucy Parkes was at World Horror the next year. Robert McCammon was receiving a much-deserved Grand Master Award, and Lucy was walking around the hotel positively beaming. Looking at her, you'd think she was the one getting the award.

To an outsider her behavior might have seemed strange, but I got it. I understood. Like so many who made it out to Salt Lake City that year, I attended the Q&A session with Robert McCammon, and listened with rapt fascination as he talked about the harsh realities of publishing for a living and all the soul searching he'd done as a result of that. Listening to him talk, I became even more of a fan than I had been, and that's really saying something, believe me. And then, the next night, I had the greatest Robert McCammon moment of my life, for my novel Flesh Eaters won the Stoker that year, and McCammon and Joe Lansdale were the ones to present me with that wicked little house. I was speechless. I had just been handed the Stoker by two of my literary heroes. I used to skip meals at school just so I could save my lunch money to buy their books. To shake their hands on that stage, and to have Robert McCammon lean in close and whisper "Great job, Joe," in my ear, was a moment I will forever cherish.

So, on Sunday, both Lucy and I were in high spirits as we rode the elevator down to our third annual Last-Day-of-World-Horror Lunch.

The elevator doors opened – and there was Robert McCammon!

He was sitting on a bench, waiting on somebody to take him to the airport.

Beside me, Lucy was about to rattle herself to pieces. She was bouncing on her toes, giggling crazily. I could feel the heat radiating off her.

"Calm down," I whispered. "You're gonna creep him out."

"I can't help it," she said between giggles. "I just want to touch him."

"Easy killer."

"Hey, get a picture of us together!" she said.

"I, well…"

"What? You know him. Introduce me."

"What do you mean? I don't know him. I just shook his hand last night. It's not like we're golfing buddies or anything."

"Introduce me," she said.

She wasn't listening to me, and I'd never hear the end of it if we didn't do this, so I sighed and gestured for her to lead the way.

What followed was about three of the most uncomfortable minutes I've ever spent. As far as celebrities go, McCammon was one of the nicest of all time. If I'd have been in his shoes, and a strange woman latched onto me the way Lucy did to him, I'd have probably gotten a restraining order. But he kept his composure through it all and even managed a sort of grin

when she sat in his lap and put her hand over his heart so I could snap a picture.

He was a good sport, even if he was glad to be rid of her.

\# \# \#

Well of course good things kept coming Robert McCammon's way, for the next year, which is this year, McCammon was honored with the HWA's Bram Stoker Award for Lifetime Achievement. At long last, it seemed, the world was taking Lucy Parkes' advice and paying attention to the legend living in their midst.

And, as for Lucy, she was simply ecstatic.

More than that even, she was manic the entire weekend. Like a child who has been given too much candy and caffeine.

We watched as Robert McCammon and Clive Barker received their awards. Over the applause I said, "I wonder when Neil Gaiman will get his." But she didn't hear me. Her face was all aglow, and there were tears of joy on her cheeks.

But as much as it pained her, she kept herself in check and didn't hound him. She kept her distance most of the weekend, waiting for the perfect time to present him with what she considered her greatest creation – a portrait of him, dressed as Matthew Corbett, studying a bloody murder scene left behind by Mister Slaughter.

"I think I'm going to do it Sunday morning," she confided in me. "Before his Q&A panel. We could watch that and then go out to lunch."

"I'll have to catch up with you after the Q&A," I said. "My zombie panel overlaps the first thirty minutes of his thing."

"Oh, that's right. Why'd they schedule it like that? Nobody's going to go a zombie panel when they can see Robert McCammon."

"Gosh, thanks."

"Well you know it's true."

"My wife will be there."

"Your wife hates my guts."

"She does not."

Lucy cocked an eyebrow at me. We both knew I was lying. "I'll see you after the Q&A," she said.

So I went off to visit the dealer's room and she went off to get her portrait ready to present to McCammon. Then, after my panel, I went over to the meeting room where the Q&A was supposed to be going on. I found a few irritated-looking folks standing around, but no Q&A. I stopped the first person I saw and asked if I was in the right place.

"Yeah, well, it was supposed to be here."

"What happened?"

"McCammon didn't show."

"You're kidding?"

"I wish." The guy looked angry. "I was really looking forward to hearing him talk too."

I wandered back to the elevators. Poor Lucy, I thought. She was going to be heartbroken. But when I knocked on her door I was surprised to hear her sounding almost musical. "Who is it?"

"It's me. You okay?"

The door opened and Lucy was standing there, the tips of her hair wet. She had a huge smile on her face. "Of course I'm okay. Why wouldn't I be?"

"Oh, well, I thought, you know, because McCammon didn't make his Q&A."

"Oh, that." She dismissed it with a wave of her hand. "That's nothing."

I nodded.

"You about ready?" I asked.

"In a minute," she said, and walked into the recesses of her room. I stepped inside and the carpet squished beneath my feet. I looked down. I could see water pooling up around the edges of my shoes. I looked into the bathroom and saw water everywhere.

"What did you do?" I asked.

She spun around suddenly, and her eyes narrowed suspiciously. "What do you mean?"

"The floor's all wet. They're probably going to make you pay for this. We had to get one of the rooms in our house cleaned after a pipe burst and let me tell you it ain't cheap." I walked deeper into the room. "It's all the way into her too. What did you do?"

"I took a bath," she said lightly. She gestured at the bed. "Come in. Have a seat. I just need to get my shoes."

She had made the bed, which was a quirk of hers I never understood. The housekeeping staff will do that for you, I had told her once. But she had just waved that away. When I pushed her on the matter she finally admitted that it embarrassed her, knowing the hotel's maids would see her room a mess. It amazed me that someone who walked around looking like a secondhand dress shop had thrown up on her could be so worried about an unmade bed, but that was Lucy, take her or leave her.

Anyway, I sat.

And frowned.

"You didn't have to sleep in this thing, did you?"

She was digging through her closet, looking for her shoes. She stuck her head back out, frowning. "What do you mean?"

"It's all lumpy," I said.

She shrugged. "It's a hotel bed. Whatcha gonna do?"

"I don't know. Get another room maybe. My bed was like sleeping on a giant pillow."

"What difference does it make? I'm usually too drunk to care anyway."

"Yeah, I guess."

She came out of the closet with a pair of black mules, slipped them on her feet, crossed the room to the desk chair, turned it so that it faced me, and sat down in it. Then she reached over and pulled her bag under the chair. Every move seemed to be performed with exacting deliberation, like she was setting up pieces on a game board.

I watched her do all this with half a smile on my face. She was acting oddly, even by her standards, though she seemed determined to put me at ease. She put her hands in her lap and smiled. She looked very prim, very proper, very English.

But then I saw her eye twitch.

"I'm surprised you're not more upset about missing a chance to see McCammon," I said.

"It's okay, really." Her eye twitched again.

"Did you at least get a chance to give him the portrait?"

"Oh, that," she said. "No, I decided it wasn't finished."

"Not finished? But you were so proud of it."

"Yes, but it isn't finished."

She glanced down at her bag, then up at me. She looked awfully pale. Her eye twitched a third time.

"Lucy, are you okay?"

"Why do you keep asking me that?" she said, suddenly in a fury. It took me aback, like rounding a wood pile and finding a snake there. I said, "Whoa! Hold on."

"I'm fine," she said. "I'm fine, I'm fine, I'm fine!"

"Okay," I said. "Jesus, stop shrieking at me."

"Now I'm shrieking?" She jumped to her feet, her hands gesticulating wildly. "I'm shrieking!"

I stood up and backed away from her, and when I did I got a glimpse behind the armchair in the corner. Her portrait of McCammon was back there. I glanced at her. Her chest was heaving, eyes wild, hair sticking up all over the place like wire. Her gaze went to the armchair and then returned to me.

Her eye twitched.

I reached behind the chair and pulled out the painting.

"That isn't finished," she said.

But I wasn't paying any attention to her words at that point. The painting was dripping red. There were gobs of red paint on the bottom of the painting. At least I thought it was paint, at first. Then I caught that familiar coppery smell.

"Oh God," I said, nearly gagging. "Lucy, what is this?"

The blood on the canvas was that deep red almost black head blood like I used to see at fatality traffic accidents. It clumps like wet slimy Jello.

"What is this?" I asked again.

"A work in progress," she said, and surprised me with a smile. But it was a grotesque smile, and it couldn't have alarmed me more if her teeth had been filed to points. "It was fine before," she said, gesturing toward the painting, "but it lacked heart. That was the problem. Right before I showed it to him, I realized that was the problem. I've always said Rick was so magical as a writer because he put his heart onto every page. That's what my painting was missing. His heart."

"His…"

I looked to the bed. Lumpy, I thought.

I threw back the covers, but the bed was clean. Glancing back at Lucy, I saw her holding her breath. She was staring at the bed, not blinking. I put one foot up on the side of the mattress and gave it a kick. It only slid a few feet but that was enough to show the hacked up body sandwiched between the mattresses. Robert McCammon's severed head stared up at me from the middle of a pile of guts.

I backed away, shaking my head in disbelief.

She moved suddenly and I spun around to face her.

She had scooped up her bag and now she was hugging it tightly to her chest.

"What have you got in there?" I managed to say.

She smiled.

"What have you got?" I demanded.

I took a step forward, my hand outstretched. She didn't move. I grabbed one of the straps and pulled it from her grip. I looked inside – and there, in a doll's display box, was a lump of wet muscle that had once been Robert McCammon's heart.

Again, I looked at her.

"Why?" I asked.

"You know why, silly. We've both said it a million times. He puts his heart on every page. But you know what's really great? When I hold it close, I can still hear it beating. And it's not hideous at all."

THE HUMAN BODY AS ART: ANDY GOLUB

By Joel B. Kirkpatrick

The human body has been an object of art and a subject of art for all of our known history. When combined with 'art', even in minimalistic ways, the human form is transformed. Age disappears, gender bends, personality is enhanced. We are never as human as when we are expressing our humanity.

That is the definition of being human— we have ideas to express.

Human art bends ideas, as easily as it bends our perception. Nudity can be covered by nothing more than brush strokes. Inhibitions can be cast off, along with clothing, by donning no more than some whimsical colors. We all love seeing ourselves in a different light; seeing ourselves from other directions.

Artist Andy Golub paints bodies. He seeks to reveal us, by covering us…with his art. He gives us something to look into—not merely look at. **"I see it as collaborative,"** he says, **"which is ironic since I'm the one doing all of the painting. The model's body and personality are the inspiration for a painting spoken in my voice."**

When multiple bodies make up his canvas, the finished

Photo: Arthur Eisenberg

painting is only 'right' when they are exactingly posed. **"If they change too much from the original position, then the lines won't match up. It's not about being perfect, but being close enough so that you can see what I'm doing with the art. Staying in position for long periods of time can be very difficult for models. Usually it involves taking a break in the middle. Then it takes a while to figure out how to get back into the same position."**

Andy does full-body paintings, and they are quite intricate, sometimes involving multiple 'canvases'. Can a person be painted head-to-toe in half an hour? Longer? What does he do with the completed models while they are merely waiting? **"I can basecoat a single color onto a model within a half hour,"** he says. **"To basecoat a multicolor design takes over an hour. When working with a large group, I often have the models help out by base coating themselves and each other, under my direction of course."**

Andy Golub has created publically all over the world. Where does he stir the most attention? Where has he been the most welcome? **"The most attention has probably been in Times Square, mostly because I've painted large groups of models there several times and also because there's been some conflicts with police. I'd say the place where people understood what I was doing the most was probably in Williamsburg, Brooklyn. There are a lot of artists and musicians there."**

In New York City, one of Andy's fully-painted but unclothed models was actually arrested. **"Two of my models and I were all arrested for public lewdness (all charges have been dropped). Then my lawyer announced to the city that I'm doing it again (which is not required) and the police were instructed not to arrest, but one cop arrested her anyway. I have a great civil rights attorney in Ron Kuby. I am very aware of the law (I carry copies of the laws in my backpack) and everything I do is completely legal. I will not allow false arrests and/or harassment to deter me from making my art and yes, in public."**

Andrew Koenig is one of Andy Golub's favorite photographers. **"He's a great guy. He's been coming to a lot of my shoots for over a year."** How much collaboration takes place at events like the Time Square shoots? Has he ever suggested changes to your art, Andy, to enhance the photos, or is he merely an observer? **"Andrew definitely understands the importance of free expression. He also has taken some great shots of the models from unusual angles."**

Andy is often drawn to Times Square. **"People from all over the world are there. It's sort of the most public place you can be. Some people are excited, a few people are offended and many people just stare and contemplate. I like that. I think it challenges people's ideas about art and the body. I also like the idea of my work, which is free expression, being a public alternative to the**

Photos: Andrew Koenig

huge billboard advertisements created by all of the marketers."

Many of the models are from the surrounding crowds. **"It's one of my favorite things when somebody from the crowd volunteers to get painted,"** Andy muses. **"It happens pretty often, both guys and girls."**

Cities the world over have always had their street art and painted living-statues. However, most of those are artists earning a living while they pose. In what way are these events earning Andy a living? **"When I am painting in public, I do not collect money. But as a professional artist, I sell prints of my work, show in galleries, paint murals and do live painting for events. I'm also starting a line of t-shirts."**

Photo: Arthur Eisenberg, Photo: Rob Ruiz

Andy has a symbolic way of looking back at the crowds, objectifying them with his art. **"From my point of view I feel like I'm pulling the inner personality of the model to the surface and the faces express that well. I try not to think too much about what my art means. It can get in the way of the spontaneity."**

Easily recognized and completely translatable from any surface that Andy paints upon, his art has a lot in common with graffiti. Has he ever been called a 'graffiti artist'? **"Yeah I get that. My lines also stretch in a graffiti-esque kind of way. But I paint with a regular brush so I think it's more tactile. I recently did a large mural at 5 Pointz, which is an amazing building covered in graffiti in Long Island City, Queens. I'm a fan of the work of many graffiti artists, so it was a great experience to be a part of that. Also, I think of myself more of a street artist and take pride in creating art on the spot, feeding off of the surrounding environment."**

Who decides if the model will be fully nude? Does such a condition even matter to the artistic outcome? **"Studio shoots are always full nude. Outdoor public bodypainting can be either full nude or in a g-string, which is up to the model. I will suggest full nude as an option, let them know that it's perfectly legal and that I have a great lawyer in case there is an arrest. But it's their choice. Some models want to do it but are afraid of getting arrested. I think it does impact the art. Having done full nude bodypainting in public several times, you can feel the surge of energy when the model removes her g-string (the way it works, the model removes the g-string after the rest of her body is base-coated and the lines are under way). More than anything, you can feel the stretching boundaries of what is allowed. It makes me feel more free in my art, more confident to trust my instincts."**

While striking, and by some design shocking, Andy's art cannot rightly be called frightening. But he has obviously wondered about a darker turn to his expressions. Are there any samples of such 'darker' creations?

"The faces I paint onto the models to me are a reflection of their inner personality. And I discover their personalities as I paint them. One time I painted a face on a girl at a party. She seemed like a completely sweet girl, but when I looked at the painting I had just made, I was convinced that she was evil." He shudders. **"I feel that the faces I paint onto people come from a pretty dark place. People often find my art to be happy because of the bright colors that I use. To me, positive and negative feelings are all connected to each other and exist in the same painting."**

People tend to lose their inhibitions, even when covered only in a thin layer of paint. Body-painting, in a tangible sense, is clothing. Does Andy have an opinion of why this phenomenon occurs?

"On some level I think it's liberating for a lot of people to be nude in public. People especially go crazy for the Halloween Parade. But on another level, I think it's about the fact that people are becoming art. Very often there is a moment when the model goes through a transformation. I make the art up as I go, feeding off the energy of the model. At some point the model and the painting become one."

Is there some grand Andy Golub event that he would love to create but has never found the exact means to accomplish? **"I'm always on the lookout to do the largest group bodypainting possible, having it photographed from high above. This is very difficult because bodypainting needs to be completed in one session. I'm not going to reveal too much, but I'm in the planning stages of a large installation that involves time-lapse video and video projection.**

"Through my bodypainting, I've connected with hundreds of people I would have never otherwise met. We've experienced these paintings together, inspired each other and spread the energy of creativity and expression onto the public streets. Wherever my art takes me next, I will always be appreciative for these experiences."

DAVID B. SILVA TRIBUTES

"As I sit down to write this, it's been two weeks since Dave Silva's death, long enough for the dizzying disorientation to pass and for the cold, hard reality to sink in. I was one of the few people who knew that Dave had been ill, and in some ways I had begun to prepare myself for the inevitable. But I hadn't done enough. I was living in my own weird little world of denial, where my inability to face the truth collided head-on with Dave's tendency to build walls and guard his privacy, which prevented him from telling most of us just how serious his condition had become.

I knew Dave for thirty years. We progressed from our initial cool, professional correspondence to a more casual, chattier sort of relationship. Dave bought the first short story I ever sold, and from there we became true buddies, the kind who, in those days long before e-mail, carried out actual conversations, talking on the phone for an hour or two every day. We visited each other's homes and took convention trips together. We shared and critiqued our stories and novels and works in progress. I became a sounding board when Dave had doubts or concerns about something with his magazine, *The Horror Show*, and he became my mentor when I started my own magazine, *Horrorstruck*, standing close by to serve as critic and comforter from the first nugget of an idea right through the mailing of the final issue several years later.

We eventually became full-fledged professional collaborators, editing two anthologies and, after taking a break for a few years, coming back to create the *Hellnotes* newsletter, an attempt to break the traditional publishing mold by delivering each weekly issue in three different formats – e-mail, fax, and hard copy. We edited Hellnotes together for five years, before finally deciding we were exhausted and needed a break, making the difficult decision to pass the newsletter on to other hands. It eventually found its way back to Dave, and he went on to transform our baby into a groundbreaking news website, but I didn't go along on that particular ride; that was all Dave. In fact, our collaboration days were pretty much over by then, although we never stopped scheming and planning.

We always had an idea for another anthology, another novel, another editing service or writers' school or horror-based social network. And by we, I mean Dave. His mind was constantly churning. He was continually tossing out new ideas. He was always inventing, always envisioning, always proposing. Even in his last few months, when his health had already taken a sharp decline and his money was so tight that he couldn't seek the medical help he needed, he was still looking to the future, talking about finishing up the novella he'd been struggling with and buying a new computer and moving on to bigger, more exciting projects. And he was still dropping me those familiar Dave Silva e-mails, those notes that said things like, "What if we tried this?" or "What do you think about that?"

I've tried several times these past few weeks to distill my thoughts about Dave down to their essence, but I haven't been able to do it. He was too much a bundle of contradictions. Friendly and outgoing. Quiet and withdrawn. Prone to hearty laughter. Prone to moody silences. Willing to give you the shirt off his back and the last crumb off his plate, but vehemently opposed to accepting help himself.

Dave's skill as an editor was legendary. His talent as a writer was awe inspiring. His insight and kindness and compassion, his knowledge and skill, his energy, have all been written about at length in recent days, and I can affirm that everything said about him is true. What I haven't been able to do is sum up the man in a coherent fashion, in a way that captures his spirit and perhaps explains it a bit, as well. Until now. Until I started thinking about all of those ideas he had over the years, that non-stop well of stories and snippets, projects and proposals, that was bubbling away inside his mind all of the time. The ideas he had – small, large, wise, dumb, profound, silly, exciting, inspiring, intimidating, and sometimes just downright ridiculous. They never stopped. I'm positive that as he laid down to sleep that last time, that sleep from which he would never awake, his mind was spinning out some brand new crazy, creative concoction of – well, something. A novel, perhaps, or the greatest anthology ever to hit the horror field, a new website, some new thing, the next thing, maybe a couple of next things.

That was the essence of Dave. He was a constant dreamer. He was a kid who never grew up – he called himself a "lost boy," after all, and lived by the motto "better weird than plastic" – a kid who always knew he was going to beat the world, if not today then tomorrow, the day after at the latest.

I'm remembering my long-ago visit to his home in the mountains of northern California. It was the mid 1980s. *The Horror Show* was taking off big time and the horror field was booming. We spent several days traveling around his corner of the state, seeing the sights, and several nights sitting around a campfire, looking up at a black dome full of fiery stars spinning overhead. And through it all we never stopped talking. Through it all the ideas never stopped coming. It was the most intense period of creative frenzy I ever experienced. We laid out ideas for books and stories, anthologies and collections. We planned special issues of his magazine. We held the first discussions of what would soon blossom into my magazine. We even cooked up a fictional publication called Iocus, which went on to become the subject of an elaborate and quite successful April Fool's prank in *The Horror Show*. We were hopped up on caffeine and salt and sugar and an even more powerful drug – invention. Dave's eyes glittered with excitement as each new idea spilled out. He would talk faster and faster, sometimes getting up to pace around the campfire, unable to restrain himself. It was thrilling to see – a dreamer in the full and uncompromising grip of his dreams.

That's the Dave I'm going to remember most. That's the Dave I'm going to miss until the day I lie down for my own final sleep. Dave, the dreamer. Dave, the guy who was always creating. Dave, the man whose mind never stopped turning, never stopped looking for the next thing. He couldn't be stopped, really, not by literary roadblocks, not by financial problems, not even by serious illness. In the end, only death could stop him.

Or maybe not.

Maybe he's still out there.

Maybe the lost boy has made it to Neverland at last, where he is marshaling all the other eternal urchins for some excellent adventure, some grand experiment, grabbing them with a grin and a laugh and a sparkle in his eyes as he says, "Hey, what if we tried this?"

– Paul F. Olson

"For many years, Dave and I talked regularly on the phone, and they were conversations full of laughter. When I wrote the introduction to the Gauntlet edition of *Through Shattered Glass*, my second goal was to praise his work, and my primary goal was to render him helpless with mirth. Praise between friends can quickly grow embarrassing, and the better gift is laughter. Our friendship was long-distance, always by phone and mail. Dave had a standing invitation to dinner, but we never met face-to-face. I will miss his laugh. He was a kind and humble man, a devoted son to his parents, and a stand-up friend."

– Dean R. Koontz

ooo

"Dave Silva created a market for horror that was outside the mainstream. He gave a lot of new and nearly new writers a paying platform for their work. *The Horror Show* was great, and so was Dave. We had not had a chance to be in contact for some time, but not due to any reason. Just life tracks running in different directions. Makes no difference. I miss him. He helped create the modern field of horror fiction and was a good guy to boot."

– Joe R. Lansdale

ooo

"In the Summer of 1984, I was a twenty-year old disullisioned college student. One afternoon, I stopped in at a B. Dalton Bookstore in an Orange County, California shopping mall. While browsing the magazine racks, something with a stark white cover with a blue border and the words *The Horror Show* caught my eye.

It was nothing like I'd ever seen before. This little magazine was sandwiched between *Rod Serling's The Twilight Zone* Magazine and something else on the rack, probably *Fangoria*. I could tell right away that it wasn't a big slick corporate production. I opened the front cover to glance at the contents – it was clearly a horror magazine, but the writers were people I'd never heard of. Right then and there, I made the decision to buy it.

I loved everything about *The Horror Show*. Its influence was immeasurable. Without *The Horror Show*, much of the small press explosion of the late 1980's would not have happened. Dave Silva showed that with a shoestring budget, one could produce a publication of high professional quality. The fact that he managed to get the magazine onto the magazine racks of large chain bookstores is nothing short of a miracle.

I was exposed to Silva's short fiction shortly after first encountering his magazine. In the years to come, whenever his byline appeared in an anthology or magazine, I knew I was in for something special. "Dwindling" was the first of his tales I encounterd, in Karl Edward Wagner's seminal The Year's Best Horror Stories. Others followed - "Ice Sculptures", "The Hollow", "Metastasis", "The Night of the Fog", "Dry Whiskey", and probably his most infamous and well-known story of all: "The Calling".

Much has been said of David Silva's kindness and generosity toward beginning writers – he was that way with beginning publishers and editors, too. Every small press editor/publisher of that era I knew – from David Niall Wilson (*The Tome*), to Mark Rainey (*Deathrealm*), to Richard T. Chizmar (*Cemetery Dance*) – readily admit that David Silva was always quick to offer advice and guidance on the ins and outs of publishing a small magazine. My early submission efforts weren't good enough to make it into the magazine, but his rejections were always insightful - some of those stories I later rewrote based on his feedback and sold elsewhere. Newbie writers: this is how it's supposed to work.

David Silva was not known for making appearances at genre conventions like World Horror, but he did show up at some World Fantasy Conventions back in the day. That's where I first met him - in Chicago, 1990. Meeting him was an honor. I met him one other time, about eight months later, when he accepted his Bram Stoker Award for Superior Achievement in Short Fiction from the Horror Writer's of America. Bentley Little was also present to accept his own Stoker for Superior Achievement for a First Novel (for *The Revelation*). Yes. I was present at a con in which two of the most reclusive writers of horror attended.

Over the next decade or so, our correspondence was sporadic. It picked up a bit when he co-edited/published *Hellnotes*. When he heard I had a brush with cancer, he called me. I was touched by his concern. That's the kind of person David was; he genuinely cared about people.

I hadn't been in touch with him all that much in the early years of this new century. It was only recently with the advent of Facebook that we were within each other's orbit again. I was surprised to hear he'd relocated to Las Vegas. Dave didn't post on Facebook all that much; most of what I learned about him was through his new writing partner on several new projects, Robert Swartwood. I knew he'd restarted *Hellnotes* as a web publication, and while he wasn't as prolific through much of the 2000's as he was in the 1980's and 1990's, I was optimistic about recent developments: he was reprinting his backlist as eBooks, and he was working on new projects. I was happy for him.

And now, he's gone. Taken so suddenly.

Dave Silva was a unique individual in a field where flash and noise have given way to substance and depth. His fiction was superior to anything being written and published by flash-in-the-pan writers who are big on promotion but short on talent. Long after their work is forgotten, I can rest assurred that Dave's accomplishments – his superior short fiction and handful of novels, his excellent anthologies, and, of course, the writing careers he cultivated and nurtured through his magazine *The Horror Show* – will live on.

And with that, I am reminded of the phrase he used to sign off on in his *Hellnotes* column in *The Horror Show* – Better weird than plastic. He started using it in the Spring 1986 issue, and continued the tradition until the final issue (Spring 1990). He never addressed what the phrase meant until the Summer 1989 issue, shortly after he'd made the decision to discontinue publishing and editing *The Horror Show* and devote more time to his own writing: "…it's an old sixties phrase we used to banter about, not all that cryptic. It means: it's better to be weird and to be yourself, than to be phony and be like everyone else."

So true, Dave. Words to live by.

Better weird than plastic."

- J. F. Gonzalez

"I didn't really know David Silva very well, but he made a huge impact in my life. I discovered his landmark magazine, *The Horror Show*, on the newsstand rack in the late 1980's. I grew up on *Famous Monsters*, *Starlog*, *Fangoria*, etc. and had found *Twilight Zone* magazine a couple years prior. So I knew professional Horror, SF and Fantasy magazines. But *the Horror Show* was different. It was published and edited by one man in his home. And yet he had Ray Bradbury, Dean Koontz, Peter Straub, Robert Bloch, Robert McCammon, William F. Nolan, Clive Barker, Joe Lansdale and many more stars in the field in there. And not only were their contributions routinely excellent, but so were the works of up-and-coming authors like Bentley Little, Brian Hodge, Poppy Z. Brite, Elizabeth Massie and others.

Plain and simple, the magazine you hold in your hand would not exist today. Sure, I was also very influenced by the aforementioned pro mags, as well as other small press publications like *Weirdbook*, *Whispers*, *Cemetery Dance*, *Deathrealm*, *Scream Factory*, *Iniquities*, etc., but *The Horror Show* was my first and embodied what I wanted to do with my own magazine. David Silva really set the bar high for quality. Not only that, but he showed me you could start a magazine on your own and grow it and make it successful. He talked openly in interviews about the ups and downs and ins and outs of small press publishing and that was invaluable to me.

I had attempted to contact Dave a couple of times many years back to thank him for his influence, but never really knew if he got my notes (the curse of cyberspace and the mail). However, last year I was fortunate to start to get to know him via email and was finally able to thank him for his impact on my life. Not only that, but he honored me by asking me to co-edit an anthology with him. We started asking people to contribute and were moving forward on it. Then this. So I'm going to continue on with it in honor of him. Thanks for the push Dave and maybe we'll finally be able to meet in person in the future."

– James R. Beach

* * *

"Oldsters like myself cherish the memory of Dave's 1980's magazine, *The Horror Show*. It was the coolest magazine of its day, and also a contender for the coolest mag of all time. *The Horror Show* ran fiction and nonfiction, and Dave's mantra in it was "Better Weird Than Plastic". Weird the magazine definitely was. No one in their right mind would have called it plastic.

The Horror Show often had theme issues. I remember one devoted to Dean Koontz. Another to Robert McCammon. One was for J.K. Potter. One of my favorites was the Skipp and Spector issue. God, those were fun, exciting times. Later superstars of the horror genre like Brian Hodge, Poppy Z. Brite, and Bentley Little had some of their early work in *The Horror Show*. Along with, of course, some of the best established writers of the time.

In the 90's, David B. Silva created *Hellnotes*, which at the time was a revolutionary weekly horror electronic newsletter. I believe that it was the first of its kind. I wasn't online for a long while, but I subscribed to the hardcopy version. I still have a lot of the issues up in my attic, boxed up. I need to break that stuff out one of these days.

Most important of all, David B. Silva was a writer. He wrote quite a few good novels, but his greatest strength in my opinion was in the short form. I remember when his story, "Dry Whiskey", ran in *Cemetery Dance* Magazine. I thought it was amazing, and I wrote a letter to Dave telling him so. In longhand, sent by snail mail. It seems like a lifetime ago.

I'm not going to stand here and make the claim that Dave Silva and I were good friends, but we corresponded quite a bit. It started with "Dry Whiskey", and went on for a long time. Dave was always friendly, helpful, and extremely informative about the genre. David B. Silva was a private kind of person. He kept out of the limelight, and you didn't see him getting into idiotic dust-ups on the internet. He was too smart and too good for that.

The genre would not be what it is today without the massive influence that Dave Silva had upon it. It would be immeasurably poorer."

– Mark Seiber

* * *

"Among Dave Silva's many talents, he demonstrated to me a couple of extraordinary gifts. First, he had great ear for fiction. While Horror Show published only one of my early short stories, whenever I sent Dave a story that wasn't for him, he invariably sent a kind rejection note suggesting an editor who might better resonate with it. He knew editors and their tastes, and I sold many short stories with a cover letter that started, "Dave Silva mentioned..."

I always enjoyed hearing from him—even if it meant a rejection with his jaunty little top-hatted skull signature. Another of Dave's many gifts was that he made me feel as though we were friends, although we never met. He was very personal, and I always thought that he liked me and my work and he cared about my career. He was never just another editor to me, and he made me feel as if I was not just another writer trying to sell a story.

Rest in peace, my friend, you left us too soon."

– Elizabeth Engstrom

* * *

"I tried to talk Dave Silva into going with me to the Killer Con convention in 2012. Since we both lived in Las Vegas, it seemed like a good idea. Unfortunately, Dave wasn't a convention goer. He told me if he could make it, he would meet me at the room where the tickets were sold that Saturday morning. After the convention, I found an email from him on my computer, apologizing for not being able to attend. That was Dave."

– Wayne C. Rogers

All the Lonely People
David B. Silva
Delirium Books
ISBN: 978-19296539-6-6
2003/2008; $45.00 Signed
HC, $15.00 TPB

This first paragraph is going to be embarrassing for me. You see, I've known of David B. Silva as a writer for twenty years; yet, I'm ashamed to say, I'd never read anything by him. Why? Hell if I know. I have dozens and dozens of books by other authors who I haven't read as of yet. I buy books I intend to read and then never get around to them because I have so many to catch up on. One day, before I kick the bucket, I hope to read everything I own.

What made me decide to finally read *All the Lonely People*? That's an easy question to answer. I tried starting a new novel last weekend by an author I'd never read before and couldn't get more than five pages into the book. I then picked up the limited edition of Silva's *All the Lonely People*, read the first two pages and found myself hooked. The prose wasn't in your face, but rather subtle and to the point. In other words, Silva was more interested in telling a damn good story, rather than sounding someone who writes literary fiction for a living. Another thing I loved about the book was its short chapters. I hate really long chapters because I read in short spurts and like to finish where a new chapter begins. You can't do that with a long chapter.

Well, when I completed *All the Lonely People*, I had a pleasant, satisfied feeling of having discovered a new author I'd been missing for two decades. I immediately started looking on the Internet for other novels by David Silva. Let me tell you, they're hard to find. I think people are hoarding them, and I can understand why. You're going to have to bonk me on the head with a frying pan to pry *All the Lonely People* out of my hands.

So, what about the book? How is it?

The story centers around Chase Hanford, who owns a bar called The Last Stop. An elderly man carrying a box under his arm enters the bar one night. None of the locals recognize him. It isn't long, however, before everyone wants to know what's in the box. Chase is the only one suspicious of the guy. For some reason he doesn't fully understand, Chase doesn't trust the old man or what's inside the box. In fact, Chase turns away when the box is finally opened and doesn't receive the full effects of what's inside of it. From that point on, everything begins to change in Chase's world and in the worlds of the locals who viewed the contents of the box.

The next day, Chase finds himself wearing sunglasses to avoid the bright light he encounters during the daytime. He can't seem to sleep or eat; yet, he zones out when least expected, then wakes up, and doesn't know where he's been. He's gradually losing all of his memories and has to constantly place Post-its around the bar and in the car to help him remember things. His wife and ill daughter don't have the slightest clue as to what's happening, and he doesn't know how to explain the transition to them. He can't even explain it to himself.

Tracking down the other people who were in the bar on that night, Chase discovers they're even crazier than he is. They think something is after them and don't know how to escape. Of course, it isn't long before he starts seeing strange, black shapes out the corner of his eye. That's when he realizes he has to track down the man with the box and find out how to reverse things.

Storytelling is what it's all about, and David B. Silva tells one dynamite story. I finished *All the Lonely People* in just four days, which is fast for me with my limited reading time. I found myself enjoying all the characters and felt like I knew them from somewhere in my past. I felt comfortable with them, especially Chase's family. At no time could I guess where the story was heading, which is the sign of a very talented writer. He keeps the reader on the edge of his seat, but doesn't allow the reader to outguess him. The prose was sharp, yet clean and simple so one didn't stumble over the words or have to re-read a sentence. Best of all, the ending was wrapped up in a way that left me fully satisfied and not scratching my head in confusion.

Most of Silva's fiction can found as an e-book, but finding the print format of his fiction is a lot harder. I'm a book person and like to read while sitting on the couch or having lunch at work. I like seeing the book up on my bookshelf. I have to tell you that a book looks much better than Kindle. Anyway, if you haven't read David B. Silva before, this is the time to start.

- Reviewed by Wayne C. Rogers

THE SLEEPING UTE

By Steve Rasnic Tem

"The old people tell stories that show that all things have life—trees, rocks, the wind, mountains. One believes that there is a cliff where the Mountain People stay and they open the cliff and talk to him."

—**an Indian Elder**

Abner couldn't remember much about that night, just that he and the old Ute had been drinking. They had to do their partaking up on the hill behind the saloon since Indians weren't allowed inside. Abner would go in and use that little bit of money left from the month's silver ore to buy a couple of jars, then climb back up the hill and they'd drink them together. It weren't exactly a polite thing to be drinking whiskey with an Indian, so he tried to be sneaky about it, paid the barkeep a little extry to take the jars out, told him he had a sick friend and he'd bring them right back. It were a lot of trouble but Abner didn't like drinking alone. And the Ute weren't a bad feller. He'd seen him around town for years doing odd jobs sweeping and mending. He didn't know how old he was—he never could tell with Indians—but his face *looked* old, like a cracked block of clay. Course he'd never talked to him much before now.

People here in town probably didn't care if he drank with an Indian anyhow. They hardly ever talked to him; in the saloon he always drank alone. He kept to himself up on his silver claim, scrabbling to make something. Some folk just didn't trust a man didn't socialize. So be it.

But that old Ute were a good listener. So good Abner didn't even know the feller's name. It weren't that the Ute didn't speak white—he had him some pretty tall tales to tell. It's just that one of them tales weren't his name. Abner didn't care. He told the Ute his own name right out. "Name is Abner," he'd said, and they shook hands.

Right around the sixth turn on the jars Abner were having a time getting back up that hill again. He done spilt about half the whiskey. He looked his mule over trying to decide if that were an option. Abner figured he could get up on that mule once, but not the couple of times up and down required. That's what told Abner he'd had enough. He figured from the way the Ute were huddled up in his blanket, holding his head sideways, like he were listening to the ground, that the Ute had had plenty too.

"Why you holding your head like that?" He didn't intend it mean but thought it prob'ly sounded mean.

The Ute didn't seem offended. "Indians like to listen to ground."

"I can see that. But what are you listening for?"

"Listening for that giant, Sleeping Ute. Big as a mountain! Oh, he's still sleeping now, after all them battles he had years ago. But someday he's going to wake up, and he's going to walk over here, and for you white fellers, that will be the end of your time."

"Why, what's he fixing to do? Eat us?"

"Eat you, pro'bly. But maybe he put you to work, first! Make you peel his taters!"

Abner thought for a second. "You know, I don't think I'd stand for that. Not at all."

"Wouldn't have a choice!" the old Ute shouted gleefully. "Better get them tater-peeling fingers ready!" Then he tilted his head sideways again, listening for the giant Indian's footsteps.

Abner walked over and swung his fist, knocked the Ute's head the other direction. The Ute fell asleep.

Abner sat down and finished off the jars. He fell asleep too.

He woke up with something wet mopping his face, looked up to see his mule looking down at him, stars in a cloud around the top of the mule's head. "Gracie, that you?" The mule licked him again.

Abner staggered to his feet. It was pitch dark and cold, the moon hanging low in the sky like a heavy ball of ice. Below him the town looked empty. He shivered, picked up somebody's dusty old blanket off the ground, wrapped hisself. He saw the Ute laying there, still sleeping. Abner never liked staying in town too long—somebody was always raring to cheat you out of yours. Time to go home.

He started to climb up on Gracie, then looked back down at the sleeping Ute. He thought about how nice it was to have somebody to talk to again, and how grand it would look to have that old Indian sitting out the front of his property, maybe smoking a pipe. Pretty classy.

It took him awhile—Abner had never been much use after drinking. But he finally got the Ute across the back of that mule. And the Ute never stirred a bit.

###

Abner woke up the next morning with a bunch of elk bugling in his head. He walked outside into the heat, figuring that would wake him up some. Gracie was tied to the fence a few feet away.

He noticed the dead Indian right away. Unless the old man was doing some kind of special Indian thing, which Abner doubted. He had his head on the ground, his neck twisted funny, the rest of him above, halfway up the fence.

Abner went over the events of the previous day. He remembered bringing the Ute home. He remembered getting off Gracie, tying her to the fence, and going inside, falling onto his bed. He didn't remember taking the Ute off the mule.

He remembered that big old ice moon and felt all cold inside. The Ute might have died after he hit him, or he might have fallen off Gracie and died here. Either way, Abner had done killed that old Indian.

Back in town they didn't care for Indians much, but they didn't just let you up and kill a tame one.

Abner went over and poked the Indian with a stick. He flopped over, his eyes wide open. Oh yeah, Abner'd done him good.

Abner didn't think he'd ever solved a problem his whole life, but he sat down and started to think about this one. He thought about putting the Indian down in the mine, but what if he finally hit a rich vein after all these years and needed some extra help? He couldn't chance some worker stumbling over the body.

But on the north edge of the property, right by that big mound of rocks, was a shaft that dropped straight down, left over from somebody's failed operation. Nobody was going exploring down that hole anymore, and even if they did, it'd look like the Indian went walking one night and didn't watch his feet none too good.

That afternoon Abner loaded the Ute onto Gracie one last time and took him up there by the hole. He tried to be respectful, but in the end he just said a couple of "God blesses" and dropped him into the hole. The Ute went straight down with nary a sound—that shaft was even wider than Abner remembered it. Abner leaned over listening for the thunk, but there weren't none.

The next morning Abner got up and found the Ute laying out there in front of his house again.

When Abner walked over to examine the body the Indian seemed some bigger. A lot bigger. Belly big around as a barrel and the whole body as long as a fallen tree. The face pretty much looked the same, but big as a boulder. Abner knew bodies sometimes swole up but he was pretty sure not like this un.

At least the big old head looked peaceful enough. It were almost smiling.

Abner didn't have time for the fine points. Now he had an even bigger problem to take care of. Not to mention that in the afternoon heat that big Ute was quite a ways on the smelly side. Abner tied a rope around the Ute's feet—it was about the only part of him he could get his arms around—and tied the other end to Gracie's harness. Gracie didn't like that none too much, but Abner wasn't going to give her a choice this time. It took a few hours, but Abner and Gracie finally got the whole load of Indian out to the abandoned shaft.

He got the Ute's legs in the hole. Then he found a piece of timber and a rock and tried nudging the head, but it kept flopping on the neck and crashing back down. Came close to smashing Abner's boots into the ground. Abner picked up the beam and whacked the big Ute in the forehead with it.

There was this loud explosion of air and the Ute sat up on the edge of the hole.

Abner stared, unable to budge. The Ute swung his huge head around and looked down, making a smile with all kinds of teeth the size of dinner plates. "Did you bring me another jar, white man?" It was said so big and yet so soft that it might have come from inside Abner's head.

Abner started to say he was going to leave, bring the Ute that jar full right away, when the Ute's legs shot down the hole dragging his belly, his arms, and even his big shoulders down into the darkness. Then the sliding suddenly stopped, the top of the Ute's head sticking out of the hole, completely filling it like a giant hairy cork. Abner could hear the Ute saying something down below, but it was all muffled by the sides of the shaft.

Against his better judgment, not to mention that he was so scared he was shaking, Abner stepped up on the Ute's head and began jumping up and down. But the Ute moved nary an inch.

Abner climbed down. Gracie was staring at him, all scornful like, like a mule would never let sech a thing happen to herself.

It wasn't easy getting Gracie up on the Ute's head, but once she figured out she could graze a bit on all the good stuff stuck in the Ute's hair she was more willing. The head still wouldn't budge. Thinking maybe a little more head whacking might help, Abner reached down to grab that piece of timber.

The earth started to shake. Abner turned around just in time to see Gracie jerk her head up from grazing and shoot Abner the awfullest look ever passed between beast and man. She bellowed once before dropping away somewhere toward the center of the world.

Sunset found Abner sitting in front of his cabin mourning the loss of his mule and his sole means of transportation into the warm embrace of civilization. He was still pretty damn shaky, too—all around him the ground appeared to quiver, the trees to sway, the horizon line to first tilt this way, then that.

He missed the damned Ute, too. He could do with a good tale right now.

At first it seemed like the top of the mountain had bent down to give him some words of comfort. Then that little ridge on the left started to move, and then that little hillock on the right. Abner tried to stand but the ground knocked him back down.

From his spot on the ground it seemed to Abner like the top of the mountain had torn itself off and was now standing over him, and looking—he'd have to say—none too happy.

Abner knew he was right about that when a clump of boulders at the end of a long stretch of red stone reached over and tore off both his legs.

"I won't be able to peel no taters!" he shouted, as the boulders came back around and pulled off his arms.

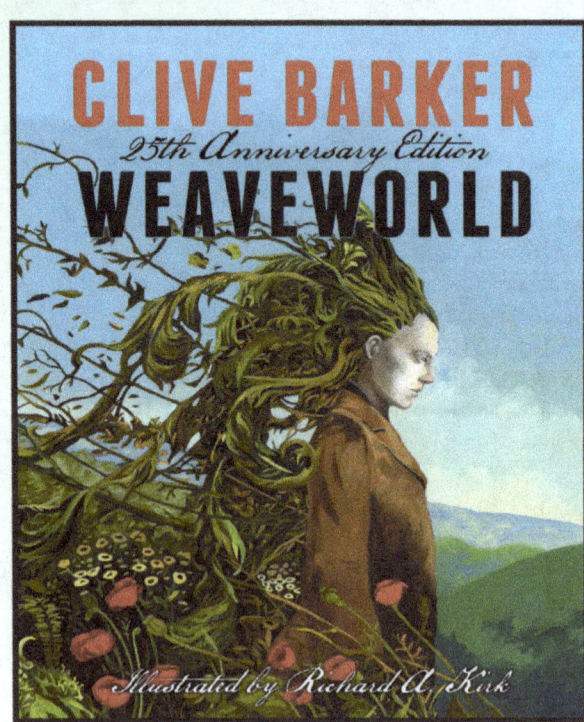
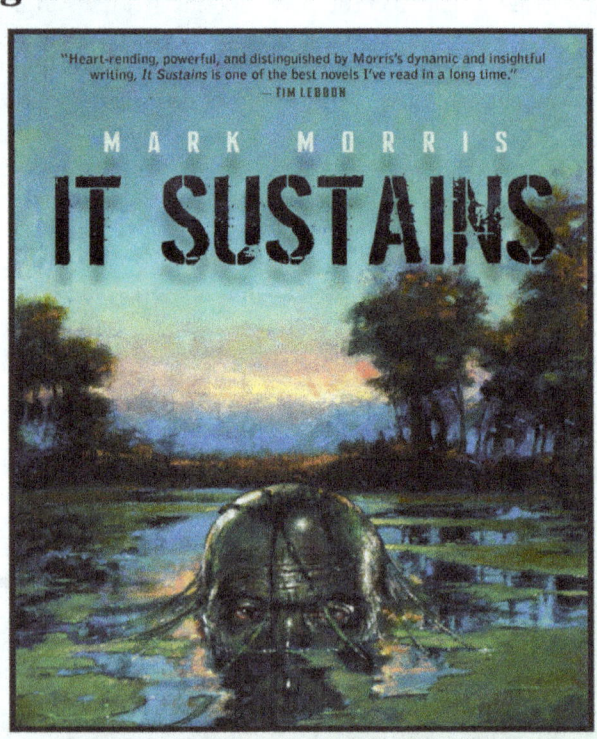

DOUBLE X CHROMOSONE:

by Yvonne Navarro

"WHY I HATE WOMEN IN HORROR"

Got your attention yet? Come on, don't jump to conclusions. I'm a woman, and I write horror. No I don't hate women, and obviously I don't hate horror. But I'm definitely a hater—

Of the stereotype.

Women in Horror. That was the name of the very first panel that I (a) was on, and (b) moderated. Yes, both at the same time, and I was terrified. I was barely published, a few short stories, and excruciatingly shy. But I digress.

That was a very long time ago, but that title—Women in Horror—has followed me around like some kind of stalker who seems harmless but in reality aggravates me enough to cause a frickin' ulcer. I've been on more panels with that title than I have fingers, and probably toes. Most have been upfront about it, but a good number have been poorly disguised with clever titles that reference different aspects of publishing or the art of writing itself. Having just searched Google for the phrase "Women in Horror" and gotten 9,110 results (I am not kidding), I suppose I need to accept that this stereotype is not going to go away. In fact, as the Internet grows ever larger, morphing insidiously toward a Skynet nemesis, it will probably only grow.

I am not a woman in horror. I am a writer, and that's what I've been for—wait for it—over thirty years. I never thought of myself as a woman writing horror, or a woman trying to write in a "man's universe." I also never thought of myself as trying to make equal pay for equal work in the writing field. If I had, I would probably be embracing this stereotype like Sally Field screamed "Union!" in Norma Rae, especially since I have been in the position where I made less money for doing the exact same unchallenging job as the male coworker at the next desk. I've never felt disadvantaged by being a woman in the writing field. An interesting aside to that is something my husband, author Weston Ochse, has noted: "There will never be an all-white-guy anthology." So when he sees an all-female anthology (among others with submission limitations), he notes that there's another anthology to which he won't be allow to submit. Not that he necessarily wants to, but it's ironic that in their attempt to be inclusive of one group, they've excluded another.

Am I going to talk about "women in horror" in this column? Sure. There are lots of great female authors to cover, actresses, etc., lots of interesting subjects to poke into. Do I know exactly what I'm going to write about? No way—it's going to be whatever strikes my fancy at the time (and I'm always open to suggestions). Life is spontaneous, and to be honest, this is probably going to be kind of stream of consciousness. My husband offered me advice about using the accepted format of articles… whatever. Not that I don't value his advice—I do. (A lot more than anyone reading this, or even Wes himself, realizes.)

It's just that he's too intellectual for my own good sometimes. That's not how I write nonfiction; that's not me. JournalStone has basically given me a license to ramble, and by golly, I am going to use it!

Years ago, maybe twenty, I was on one of those never-ending (that's how they feel to me) Women in Horror panels at a convention. One of the all-female panel members made the statement that she "had to write like a man" in order to be taken seriously. I was so ticked off by that statement that I snarled "Give me that microphone!" to the woman next to me (not the one who'd said those words) and snapped out "I don't write like a man. I don't write like a woman. I write like a writer." And that, dear readers, got me a standing round of applause from what until then had been a fairly bored audience.

Still, I have to remember that Women in Horror is akin to vampires, or zombies, or ghosts, or writing advice in general. Old stuff, right? Wornout, overused, neverending. But only to those of us who've been around for awhile. Think about it: I read my first vampire story—whatever it was—way back in the sixties. It might have been from the library (I was notorious for taking a wheeled shopping cart to the library and filling it up), or it might have been in the pages of an Eerie or Creepy magazine. Old to me? Obviously. Old to the kid who's just watched her first classic black and white Dracula movie starring Bela Lugosi? Not even—here the old becomes brand new, the stepping stone all the way up to Thirty Days of Night and beyond. It's the same with Women in Horror as a high school girl pens her first horror story, pokes around on the Internet to find out how to get it published, and sees all this info that suddenly makes her wonder if she's going to have to work twice as hard to do that, just because she's a female.

I'll take heat for it, but I'll stand by my solid answer of "No." If—when—she gets published, it won't be because she had to submit to twice as many markets, or because she knew someone, or because she had to write like a man.

It'll be because she wrote a great story. **Period.**

Comments? Questions? Suggestions? Yvonne Navarro can be reached via her website (www.yvonnenavarro.com) or Facebook page. (http://www.facebook.com/yvonne.navarro.001)

WHAT THE HELL EVER HAPPENED TO…?

By Robert Morrish

Welcome to the latest reincarnation of the column that refuses to die. Let's quickly recap how we got here…

I've always been fascinated by individuals, particularly authors and artists, who achieve a degree of notoriety in their field only to later vanish from view. I thus launched the column "What The Hell Ever Happened To…?" in issue #8 of *The Scream Factory* (way back in Winter 1991/92) in order to track down some of the horror genre's former luminaries who had since gone underground. A total of nine installments of the column appeared in the pages of *The Scream Factory* before that magazine ceased publication with issue #19 in 1997.

The column's concept continued to resonate with me, however, and in the latter stages of my tenure as Editor of *Cemetery Dance* magazine, I asked Rick Kleffel to resurrect the column under the slightly more PC title "Where Are They Now?" Rick authored two installments before I took the reins again myself for a final column in *Cemetery Dance* #63.

At that point, I wanted to fully revive the column and publish installments on a regular basis, but *Cemetery Dance's* already full slate of columnists meant that "Where Are They Now?" would only be able to appear on an irregular basis. I thus secured *CD*'s blessing to find a new home for the column, and my search quickly led me here to *Dark Discoveries*.

To complete the picture, here's a list of prior appearances of the column, and the individuals profiled.

As "Where Are They Now?" in Cemetery Dance magazine:

Cemetery Dance #63: Ken Eulo
Cemetery Dance #58: Daniel Rhodes (column by Rick Kleffel)
Cemetery Dance #53: William Schoell (column by Rick Kleffel)

As "What The Hell Ever Happened To…?" in The Scream Factory magazine:

The Scream Factory #17: Louise Cooper (guest column by Stan Nicholls)
The Scream Factory #16: Gerald Page
The Scream Factory #15: Galad Elflandsson & Leslie Whitten (two profiles)
The Scream Factory #13: Don Glut
The Scream Factory #12: Stuart David Schiff and Whispers Press
The Scream Factory #11: Gerald Kersh
The Scream Factory #10: Michael Avallone
The Scream Factory #09: Jack Cady
The Scream Factory #08: Jere Cunningham

If you'd care to explore any of these past installments, you can find them archived on my TwilightRidge.net website. Now, without further ado, let's move on to our new profile.

SEAN COSTELLO

The late 1980s and early 1990s were quite literally a dark time for horror fiction, with the prior boom era producing countless formulaic titles that led to the genre's popularity bottoming out, and many established authors being cut loose by their long-time publishers. Against this backdrop, Canadian author Sean Costello not only produced three novels – *Eden's Eyes*(1989), *The Cartoonist*(1990), and *Captain Quad*(1991) – that were refreshingly original in concept, but also achieved sufficient commercial success to be offered another three-book contract by his publisher, Pocket Books. In the following interview, Costello talks about why he declined the offer from Pocket, and why, after almost 20 years, he has recently returned to writing horror.

RM: From the research I've done, it would seem that the birth of your son, combined with a demanding "day job" as an anesthesiologist, led to the prolonged quiet period after your third novel, but could you describe it in your own words for us?

SC: By the time my son Steve was born in 1992, Pocket Books had already offered me a 'book-a-year for the next 3 years' contract; but given the fact that I was putting in a 60-80 hour work week in anesthesia, and had vowed to be as present a father as I could possibly be, I declined the offer from Pocket and decided to concentrate on being a dad. In retrospect, had the money from writing been sufficient to support a family, I believe I might have considered writing full time.

RM: When you returned to publishing 11 years later, your next two novels – *Finders Keepers* (2002) and *Sandman*(2003) – were thrillers. Was the change in subject matter more an acknowledgment of the marketplace, or a personal change in taste?

SC: The change in direction had more to do with feeling tapped out in terms of fresh ideas in the horror genre. In the interim I'd begun reading some of the great thriller writers, and when the itch to write again came along I thought it might be a fun canvas to scribble on. From the outset I've written for my own pleasure, and the thrillers were just what I felt like doing at the time.

RM: How did you connect with the publisher Red Tower for those two books?

SC: Red Tower was actually my own invention. I'd built up a fairly solid local following, and by that point in time had decided to cater only to them. I had the books printed by a POD outfit called Lightning Source, and the Chapters outlet in town was kind enough to market them for me. As a hobby writer it suited me quite well and I had a lot of fun with it. I sold about 2000 copies of each title and even made a few bucks.

RM: The plot of *Sandman* involves an anesthesiologist... would it be accurate to say that that book is in some way your most "personal" novel?

SC: The book that feels most personal to me is *Here After*. *Sandman* was just an obvious place for an anesthesiologist with a slightly bent mind to go. I used to call it "the definitive autobiography."

RM: After those two books, you returned to horror with Here After. Why the switch back?

SC: Since I've got more fingers than good ideas, I believe in taking what the muse has to offer.

RM: I believe that *Here After* had a 2nd printing... is it safe to say that the book has done fairly well commercially?

SC: *Here After* was another book that felt more at home locally, and I was fortunate enough to have this one printed and distributed by Your Scrivener Press, which is owned and operated by Laurence Steven, a university professor here in Sudbury. I thought he did a marvelous job of it and it's still the book I'm most proud of, both for the storyline and for how great it looks on the shelf.

RM: How did the decision come about by Your Scrivener Press to reprint *Captain Quad* after 20 years?

SC: I had reprinted the other two Pocket Book titles myself under the Red Tower logo, but had never gotten around to doing so with *Captain Quad*. Scrivener thought it might be a good idea to complete the sequence with one of his gorgeous trade paperbacks. I'm glad he did.

RM: In your acknowledgments for *The Cartoonist*, you mention Richard Curtis... I assume he was your agent? How did you initially connect with him? Did you just send him a manuscript "over the transom," or did you have a referral or connection?

SC: Richard Curtis was my agent on those first three novels and I was fortunate enough to have been referred by another of his clients.

RM: Do you have any unpublished "trunk" novels that might see the light of day?

SC: Not so far.

RM: As far as I know, you haven't published any short fiction... is that more of an economic decision or do you just lean more towards longer works?

SC: When I started out in the mid-eighties I wrote a bunch of short horror fiction and had two or three titles published in small press magazines. I guess I lost the taste for it once I realized I could muddle through an entire novel.

RM: I've seen your current status described as semi-retired... for an anesthesiologist, what exactly does that mean?

SC: I've stopped [being on-call] and have been able to limit the degree of complexity of the cases I do, making the work-week much shorter and much less stressful.

RM: Now that you have a little more time on your hands, how ambitious are your plans for writing? To put it another way, what are you working on?

SC: I've been fiddling with a new novel, a dark-comic thriller called *Squall*, and am currently negotiating an option agreement for the making of *Here After* into a feature film.

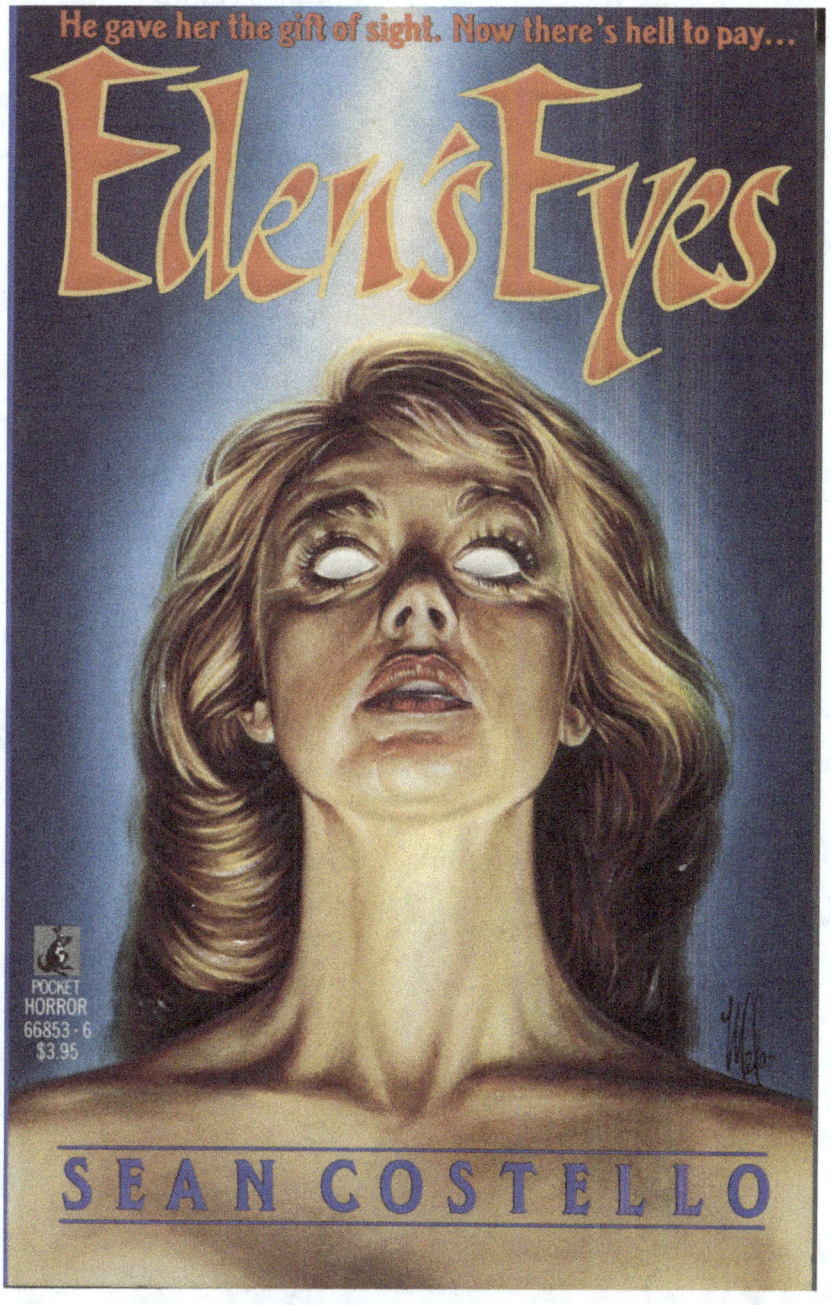

By Michael R. Collings

Multiverse: "The hypothetical set of multiple possible universes (including the historical universe we consistently experience) that together comprise everything that exists and can exist: the entirety of space, time, matter, and energy as well as the physical laws and constants that describe them."

I've been thinking a bit about the *multiverse* recently, as a thought-experiment, as a cosmological possibility, as a theological construct. The idea of an infinite number of universes—and concomitantly an infinite number of earths, each differing from the next to an infinitesimal degree—is one of those mind-bending concepts that makes science fascinating, seductive...and ultimately unfathomable.

Carried far enough, the idea of a *multiverse* suggests that all things are eventually related, connected in ways that—on the surface, at least—make sense but that become increasingly convoluted the deeper we think about them. There is even a philosophical mode that opens the multiverse up to fictional characters and events, making them essentially more 'real' than our imaginations can make them—perhaps a justification for all of those shelves of academic studies devoted to understanding Hamlet's psychological problems. In *this* universe, at least, Hamlet is nothing more or less than a series of marks on a page, and as such actually has no psyche into which to delve. But elsewhere/elsewhen?

New thought: a short while ago, I attended the 31st annual "Life, The Universe, and Everything" SF/F Symposium in Provo, Utah (my 28th year, which makes me one of the old-timers in multiple senses). Most of the panels I participated in dealt with horror: horror and religion, modern horror, horror in poetry. And some of the most frequent questions concerned boundaries.

"What is the difference between 'adult' horror and YA horror?"

"How does Modern Horror differ from Classical Horror in the manner of Poe and Lovecraft?" (As if those two could readily fit into the same little pedagogical box).

And that led to even broader questions of definition: "How do you know when a work is science-fiction, fantasy, or horror?"

There were (and are) any number of answers to that last question, but almost all of them ultimately beg the question. Science fiction, some say, is about the ramifications of technology on human existence; what, then, about the many SF stories that avoid the question of technology altogether and simply put characters onto rocket ships or alien planets without any consideration of *how* they got there. According to Tzvetan Todorov's famous conjecture, Fantasy concerns the intrusion of what *seems to be* the supernatural into the natural. If, upon closer inspection, the intrusion actually follows natural laws, it is deemed *uncanny*; if it does in fact break natural laws, it is *marvelous,* and the *fantastic* in fact only exists so long as readers do not yet know which is the case. Horror seems the simplest of the three: it consists of fictions designed to elicit a shiver along the spine, a frisson, a physiological clenching of the gut as the reader encounters something monstrous, terrifying, horrific.

Yet what about non-horror tales that include monsters—perhaps the ubiquitous dragons of pseudo-medieval fantasies or the unspeakably gruesome aliens that haunt much SF? Where is the dividing line among genres? I mentioned Hamlet earlier, the star of the greatest tragedy in the English language...and also of a ghost story at a time when people seriously believed in ghosts. Does that make the play horror? or fantasy? or realism? And what about *Beowulf,* which has a definite *monster* but was in some senses more history than fiction, at least for its original audience?

The answer to the question of boundaries is perhaps easier than at first appears: the lines exist in the minds of booksellers who are determined to put every book on the appropriate shelf, even when that shelf might not actually be that appropriate. A personal example: one of my novels—an excursion into ghosts and revenants of varying sorts—was just reprinted by a British publisher. In the process, the publisher gave the book a remarkably evocative cover, changed the title from simply *Shadow Valley* to *In Shadow Valley*...and marketed it as part of their Mystery Library. Granted there is a mystery in the book, but the core is horror. Who is right? the author? or the publisher?

All of this leads to a point that actually brings

the disparate parts of this essay together.

What if?

What if such things as multiverses—metauniverses, to use another term—exist. Wouldn't that mean that, in some esoteric sense, the whole idea of genre in literature is little more than an intellectual game, that stories *exist* and that we, through an unchallengeable need for categorization, impose labels on them: Science Fiction, Science Fantasy, High Fantasy, Epic Fantasy, Sword & Sorcery, Weird Fiction, Dark Fantasy, Urban Horror, Supernatural Horror, Ecological Horror, Eschatological Horror, and many other variations on the same themes.

It makes more 'sense,' if you will, to suggest that there is a multiverse of speculative fiction (and of all fiction), each tale differing infinitesimally from the next until at some point, the tales seem to *shift* into another genre, when in fact they actually might not.

Case in point: I've read a number of "shared-world anthologies" recently, including several that were on the preliminary ballot for the annual Bram Stoker Award® from the Horror Writers Association. Most of them had one thing in common—the worlds of the fictions were essentially the same one. Usually something like *our* world, with one major change. Perhaps it was the presence of a black hole over central Europe that devastates civilization. Or a Zombie apocalypse of one sort or another. In most cases, "shared-world" meant multiple fictive versions of the same place.

But *what if* there were a "shared-multiverse"?

In 2011 and 2012, Paul Genesse edited several volumes of *The Crimson Pact.* Each story in each volume took as its starting point a single event in a single 'reality'—a cataclysmic battle against demons that resulted in the defeat of the demons…and their expulsion from that reality into the multiverse at large. Which in turn meant a theoretical infinity of stories about demonic incursions that shared elements of the supernatural, the science-fictional, and the horrific, depending upon the milieu of the world involved. In practice, stories ranged from mythological to space opera to SteamPunk and everything in between, but at the core of each was that historical battle in one reality and its ramifications in other realities. (For my review, see: http://michaelrcollings.blogspot.com/2012_10_01_archive.html).

That is the way I also choose to think about *Limbus, Inc.,* an anthology edited by Anne C. Petty that I recently reviewed (http://michaelrcollings.blogspot.com/2013/02/limbus-inc-worlds-within-worlds.html). A collection of tales by five highly talented authors—Benjamin Kane Ethridge, Jonathan Maberry, Joseph Nassise, Brett J. Talley, and Anne C. Petty—the anthology pivots around the existence of a corporation, Limbus, Inc., that initially seems to be an employment agency on *this* world. Then things shift. And abruptly we find that there are no boundaries as to where the stories might lead. The universe depicted allows for science-fiction through the involvement of aliens and such technological innovations as transport through time and space; for the fantastic in which elements *seem* to be supernatural until readers discover that the definition of *natural* has been infinitely expanded and includes, well, just about anything; and for horror that ranges from the cosmological vastness of Lovecraft's Great Old Ones to the ancient tales of bloodthirsty gods and their hideous appeasement ceremonies…or would that last one be more Religion? Or Folk Tale? Or anthropological study?

In one sense, it doesn't make any difference what one chooses to call it. Like *The Crimson Pact, Limbus, Inc.,* simply posits a *multiverse,* with a sole constant—in this case the company itself. It presents a virtual view into five realities—six if one counts the linking story—each one of which has its own physical laws and constants, as supernatural-seeming and as fluid as they may seem at first glance.

Now, back to the first point: *multiverse*—"The hypothetical set of multiple possible universes (including the historical universe we consistently experience) that together comprise everything that exists and can exist: the entirety of space, time, matter, and energy as well as the physical laws and constants that describe them." In fiction, this hypothetical set *can* in fact exist. It can become the basis for stories and series of stories that explore beyond what it known, often beyond what is *knowable* and at the same time asserts that *all story* is essentially about us, about the readers, thoroughly enmeshed in *our* reality (or would that more accurately be *realities*) even as we share the experiences of intangible constructs that take us, willingly or no, into the *multiverse*…and beyond.

Level 2 Multiverse courtesy of Silver Spoon

YA Horror

By Amy Shane

Isn't it amazing how the young adult industry has swept into our society? This genre is captivating hearts both young and old, pulling us into its spellbinding allure. Tempting us with magic and mystery and capturing a time of new awakening and innocence. From *Harry Potter* to *Hunger Games* and of course the *Twilight* series to the newest movie in theaters, *Beautiful Creatures*. Characters overcoming and conquering predicaments with perseverance, magic, or with the fortitude of amazing heroism found in teenagers. Young adult books are written in a style meant to instantaneously transform you into a world of intrigue, fantasy, horror or love. Tapping into a fresh perspective using some of the same fears we have as adults presented in a simpler manner.

Because as adults we get caught up in our daily lives and long for the nostalgia of simple times. We often search for a way to feel the familiarity of slipping into a simple horror, the paranormal, or just falling into the dark recesses of the mind. Searching for ideas that are so pure and untainted, where violence, lust and sex are downplayed, so that the storyline takes center stage. That's when I grabbed onto my childhood roots and picked up a young adult book. Longing for that feeling I had when I was first introduced to reading. With the cracking open of that very first story book, I lay awake caught up in wonderment, hanging on every last word, not wanting the magic to end. As soon as I was old enough, I searched for a way to feed my imagination and discover that magic. Hoping to feel that same enchantment, I sat and watched the movie, *Something Wicked This Way Comes*. As my pupils constricted and dilated and my body pumped with adrenaline, I was hooked with that wicked horror. I was delighted by the storyline and became transformed as the carousel spun into wicked darkness, starting a carousel ride in my mind, bestowing me with a love for fantasy and horror. That's when I knew where my passion would take root and thus I came upon my first horror book. With a flashlight on and the covers pulled over my head, I had the confidence to face that scary book. Characters suddenly came to life and scenes unfolded before me like a popup book, proving that fascinating stories can mean it is possible to live a magical life and give wings to the imagination.

Through young adult books, we can discover eloquently and artfully written words filling the pages and capturing the core of our innocence. Books that can tap into our fears and take root in our passion. They can pull us under their spell leaving us completely hooked, with the residue of their magic permanently etched in our hearts.

Young adult authors have a challenging task ahead of them, one that differs from that of adult writers. By taking the responsibility of sowing the seeds of our youth they are left with the responsibility of teaching and inspiring with their imagination. The more I read, the more my respect profoundly grows for the imagination and magnitude that these authors will utilize to dive into the depths of fantasy. As Neil Gaiman said, "Fairy tales are more than true: not because they tell us that dragons exist, but because they tell us that dragons can be beaten."

If you have never thought of taking on a young adult novel, purely because of its subject matter, target audience or genre, I challenge you to take a leap of faith, trusting that these authors will guide you on a fantastic journey. You might even be surprised by their depth.

In this special issue of *Dark Discoveries*, dark fantasy takes the driver's seat. The topic of dark fantasy thrills me; it is the definition that sets those of magical sweet fantasy into something that may be dark, horrific, morbid, or even peculiar. Taking characters from the darker side of the writer's mind and bringing them to the forefront, even if only for a mere moment, allowing these characters a chance to be heroes instead of villains. Many young adult titles come to mind when I think of dark fantasy but there are two that remain at the top of my list: *Splintered*, an *Alice in Wonderland* fantasy filled with the darkest and most morbid creatures of Wonderland, along with *Miss Peregrines Home for Peculiar Children*, an echo of fact and fantasy relating the horrors of monsters to the horrors of mankind.

So if you're ready to dive into a tempting read you're not alone. To the outside world it looks like adults reading YA might be the next big thing; Bowker published a report in September of 2012 that stated that 55% of young adult books are purchased by those 18 and older with the largest group being ages 30-44. So, take a collective sigh, take that leap, put down the remote, and sit down with a good YA book. You might just be pleasantly surprised. To help guide you on a dark fantasy journey here are a few great titles that I recommend: *Incarnate* by Jodi Meadows, *Falling Kingdoms* by Morgan Rhodes, *Shadow and Bone* by Leigh Bardugo, *Carnival of Souls* by Melissa Marr, and if you happen to be a fan of *Game of Thrones*, try *Throne of Glass* by Sarah Maas. I hope you have a magical journey.

Miss Peregrine's Home for Peculiar Children
By Ransom Riggs Quirk
Hardcover, $17.99, 348 pages,

Miss Peregrine's Home for Peculiar Children is dark, intense and wonderfully strange, delightfully filled with the creepiest and most intriguing vintage photographs, all marvelously crafted into a peculiar tale of dark fantasy and intrigue.

As a young boy, Jacob lived for the nights that he would sit curled up at the edge of his bed listening to his grandfather's spellbinding tales. With stories from an enchanted orphanage designed to take in the oddest, strangest and most exceptional children and keep them safe from the monsters of the world.

Stories filled the air of a girl who could fly, a boy filled with live bees, an invisible boy and even a girl who could create fire in the palm of her hand. His grandfather would tell him that these stories were as true as the Holocaust but as Jacob grew older, the doubts began to settle in his mind. Even with the cigar box of photographs used as proof, they were not enough to make him believe.

Then something extraordinary happened; extraordinary and terrible all at the same time and that's where Jacobs's life truly began. Starting an adventure of a lifetime, haunted with the stories and his grandfather's last words, he heads to a small island on the other side of the world. With his aim to find the truth behind Miss Peregrine and the home that sheltered his grandfather along with the peculiar children.

This amazing book weaves you through the echoes of before and after, dappling in time travel and temporal loops, constantly thrusting you from the same day in the past to the present day, over and over. Taking readers on an adventure of a lifetime, giving you time to discover each peculiar child and the mysteries of their secrets. As this book delicately weaves in the tragedies and fears of the Jews in the time of World War II you are chased by monsters reminiscent of the Nazis, monsters they call hollowgasts. Horrors in their own right, with pungent rotten flesh and gnashing jaws, filled with grappling tongues, ready to devour their innocence. This is not only just a story with echoes of monsters seen as beasts, but that of monsters made of humans. Leading you to believe that this story is not only about a safe house for wayward orphans with magical powers but one that was created to be a vault for the horrors of a war era.

Ransom Riggs is a mad genius. From taking the time to transform photographs from a lost era and fabricate them into such a mysterious tale, to the way he delicately weaves history and heartfelt sensitivity all with in your face intensity. A book written with a boy's perspective and made to identify with a boys mind. Filled with delightful lines and funny quips; taking a refreshing spin on magic, dark fantasy, time travel and history. Highlighting the worst of humanity and making a way for a person to emerge from those ashes as brave, honorable and even magical.

Splintered
By A.G. Howard
Abrams-Amulet Books
Hardcover, $17.95, 384 pages

Splintered is an enchanting read, capturing the grotesque madness of Wonderland's creatures.

When I received this book I immediately and willingly dove head first into the rabbit hole, relishing with open eyes all that Wonderland would behold for me; and to tell you the truth, there wasn't a moment that I was disappointed. Never has anyone captured so beautifully the tale that Lewis Carroll spun like a web into an innocent child's heart like A. G. Howard.

I have been captivated by Alice in Wonderland for as long as I can remember and never has there been a tale to feed both the adult and young adult heart. *Splintered* is a breath of life for fans of all ages. This story transcends time and generations and splendidly fills in the gaps of time.

What if Alice was still tied to Wonderland once she returned awakened from her curious dream? Did she pass the magic on from generation to generation? What would it be like to be Alice's great- great- great granddaughter? Would the pull from Wonderland still be able to stir in your heart? If you listened to that whisper, would it cause you to remain sane, or thrust you into the walls of a padded room gently nestled inside a mental hospital? This haunting tale answers these questions, spinning the reality of what you thought Wonderland was like and fills your head with a new and darker Wonderland. I hope you take a leap of faith into the rabbit hole, trusting that A. G. Howard will guide you on a magical journey. You might just find yourself in love with Alyssa from the first page as I did. From the moment the bugs buzz their first word and flowers chastise Alyssa, I was hooked.

There is not one character left out, as the author gives each one its own right and moment in the spotlight. Sometimes Alice's tale got the story right and sometimes she got their descriptions morbidly wrong. Only to find your mind racing back to the classic tale, searching the recesses of your brain for every detail, drawing up their description and anxiously reading for the new description.

Alyssa's beautiful, dark and magical love story grapples with you, as her conflicted feelings are divided between Jeb, who is flawed and often emotional and Morpheus, her Netherling guide who is darklymysterious and often seductive, winding you into an unavoidable paradoxof love and hate. With adventure and love this story captured my heart. The mind of A. G. Howard is a fantastic thing. Even though this story took years to be penned, it was worth every moment. A. G., I hope your mind is still spinning new tales and that we have only seen the outskirts of the magnificent web that you can weave. I delighted in the magical release of this tale and wait on the wings of a moth for another tale so sweetly wicked.

Seated on a Bony Throne: The Work of Brian McNaughton

By Aaron J. French

In 1997 a collection of fantasy/horror stories entitled *The Throne of Bones* was published by Kenneth E. Abner's Terminal Fright Press with an extremely moody cover art piece done by Jamie Oberschlake. Less than a year later the book had won the World Fantasy Award for Best Collection and was nominated for the Bram Stoker Award for Best Fiction Collection. The (at that time) little-known author, Brian McNaughton, was suddenly thrust into the genre spotlight, introducing a whole new generation of authors and fans to McNaughton's seminal work.

Brian McNaughton was born in Red Bank, New Jersey, where he attended Harvard and worked as a reporter for the Newark Evening News for ten years, before pursuing his writing career in the 1970s, penning several erotic Lovecraftian thrillers such as the *Satan's Love Child* series (1977-1981), and the highly obscure *The Poacher* (1978).

But the gradual decline of horror fiction after the explosion of authors Stephen King and others in the late 1970s took a toll on McNaughton, and his subsequent frustration almost caused him to give up his writing career. Thus his bibliography remains eerily vacant for the mid-period of the 1980s. Finally in the late '80s/early '90s he returned to his typewriter and started penning the creative fiction that would eventually become *The Throne of Bones*.

This is the reason why only old timers and genre mainstays knew who he was when *The Throne of Bones* won the World Fantasy Award in 1998. I'll confess to abiding in ignorance as well, though I'm a generation yet removed from these events. I almost magically stumbled upon a first edition of the Terminal Fright incarnation at a local used book store and snatched it off the shelf based on its cover art alone. I flipped through the pages, generally liking what I read, and purchased the copy for an agreeable five dollars.

I'm very happy that I did.

Many of the stories in *The Throne of Bones* could easily fit together into a kind of horrid mosaic, however they are not technically related, having been published separately in venues like *TEKELILI!*, *Lore*, and *Weirdbook*. At once dark, fantastic, and highly sexed, the consistent mood of the writing immediately draws you in, making it easy to get lost in McNaughton's worlds for a long time. With these stories, he successfully married elements of horror, erotica, and fantasy in new ways that had never before been seen.

The first story in the collection, "Ringard and Dendra," will appeal to the most people, as the elements of Lovecraftian horror and fantasy work together to create a wonderful tale. But the next six, which are a connected set and make up the *Throne of Bones* sequence, will prove weird and jarring even to the most mature dark fantasy readers.

Imagine if you could find out what all the orcs in *The Lord of the Rings Trilogy* got up to in Mordor's red-light district and you have an idea of what the *Throne of Bones* sequence is like. These stories wind down an increasingly dark road of the Necromantic, and truly push the reader into unknown limits of sanity, morality, and desperation—all done within a fixed fantasy setting, assuring that any semblance of recognizable reality will be withheld. You've really read nothing quite like it.

Once this harrowing trip is over, the remaining eight stories continue the theme of fantasy and horror, throwing in some grotesque humor as well, and combing elements of H.P. Lovecraft, Robert E. Howard, Clark Ashton Smith, and J.R. R. Tolkien. These stories make up some of the best weird fiction and dark fantasy ever written, causing S. T. Joshi, renowned literary scholar of this material, to exclaim in his afterword for *The Throne of Bones*: "…Brian McNaughton seems to have mastered one of the most difficult of literary arts: to draw upon the classics of the field without losing his own voice" (338).

Unfortunately McNaughton left us in 2004, producing only two additional short story collections: *Nasty Stories* (2000) and *Even More Nasty Stories* (also 2000). Neither collection managed to achieve the same notoriety as *The Throne of Bones*, yet in addition to his multiple novels McNaughton successfully published over 200 stories throughout his career, so there is plenty of material out there for those who are interested.

My advice to you?

Start with *The Throne of Bones*.

Become entranced.

Then dig a little deeper.

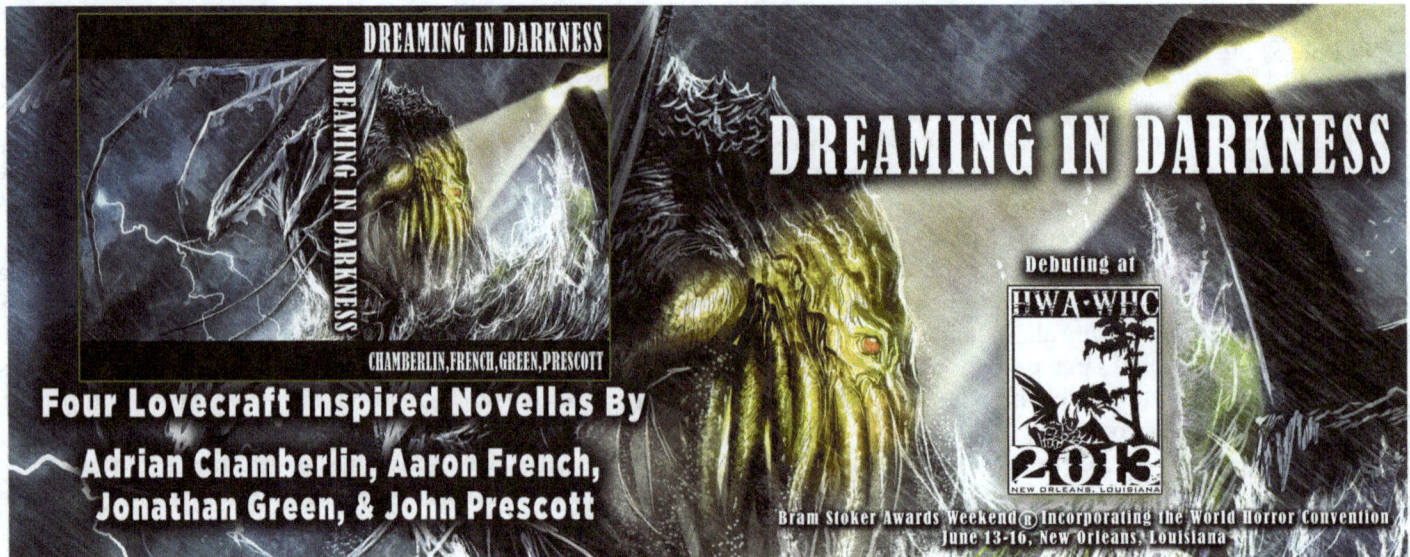

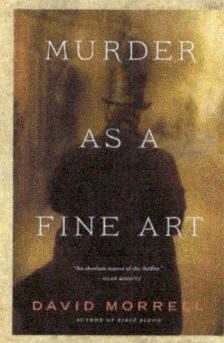

Murder as a Fine Art
By David Morrell
Mulholland Books
ISBN: 978-03162167-9-1
May 2013; $25.99

Remarkable. Compelling. Intriguing. These and other words appear (perhaps too frequently) in review after review. I try to avoid them as much as possible since they suggest an unusually high level of achievement and should be reserved for such. But in the case of David Morrell's Victorian masterwork, *Murder as a Fine Art*, they are entirely appropriate.

The novel is a foray into history-as-fiction, with a foundation in carefully researched, highly informative (and relevant) historical data and a superstructure of meticulously crafted fiction. It brings together two sets of individualized characters that would, in the year 1854, normally have had little to do with each other.

The first is an official duo: a detective in the London Metropolitan Police, trained in the latest techniques of observation and focus; and a constable assigned to him, whose heartfelt wish is to prove himself worthy of eventually becoming a detective himself. The two of them undertake an investigation of a particularly grisly, brutal series of murders that—point by point, almost beyond the limits of belief—mimic one of the first mass murders in modern England, the Ratcliffe Highway murders of 1811. Forty-three years later, it seems, the killer has returned to add to his list of victims.

Detective Ryan and Constable Becker arrive at the scene where a crowd—soon to be a mob—has already gathered in the full heat of panic. Step by step the two officers work their way through the crime scene—itself something of a new concept at the time—simultaneously revealing crucial elements relating to the murder and illuminating Victorian sensibilities toward crime, criminals, the police, and life in general. The scene ends, almost comically, with Constable Becker manfully struggling to maintain the integrity of several footprints that certainly belong to the killer. Unfortunately, two pigs, one on each side, take it into their minds to attack him. What follows is, again, almost comic: *almost,* because the slime containing the footprints is polluted with human waste—common at the time—and should Becker be injured, he would run the serious risk of infection at the least, cholera at the worst. In Victorian England, nothing is as simple as it seems.

Eventually, Ryan and Becker realize that the murders follow precisely not only the 1811 tragedy but also the explication of it in a recent essay, "On Murder Considered as One of the Fine Arts," by the notorious writer and opium-addict, Thomas de Quincey. While still trying to find out how to bring de Quincy to London from Scotland, Ryan discovers that the writer and his daughter, Emily, are already in London—and thus the second set of characters. Ryan initially decides that de Quincey must have more to do with the crimes than merely writing about them and is in fact deputed by the Home Secretary to place de Quincey under arrest.

Instead, Ryan, Becker, de Quincey, and the indefatigably independent and open-minded Emily join forces to uncover the identity of the killer, to determine why the recent spate of deaths so closely follows that of 1811, why the killer has secretly decoyed the de Quinceys to London, and why he persists in mercilessly and bloodily baiting both the police and the de Quinceys with their inability to capture him.

By concentrating on these four characters, Morrell deftly juxtaposes two modes of thinking and understanding. The detective and the constable see themselves as objective; they base their actions on perceived evidence and reason. They think things through according to their understanding of the world in which they live, the society that surrounds, and the backgrounds they bring to the task. De Quincey, on the other hand, is uniquely—and, for those around him—disquietingly subjective.

Part of the time, when he is under the influence of his 'medicine,' copious doses of the opium-based *laudanum*, de Quincey functions in something like a fugue state, acting on visions and conclusions that seem not to have any basis in 'reality.'

The disjuncture between the two modes of knowing forms one of the continuing themes of *Murder as a Fine Art*. Stolid Victorians to the core, the police officers rely on what they consciously know. Visionary and philosophical, de Quincey often acts on "thoughts and emotions we don't know we have," on a dissociation of the mind into two parts that prefigures Freudian concepts by over seventy years; in a word, on the *subconscious.*

The conflicts between conscious and unconscious, between social mores and expectations and human impulses and urges, between drug-induced possibilities and accepted actualities provide much of the impetus for the novel. The crimes are simultaneously conscious acts and unconscious acting-out. The characters—both heroes and villains—persistently confront the disparity between Victorian ideals of action and expression and the realities of 1854 London.

And over-riding all is the presence of the ultimate villain (no spoiler here): Opium itself. The drug that makes life bearable for some, agonizing for others. The source of the wealth that supports the London upper-class, with all of its predilections and assumptions; the source of the poverty that drives the lower classes to crime and death.

Before I begin to sound as if *Murder as a Fine Art* is some kind of historical tract, let me be clear. Morrell incorporates vast quantities of history into his story, but it nonetheless remains a *story.* As such, I found it immensely readable and simultaneously enlightening.

Highly recommended.

- Reviewed by Michael R. Collings

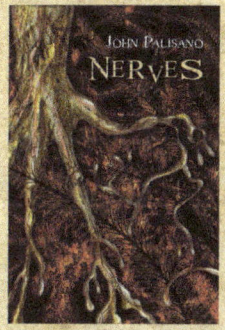

Nerves
By John Palisano
Bad Moon Books
ISBN: 978-09851940-0-0
2012; $18.95 TPB

The debut novel by John Palisano, *Nerves,* is a story of witchcraft, magic, faith, and oddity. It's also a story of brothers and of family. The plot centers around Josiah and Horace, two brothers, each of whom have been granted special gifts: the former the ability to extend his nerves through his fingertips (and do all sorts of cool stuff with them, like restoring life to the dead), while conversely the latter seems to suck the life out of anyone he's in contact with, until eventually that person dies. The two are being pursued by a witch named Ogam, one of the most interesting villains I've encountered in a while, who is wanting to collect on a debt that's owed.' Meanwhile, the brothers are trying to escape and make it back to their sick mother, a white witch in her own right, who lies in a bed back at home. This all culminates in a fantastic climax that's really the highlight of the book.

Nerves has its ups and downs moments, but for the most part it's very fast-paced, and allows for quick reading that is also deep in content. Palisano draws from a variety of different sources to create his interesting milieu: spirituality, myth, magic, and even rock and roll. His characters are well-drawn without being too self-absorbed as to hinder the flight of the plot. The result, for me at least, is around Clive Barker meets "The Stand," with plenty more attention given to the underlying current of spiritual and philosophical ideas—however this never overshadows the entertainment value of the book. And let's get this straight, *Nerves* is action-packed! The first scene alone is enough to get any action junkie on board.

Overall a great book, with only a few small criticisms not even worth mentioning. *Nerves* is readymade to enjoy, and anyone who gives it a chance will not be disappointed. Recommended!

- Reviewed by Aaron J. French

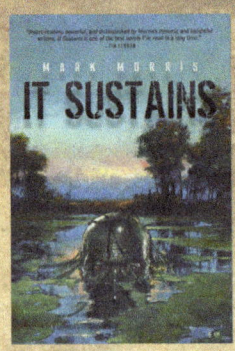

It Sustains
By Mark Morris
Earthling Publications
ISBN: 978-0-9838071-3-1
May, 2013; $35.00 Signed HC

Mark Morris is a British Horror writer who started out back in the 1980s. His first novel, *Toady*, garnered favorable reviews and he's steadily continued on since then. His latest is a short horror novel/novella from Earthling Publications titled *It Sustains*.

The story is about a teenager named Adam who has a traumatic event happen in his life when his mother is killed. He and his father move away to another town to try and move on and restart their lives, but something doesn't want Adam to do that. His new friends are quickly starting to reveal that their motives may not be what they seem, and they may have some connection with what happened to his mom. You can't escape your past, they say. And as the story moves forward that becomes very apparent.

It Sustains is a fitting title as Morris carefully builds suspense and tension as the book moves toward the climax. A subtle, disturbing story that has its roots firmly in the realm of works by authors like Ramsey Campbell and Glen Hirshberg. Morris ranks up there with some of the better writers working in the horror field today and It Sustains is another notch in his belt. Features an introduction by Sarah Pinborough and artwork by Edward Miller. Highly recommended!

- Reviewed by Trever Nordgren

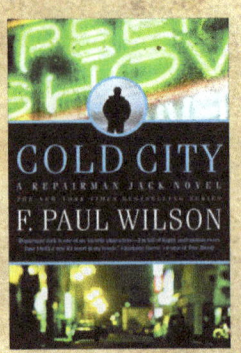

Cold City
By F. Paul Wilson
Tor Books
ISBN: 978-0-7653-3014-7
November, 2012; $25.99

F. Paul Wilson's *Cold City* is the first Repairman Jack novel I've read, and it makes me want to read the rest of them. The series follows Just Jack, a self-styled "repairman"—but he doesn't fix electronics. He fixes situations. Your boss is using your illegal cousins to blackmail you? Call Jack. All of the Christmas toys from the toy drive for Children with AIDS go missing? Call Jack. *Cold City* is one of a trilogy of prequels dealing with how Jack became Repairman Jack.

Jack pulled me into his story from the first line. It drew me along as he loses his job, acquires a gun, and stumbles onto a slightly illegal (but better paying) job. During this we meet Abe, your usual Jewish New Yorker, Julio, a Puerto Rican bartender, and Cristin, the obligatory sexual relief character. I'd be more pissed off about her except she does serve a purpose other than banging Jack. Through her we find out more about Jack's parents, the death of his mother, and part of why he decided to fall off the grid. But Jack's plot arc is just half of the story—we also flip between him, a young Palestinian jihadist named Kadir, Nassar, an employee of a mysterious organization, and various minor characters. Nassar is looking to tempt Kadir and his friends into joining him in an endeavor to "further the jihadist cause" while looking to his own interests. Sayyid, the leader of Kadir's group, has big plans for New York City. Jack's just chugging along, completely oblivious to them until a fiery and satisfying collision. It's not the climax of the book, however. There doesn't appear to be one and the end sets up to flow directly into the next book.

The writing itself is amazing. The action is smooth and realistic. Jack doesn't jump off of buildings or defeat his kidnappers with both hands tied behind his back. He just shoots people, or beats them up with a pipe. The perspective flips between the characters are superbly done. You see what each character is doing and they don't have some mysterious second sense for what's going on with the other narrative characters, as you find in some other books. For example, Jack goes to a bar after a job—*but two of the bad guys are going to that same bar*. What's going to happen? Will there be a shoot-out? I found myself concerned for Jack's well-being, and applaud Wilson for his excellent writing. I did have some issues with the ~mysterious cult~ until I did some googling and found out that the series is paranormal with emphasis on the normal. After that, the bad guys came off as bad guys instead of a high school drama club who never took their capes off.

All in all, *Cold City* is a good read and I recommend it.

- Reviewed by Kirstin McKinney

Peep Show Volume 2
Edited by Paul Fry
Short, Scary Tales Publications
ISBN: 978-09542523-6-6
November, 2012; $14.95 TPB

Back in the early 2000s, *Peep Show* was a small-press magazine based in England that was run by Paul Fry. Only five issues were published, but in that short time, there were a lot of great authors featured in that 'zine. You'll recognize such names as Graham Masterton, Ronald Malfi, Wrath James White, Alex Severin, Christopher Fulbright, Ray Garton and Mike Bohatch. But in the small-press world, 'zines usually have a short life, and *Peep Show* was no exception. Many of the small-press magazines in the day of snail-mail submissions are gone. However, Paul Fry has resurrected *Peep Show*, only now it's an anthology instead of a 'zine.

Volume 2 features several known authors, as well as a few newcomers. The anthology starts off with "The Farm House" by Jeremy Terry. It begins a little "Rocky Horror-esque," but quickly gets creepy and spooky, as well as erotic.

When Gene O'Neill is included in an anthology, you know you're in for a treat. In "The Silkworm Moth Effect," Dr. Seamus Chacon has discovered a way to make women desire him. Of course, he takes advantage of this, but doesn't expect the end result.

Ben lusts after his next-door neighbor Candy, much to the disapproval of her father, in the story "Curfew" by Eric Red. Although Candy's dad warns Ben to stay away, the teenager can't resist her. He becomes obsessed with her, to the point of sneaking in her room. Candy likes him, too, but her love is not what Ben is looking for. This was a nasty little story I really enjoyed.

There have been many stories about the girl in the trailer park who takes on all the boys. But Walter Jarvis's "The Line-Up at Buddy Milam's Trailer" takes the trope to another level, a horrifying level.

There are several more stories. Not all of them are great. But overall, *Peep Show Volume 2* is a fun, shocking ride through sex and death. This anthology is very diverse in its authors and tales. If you're someone who likes his or her erotica on the dark side, *Peep Show Volume 2* will be a very satisfying read.

- Reviewed by Sheri White

Milton's Children
By Jason V Brock
Bad Moon Books
ISBN: 978-0-9884478-5-1
2013; $15.95 TPB, $25 Signed HC

Former *Dark Discoveries* Managing Editor and Designer Jason Brock is a busy guy. Besides making documentaries on SF and Horror luminaries, publishing landmark limited edition anthologies and editing and publishing his own magazine *Nameless*, he also finds time to write a bit here and there. He's had a number of short stories published in various venues (including a couple excellent ones I ran in DD a while back) and now he's done something a bit longer in the novella *Milton's Children*.

An interesting fusion of *Paradise Lost* and Lovecraft, it focuses on a team of Military Personnel who assemble for a trek deep into Antarctica to explore something amazing recently discovered. The incorporation of the main protagonist's beliefs into the plot (via a defense at the start) is an interesting move and helps to bolster both the scientific background as well as the irony of the following events in the story. It's easy to become preachy with this kind of thing, but Brock succeeds in avoiding that quite well.

Milton's Children is a brisk, action-filled read - a nod to the classic ecological monster movies of the '50s, '60s and '70s with modern-day knowledge and scientific information factored in. It really gives the reader food for thought about our own actions and presumed domination of the planet. In reality, there is a lot we still don't understand and our grasp of being the "head" species is tenuous at best. I enjoyed it very much and with the issues brought up and the possible implications and outcome, I could easily see this becoming a much longer piece (or a sequel? Word is that might well be on the horizon actually).

Highly Recommended!

- Reviewed by Trever Nordgren

Ink
Damien Walters Grintalis
Samhain Publishing
ISBN: 978-16192107-2-1
2012, $16.00 TPB

Ink is Damien Walters Grintalis' first novel, and it's an excellent horror story with precision writing, a different concept that's both refreshing and utterly intriguing, and edge-of-your-seat suspense that builds slowly to a fever pitch, until it finally explodes with its intense ending. Needless to say, this is an author to keep an eye out for.

The story centers on Jason, whose wife Shelly just left him for a woman. Jason's life with her wasn't all that great to begin with. While he misses her, but his mind is secretly shouting out FREEDOM! like Mel Gibson did in *Braveheart*. All it takes is a few hours before Jason figures out that his life is much better off without Shelly.

To celebrate, he decides to get drunk and get a tattoo since these are two things that Shelly frowned upon. While in the bar that night, he meets a tattoo artist by the name of John S. Iblis, who likes to occasionally sing a tune, "Had a girl and she sure was fine." Iblis quickly talks Jason into letting him do a tattoo for him. Once the artist has him back in his shop, he swiftly designs one of the most beautiful tattoos Jason has ever seen. It's the tattoo of a magnificent, rather majestic griffin.

After the art work's completion, Iblis gives Jason a card with his number on it and tells him if he ever wants the griffin removed, to give him a call.

Things go fairly well for Jason after that … at least for a little while. He meets a lovely blonde woman named Mitch who immediately likes him. His wife has set the divorce proceedings into motion so he can begin a new life. And his family has accepted his divorce, though it was clearly a struggle for his mom, who'd liked Shelly.

Then, things start happening.

It starts out in a small way when the pets of neighbors go missing. He thinks it's the strange kid who lives down the street doing the evil deeds and even catches the runt peeking through the front window one night when he's getting it on with Mitch. There's also a continuous pain in Jason's arm where the tattoo is, and he's starting to have very vivid nightmares that won't go away.

Things in his life, however, don't get better. In fact, they eventually spiral downward at a rather alarming pace as he and Shelly have a confrontation. A few days later he finds her hand on his doormat. The griffin finally reveals itself to Jason, and he realizes that if he's not crazy and he's in some very deep trouble. After that, the police come knocking on his door about the death of Shelly and her girlfriend, who have had their bodies ripped apart.

The tattoo artist, John S. Iblis, knows exactly what's going on and expects Jason to come crawling back to him, begging to have the griffin removed from his arm. Iblis will be more than happy to remove the tattoo, providing Jason accepts his conditions on doing it.

It's difficult to believe this is the author's first novel. *Ink* is so well-written it's as if this is her fourth or fifth novel. This is definitely a pro at work, a writer who's going to be soon making a big name for herself. I guarantee you that *Ink* will be winning all sorts of awards in 2013 for best horror novel of the year.

Great reading!

- Reviewed by Wayne C. Rogers

Fungi
Edited by Orrin Grey & Silvia Moreno Garcia
Innnsmouth Free Press
ISBN 978-0-9916759-1-3
2012; Hardcover $28.00, Paperback
$15.00, e-book $ 8.00

If you're wondering about the title of this book then you're probably not familiar with the seminal story by William Hope Hodgson "The Voice in the Night" and all the subsequent works of horror and SF where fungi, mould, mushrooms and yeasts had a pivotal role (for an exhaustive list see the appendix at the end of the present volume). Editors Orrin Grey and Silvia Moreno Garcia must be congratulated upon their excellent and original idea of assembling a hefty collection of twenty-six stories along that line, mostly constituted by brand new tales.

John Langan sets the tone with "Hyphae," a terrific and terrifying piece where a man goes back home to find his father transformed into a living horror. Kristopher Reisz provides "The Pilgrims of Parthen" a SF tale about hallucinogen mushrooms able to transport people to an imaginary city belonging to an alien world. Jane Henterstein's "Wild Mushrooms" is the affectionate diary written by the daughter of a couple of Czech immigrants whose life was deeply marked by some odd mushrooms.

The superb "Our Stories Will Live Forever" by Paul Trembley painstakingly depicts the events occurring during a doomed air flight and the helpful involvement of mysterious mushrooms while "Go Home Again" by Simon Strantzas effectively describes how the mould infesting an old family house triggers painful memories and discloses unspeakable secrets from the past.

Ian Rogers contributes "Out of the Blue," an entertaining supernatural noir where a fast-spreading mould plays a major role and Nick Mamatas pens an accomplished, well-crafted tale of witchcraft and supernatural horror set in an entirely urban context.

Another excellent story well worth a special mention is "Dust From a Dark Flower" by Daniel Mills. It's an extremely creepy tale where a destructive rot attacks both graveyard and population of a small village (also a physical allegory of spiritual corruption?)

Next time you're taking a stroll in the woods if you happen to find some mushrooms just turn around and go the other way…

- Reviewed by Mario Guslandi

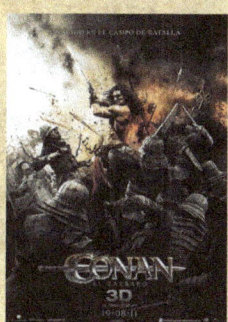

Conan the Barbarian
Nu Image/Millenium/Lionsgate Films
Director: Marcus Nispel
2011

Let me tell you where I'm coming from here. The original Arnold Schwarzenegger movie was my first exposure to the savage world of Conan and I loved it. Later I would devour all of the Robert E. Howard stories, and while I found them superior in every way to that movie, I still loved that first film. So I admit, coming into this 2011 remake, I was dubious. I liked Jason Momoa well enough as Khal Drogo in *Game of Thrones*, but could he even begin to fill Conan's big boots? What of the director, the high lord of so-so at best remakes (The Texas Chainsaw Massacre, Friday the 13th), Marcus Nispel? Then there was the fact that it took three people to write this (never a good sign) movie with combined screenwriting credits of some absolute stinkers like Halloween: Resurrection, The Crow: Wicked Prayer, Dylan Dog: Dead of Night, and A Sound of Thunder.

Gee, I wonder why I was ever worried?

But let's tackle my worries one by one and see how the movie turned out.

Jason Momoa actually made an okay Conan. He was a bit too smirky at times and played things more for laughs than he should have, but that last bit could be laid at the writers or director's feet. At least he wasn't monosyllabic and limited to a dozen or so spoken lines like Arnold was. He also moved well and twirled a sword like a beast. You really got the impression that he was deadly. I am also secure enough in my manliness to admit that Jason is a good looking man, so you could see why every princess he met wanted to fall into his bed.

On to the direction by Nispel. First, the movie relied far too much on crappy CGI and over-the-top silliness. The original movie didn't need all that crap, neither did this one. It is also a victim of modern action movie making, that being 100 edits per minute. The camera moved in too close to really see the action, and the whole "doing cool things for the sake of doing something cool even if it makes no sense."

Like when Conan battles CGI sand warriors, or when Conan fights a giant CGI octopus-thing, or just an over the top wagon chase that somehow gives physics the middle finger and sends a wagon flying. Why? But all in all, the direction is serviceable, yet uninspired. The action set pieces are either ridiculous or are so overly CGI saturated that they seem right out of Play Station.

As for the story, it's a generic revenge tale, and once again the moviemakers felt the need to modern it up. Yep, modernizing a character that first saw print over seventy years ago, why not? Just like so many other remakes, here it seems that Conan was picked just as a familiar namedrop.

I could go on and on, but here is the long and short of it: this is just not a good movie. It feels hollow, made by people who were just working a job and had no real passion for the source material. Jason Momoa tries his best, but he's forever in the looming shadow that Mr. Schwarzenegger cast, mostly because the Austrian muscleman was simply in a much better movie. There's nothing memorable in this remake, nothing that stands out. At least, nothing that stands out for being good. Rose McGowan, CGI octopuses, and far too much smirking and winking at the camera definitely stands out as bad. If you are a fan of the original *Conan the Barbarian* movie, I can't imagine you'll like this one. If you are a fan of the Robert E. Howard stories, you may think Jason's Conan is a little bit more like the Conan from the original tales than Arnold was, but the rest of the story and supporting characters are either so bland or bad that they easily overshadow any good that Mr. Momoa is trying to do. If you have never seen a Conan movie, I hope this is not your first exposure to the iconic character. Do yourself a favor and watch the original film, or better yet, read the stories. Either of those will be far better than this tepid, soulless, cynical cash grab remake.

- Reviewed By Brian M. Sammons

Sinister
Alliance Films/IM Global
Directed by Scott Derrickson
2012

Sinister is a terrifying horror film that knows how to scare you. From the moment the film begins the gruesome atmosphere surrounds us like a straitjacket from which we cannot escape until the final credits begin to roll. From the first frame to the last our bodies are tensed wire tight. This is one of the most potent horror exercises in decades.

Directed by Scott Derrickson, who made the very good *The Exorcism of Emily Rose* and the astoundingly awful remake of *The Day the Earth Stood Still*, *Sinister* tells the story of a true crime writer, played by Ethan Hawke, whose quest for fame leads him to move his family into a house to be closer to the scene of the murders he is currently writing about. He keeps quiet the fact that the house is the crime scene where a family was brutally hanged to death months earlier.

Hawke finds a box of old home movies in the attic and his curiosity gets the best of him. Late at night while his family sleeps, he watches the films. What he sees is gruesome, terrible, videos of the murders of not only the family who were hanged but of three others families who met horrific and violent deaths. He and we assume the films were purposefully left there by the murderer, but Hawke is seeking fame and fortune. He risks danger as he feels he is onto the makings of a best seller.

The murders appear to be ritualistic and, in the films, Hawke's character sees something or someone lurking in certain frames. This leads us to the introduction of "Mr. Boogie", who is one of the most terrifying horror film creations in years. The director uses him sparingly, but he is potent enough to haunt our thoughts throughout the entire film.

Hawke's search for the truth behind the murders leads him to terrifying nights, alone in his study watching the films and subjecting himself to brutal terrors. This is where the film is truly scary. The images that we are witness to are the stuff of the most frightening nightmares. They are unsettling and truly haunting. The director knows how to creep us out, and he uses these moments to terrify us beyond belief as Hawke's study, and the entire film, is shrouded in black. The film seems to have a fascination with darkness as even the daylight scenes are filled with shadows and dark corners of rooms. We know that in the dark that we are not safe and the filmmakers force us to "white knuckle" our way to the end of the film.

The filmmakers balance a fine line of "less is more" while still allowing us a couple of jump scares, but they are not used in a cheap way. We are already sitting in sheer terror when they arrive and we jump at the audacity of the truly frightening image that comes at us. Director Derrickson toys with us in a very dark and macabre way while keeping us in wide-eyed horror. There is a pervading sense of dread and extreme claustrophobia that is laid out by the director's utilizing darkness and shadows in lieu of excessive visual tricks. He allows the film to confront the darkness of the story without becoming exploitative and in doing so has created an original and supremely scary horror film.

As far as the acting, Ethan Hawke has always been an actor whom I admire, and he does solid and believable work here. He is fascinating to watch as he shows us a man who loves and wants to protect his family, but can't stop his obsession for seeking the truth, even as he discovers that he may be dealing with something that is beyond human. It is solid work, as Hawke carries the film and is in every scene.

The supporting roles are well cast and played including Juliet Rylance as Hawke's wife, James Ransome as "Deputy So and So" (a great in joke), and the great character actor Fred Dalton Thompson as the local sheriff who is offended by the mere presence of Hawke's opportunistic writer.

Sinister is an extremely well executed horror film. Not since Neil Marshall's surprising film *The Descent* in 2007 has a film given us such a brilliantly created atmosphere and scared us so viscerally. *Sinister* is truly one of the finest horror films in recent years and one of the best films of 2012.

- Reviewed by Anthony C. Francis

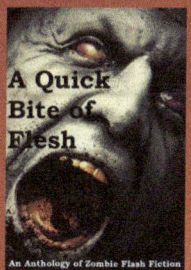

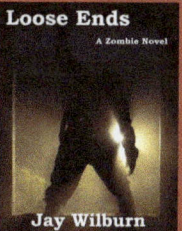
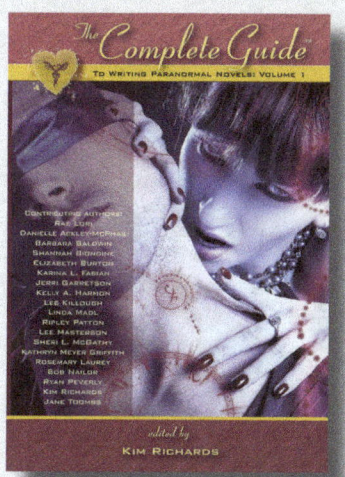

Damnation Books

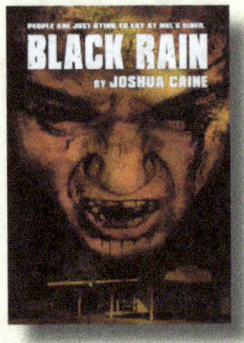
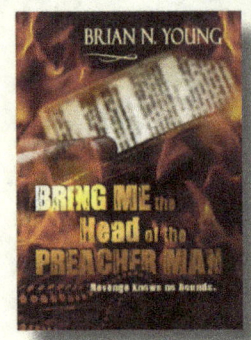

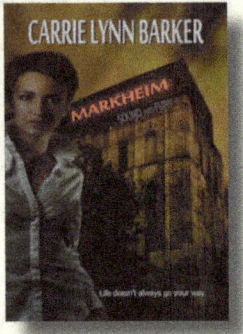
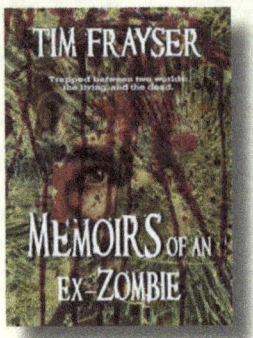

Damn Good Dark Fiction

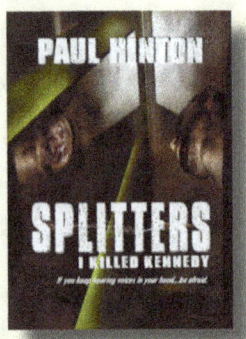

www.damnationbooks.com

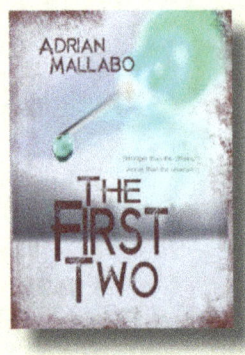
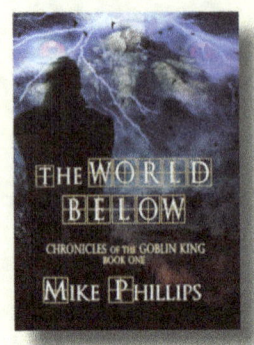

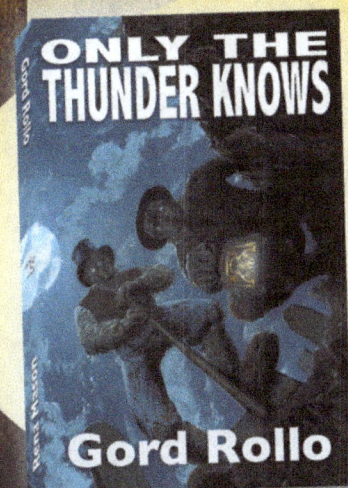

LIKE DARK DISCOVERIES?

UNSETTLE... EDIFY... INVOLVE...

Then **SUBSCRIBE** and never miss another issue of...

FEATURES:

Weird Fiction & Film, Extreme Horror, Comics & Pulps, New Blood, Dark SciFi,

Twilight Zone, H.P. Lovecraft, Horror in Rock, Forgotten Horror & SF TV...

INTERVIEWS:

Ray Bradbury, Bruce Campbell, Christopher Lee, Joe R. Lansdale, William F. Nolan,

EC Comics Al Feldstein, Brian Keene, Jack Ketchum, David Cronenberg...

FICTION:

Richard Matheson, Ray Bradbury, Thomas Ligotti, Richard Laymon, John Shirley, William F. Nolan, Ramsey Campbell, Joe R. Lansdale, Lisa Morton, Edward Lee...

"Dark Discoveries is a very handsome publication..."

--Dean Koontz

"A bright new force in Dark Fantasy."

--William F. Nolan

"Dark Discoveries is a high quality mag... and it keeps getting better..."

--Horror Fiction Review

PRINT SUBSCRIPTIONS

4 issues (1 year): US ($37.95) Canada ($46.95) Overseas ($69.95)

8 issues (2 years): US ($74.95) Canada ($92.95) Overseas ($139.95)

(*Shipping is included on print subs)

DIGITAL SUBSCRIPTIONS

4 issues (1 year): $19.95

8 issues (2 years): $39.95

Payment accepted via PayPal:

christophercpayne@journalstone.com

Also by Check/M.O. (Payable to) JournalStone

199 State Street, San Mateo, CA. 94401, USA

ON THE WEB:

www.darkdiscoveries.com

ADVERTISERS!

Inquire via E-mail for rates!

Please Note: Future content subject to change without notice. All rights reserved.

JOURNALSTONE
YOUR LINK TO ARTISTIC TALENT